Six Tricks

Doggone Disaster
Book Six in the Val Fremden Midlife Mystery Series
Margaret Lashley

What Readers are Saying about the Val Fremden Midlife Mystery Series

"Hooked like a fish. OMG Margaret Lashley is the best! Val could be Stephanie Plum's double!! Phenomenal writing."

"If you enjoy Janet Evanovich you will love Margaret Lashley!"

"If you need a good laugh, this is the series for you! Very well written, with a fun plot and a multitude of zany characters."

"I'm not sure how Margaret Lashley does it, but she can take the average situation and turn it into a laugh-out-loud adventure."

"You might also want to make sure you are somewhere private so you don't get funny looks when the tears are rolling down your cheeks and your stomach hurts from laughing so hard."

"I absolutely love this series and Margaret Lashley has a way of making real life shenanigans even more hilarious."

"Whether this is your first or sixth book with Ms. Lashley you will become hooked on Val and her pals."

"Love, Love! Funny, quirky main character that makes every one of these books a delight to read!"

More Hilarious Val Fremden Midlife Mysteries

Absolute Zero
Glad One
Two Crazy
Three Dumb
What Four
Five Oh
Six Tricks
Seven Daze
Figure Eight
Cloud Nine
And the New Val Fremden Strikes Again Series!

"I got a dog for my boyfriend. It was a good trade."
Val Fremden

Chapter One

"I'm too old and set in my ways for this crap," Laverne said. She rolled her big, bulgy eyes and handed me a Tanqueray and tonic. It was in a highball glass she'd filched from the Flamingo Casino decades ago, back in her Vegas-showgirl days.

"Tell me about it," I groused, and took a sip from the glass. The cartoon caricature of a cross-eyed, long-necked pink bird stared back at me. Its expression seemed oddly appropriate. "What are we gonna do?"

"I don't know," Laverne said. "But we better think of something fast. It's driving me crazy!" The old woman pursed her thin lips, then threw back her horsey head and chugged her Dirty Shirley like a merchant marine at last call. She slammed the glass on the counter and said, "Come with me, Val. I got something to show you."

I followed Laverne's shriveled, brown butt cheeks down the hall toward her bedroom. As I watched her two raisin-like buttocks wobble back and forth, I couldn't decide which view of the tall, skinny, seventy-something woman in a gold thong bikini was more disconcerting, the front or the back.

"Get a look at this," Laverne snarled. She threw open her closet door, spun around to face me, and stabbed a red-lacquered fingernail at the source of her distain. "He's commandeered nearly *half* the lower rack!"

I followed the trajectory of her high-gloss fingertip to a spot about midway down the closet wall. Hanging on the bottom rung of Laverne's huge walk-in closet were about a dozen diminutive men's shirts and pants, along with a sweater and a sport jacket. Together, they were eating away at well over a foot of precious closet space. It was a single woman's worst nightmare. And soon, if Tom had his way, it would be my nightmare, too.

"Geez!" I said. "That's the most disturbing thing I've seen since Uncle Jack's comb-over!"

Laverne scrunched her red lips into the shape of an inflamed sphincter. "That's not even the worst of it."

"What?" I tore my eyes from the horrific scene. "I mean...how...what?"

"J.D. doesn't like me sunbathing," Laverne complained. "He says it wrinkles my skin. And...you're not going to believe this." Laverne stared into my eyes. Her penciled-on eyebrows formed twin pyramids just below her strawberry-blonde curls. "He *hates my gold thong*, Val!"

Laverne straightened her back and stuck out her pendulous boobs, clothed only in two woefully inadequate triangles of glittery, gold fabric. "J.D. says it's not dignified. Can you believe it? If I wanted to be *dignified*, don't you think I'd have gone and done it by now? I'd have moved into one of those blasted...what 'cha call 'em? *Anal-retentive* communities."

"I believe the term is *deed restricted* communities."

"That's it!" Laverne's angular eyebrows rounded themselves into McDonald's arches. "I don't want to be deed restricted, Val." She pouted as her shoulders slumped. "I love J.D., but it ain't worth it if I have to give up *myself* in the process."

I bit my lip and looked down. I couldn't have said it better myself. But maybe my mom, Glad Goldrich, could have. Glad once told me that no one could stop change. And whether a particular change *itself* was good or bad depended on your perspective. Well, the way I saw it, the changes hurtling toward me and my neighbor Laverne were neither good *nor* bad. They were downright, gut-flopping *terrifying*.

The night of Vance and Milly's wedding, I thought I'd dodged the bullet and put the whole matrimony debate between me and my boyfriend Tom to rest. When he'd flung our cursed engagement ring in the ocean, I'd thought that meant my troubles were over.

Boy, had I been wrong.

Right after he'd tossed the ring, Tom had explained to me that he could live with the way things were...the operative term being *live with*. He'd told me he wanted us to play house. As in *live together!* Crap on a cracker! The way I saw relationships, marriage was just a ceremony. The *real* work was surviving *cohabitation*. Misery didn't love company. Misery *was* company—if you had no choice in the matter.

The mere thought of coming home to find Tom in my space *every single blasted day for the rest of my life* had set my teeth to gnashing. But if there was one consolation—ironic as it was—it was the fact that *I wasn't alone* in my dilemma. Laverne was trying to bail her way out of the same sinking boat. Mr. J.D. Fellows, Esq., it seemed, had his eye on moving in with *her*.

"You got any ideas how to deal with this catastrophe?" Laverne asked as I stared blankly at the man-infestation slowly taking over her closet.

"Not a dang clue," I muttered.

"Aww, crap," Laverne said, and slammed the closet door shut.

BACK HOME, I TIPSILY eyeballed my *own* bedroom closet. It was half as big as Laverne's. And Tom was twice the size of J.D. Fellows. I didn't like the way the math was adding up....

I heard a light rap on my front door. I closed the closet and padded barefoot down the hall. But before I could answer the door, it opened on its own. Tom strolled in like he owned the place.

"Hi there, cutie!" he said, and gave me one of his irresistible winks.

For the first time, Tom's handsome, blond, sea-green-eyed magic didn't work on me. It had been rendered powerless by what he carried in his left hand.

"What have you got in the duffle bag?" I asked, and eyed them both suspiciously.

"Just a couple of things," he said, and kissed me on the lips.

My heart skipped a beat. But not from his kiss.

Just a couple of things, my behind! Thanks to my earlier pow-wow with Laverne, I knew what this was. It was the first step in Tom's insidious plan to...to...to *what*? Invade my space? Take over my life? Destroy my world as I knew it?

Well, that was the million-dollar question, wasn't it? Only this time, I didn't have a million dollars to lose.

Chapter Two

For the past two weeks, I'd been pretty much holding down an abandoned fort at the accounting firm of Griffith & Maas. My best friend and boss, Milly Halbert, was gone on her honeymoon to Hawaii with her new husband, Vance Pantski. That had left just me and old man Griffith to totter around the empty place.

It was the middle of May. Peak tax season was over. That meant there'd been hardly any files to file, and barely a handful of visitors to greet from my post at the reception desk. After making the morning coffee for Mr. Griffith, there wasn't much else to do except read romance novels and become increasingly disgruntled over the level of romance in my *real* relationship with Tom.

Tax season wasn't the only thing that was over for another year. So was any hope of a good hair day. Over the past week, summer and all its unwelcome humidity had arrived in St. Pete with a vengeance. This morning, as I drove to work with the top down on Shabby Maggie, even the fifty-mile-an-hour breeze swirling around me couldn't keep the sweat from trickling down my back and running in rivulets right into my butt crack. So much for that fabulous, fresh feeling.

To try and cope with the heat, I pulled off my pantyhose as soon as I got to work. I put on a pot of coffee for Mr. Griffith, kicked off my heels, and hoisted my bare feet up on my desk, my legs just wide enough apart to allow for air circulation. With nothing else to do at the moment, I decided to re-read a particularly engrossing scene in my book, *Love's Lusty Love*. It was about Carlton's throbbing manhood....

"Ms. Fremden?"

I nearly jumped out of my chair. I gasped, slapped my book closed and swung my legs off my desk. My right foot caught on the open file drawer, causing me to lurch forward and knock over my mug of water with my right elbow. I watched as water cascaded over my desk like a tiny tsunami.

"Ms. Fremden?" repeated the ancient man in a three-piece suit. He stared at me from a most inopportune angle. I squeezed my thighs together.

"Mr. Griffith!" I yelped. I bolted upright, tossed my book on my desk and kicked the file drawer closed. "Can I help you, sir?"

"Yes," he replied in the calm, reassuring tone of a seasoned psych-ward nurse. He removed his thick glasses and wiped them on a hand-kerchief. "You can help me with three things, actually. First, we're almost out of coffee creamer."

"Oh. I'll pick some up tonight, sir."

"Good. Second, Milly called. She won't be coming in this morning after all. She said she needed one more day off to take care of something 'important.' So I guess the mothballs will have to wait for me for one more day, eh?" Mr. Griffith chuckled as he put his glasses back on, but the distant look that accompanied his faded smile seemed incongruent. He lingered by my desk. "Honeymooners, eh?"

"Yes, sir," I answered. I smiled at the old man who'd won my admiration the first day I'd met him. It was, of course, in this very same office. Last year, Milly had proffered me for an open position at the accounting firm. But it was Mr. Griffith who'd approved my hiring—against all odds in the known universe.

Due to mitigating circumstances probably *not* beyond my control, I'd shown up for my interview with him late, half-drunk, and inappropriately dressed. Then I'd proceeded to let go of a long, squeaky fart that couldn't be explained away by leather seat cushions. To his credit, Mr. Griffith had borne it all without a hint of disdain or disgust.

Looking back on it now, there was something to be said for setting the bar low at the very beginning. By comparison, everything I'd done since had been deemed by Mr. Griffith as nearly miraculous.

"And the third thing, Mr. Griffith?" I asked.

"That third thing...what was it now?" Mr. Griffith reached a skeletal, nearly mummified hand across my desk and picked up my book. "*Love's Lusty Love*," he read aloud. He looked me in the eye and my face grew hot.

Mr. Griffith smiled. "How about that Carlton, eh? One of my favorites."

I grinned. "And you, Mr. Griffith, are one of *mine*."

He smiled and chuckled softly. Then he touched a forefinger to his gray temple, turned, and wandered slowly back to the brown-paneled box of an office where he'd spent the better part of the last forty-five years.

I shook my head in wonder. Dressed in a formal business suit, I couldn't fathom how the old man survived the heat. Especially when he insisted on setting the thermostat to eighty degrees. But I didn't ponder the thought long. I had other things pressing on my mind. As soon as Mr. Griffith rounded the corner and headed down the hallway, I grabbed my cellphone and punched speed dial. Then I waited impatiently until Milly finally picked up.

"Why aren't you coming in today?" I teased. "Too sore to walk?"

"Who is this?"

"Milly! It's me."

"Val," Milly said absently. "Hey."

"How's married life treating you?"

"Oh," Milly said, practically swooning. "Hawaii was like heaven!"

"So, you two are still getting along?"

"What? Yeah. Why?"

"No reason." I should have been happier for Milly. But I found her response more irritating than anything else. Some people like Milly and Vance just seemed to click together. Why did I always have to clack?

"Val, I have some exciting news!"

"You're pregnant," I joked.

"What? No. But almost! While we were in Hawaii, Vance and I decided to adopt!"

"Adopt *what?* A native lifestyle? Cannibalism?"

"What?" The perturbed tone in Milly's voice hinted that she no longer missed me as much as she had a moment ago. "No, Val. A little girl."

My gut hit the floor. "You're kidding!"

"No. And I want you to come by and meet her tonight."

"Wait a minute. You've already got her?"

"Yes. She's six months old. She's an orphan, Val. We found her in Hawaii. And since no one...." Milly paused. I heard a baby cry out in the background. "Listen, I'll fill you in with the details. Come by tonight and meet her! Her name is Charmine. Val, she's so adorable. She's changed my whole world!"

Stunned, all I could manage to say was, "What time?"

"Make it early. Six-thirty? Charmine needs her sleep."

I clicked off the phone. *A kid?* I ran down a mental list of my friends who had children, and came up with exactly zilch. No one I knew had *a kid.*

Crap! What was I supposed to do with a kid?

WITH NOTHING ELSE TO do, I surrendered again to Carlton's mating call. I read a few more chapters and went to lunch. After lunch, I read a couple more. The next time I looked up, Mr. Griffith was at my desk, telling me it was time to call it a day. I grabbed my purse and my book and followed him out the door. I was in my car when I realized I'd forgotten to call Tom with the news.

"A baby girl?" he said, incredulous.

"Yes. Can you believe it?"

"No. Not really," he said. "Wow...what did Vance say?"

"Haven't talked to him. I guess we'll find out tonight."

"See you at home, then," Tom said. "Bye." He clicked off.

See me at home? *What did he mean by* home? My *home?* His *home?* Our *home?*

I shoved my phone into my purse and hit the ignition on Maggie. Her twin glass packs rumbled as deep and dark as my mood. I imagined Tom at my place, busily hanging up his clothes in my closet. Rummaging around in my fridge, drinking my beer. Eating my chips. *Argh!* Home had been my sanctuary from work. My place to be *me*. Wearing sweatpants all Saturday. No makeup. Candy bars and cocktails for dinner. If he moved in, all that would be history!

And once he'd moved in, how long would it be before *work* became my sanctuary from *home? How long before* home *became just another four-letter word?*

I mashed the gas pedal and clamped my jaw tighter than my ex-husband's wallet. My teeth were about to crack under the pressure when I spied something odd. It was one of those inflatable, side-of-the-road puppet-things that danced maniacally to the beat of an air compressor. This one happened to be a stork with a diapered baby-doll suspended in its beak.

Whoever'd come up with *that* bright idea obviously hadn't thought it all the way through. Instead of soaring gracefully through the air to deliver the baby, the murderous, flailing stork was slamming it against a light post like an episode of *Animal Planet* gone horribly awry.

But I had to admit, the homicidal stork had performed its job. It had definitely gotten my attention. I slammed on the brakes. Maggie's tires squealed as I pulled a one-eighty and lurched into the parking lot of the new Baby Bonanza Boutique. I wanted to pick something up for Milly's new, baby daughter.

When I opened the door to the boutique, it was like entering another portal of existence. In that strange, new world where pastels ruled and babies drooled, I felt as out of place as a chili-cheese dog on a vegan buffet. I looked around at all the baby paraphernalia and the room began to spin. *Poor Milly! Tom may be invading my space, but at least he doesn't come with a stroller, a playpen, a diaper bag, a swing set, a bassinet, a crib....*

"Welcome to Three B's!" a piercingly perky woman's voice rang out. Given my current mood and state of disorientation, her high-pitched cheerfulness nearly gave me a seizure.

"Uh...thanks." I turned to face her and glanced around the disorienting land of teddy bears and hearts and rainbows. I blinked hard. I was about to drown in all the baby stuff swimming around.

"Can I help you find something?" the woman chirped.

"Uh...yes. I need something for a six-month-old girl."

The woman's face melted into materialistic ecstasy. "Oh! A little girl! How precious! I have just the thing!" She practically sprinted to a rack. A second later, she shoved a handful of pink satin and lace in my face. "Look at this! Direct from Paris!"

I ran my eyes over the frilly dress. Even *I* had to admit it was gorgeous. When the woman twirled the tiny dress around to reveal a pink satin tieback bow, my heart melted and my wallet opened. "I'll take it," I said.

"Excellent choice," the woman cooed. "That will be $145.79."

My heart began to freeze over again. Then I thought about Milly. And Charmine. I was going to be an aunt...sort of. "Okay," I said, and handed over my credit card.

"Would you like it gift wrapped? It's just $5.99 extra."

Comparatively, that sounded like a bargain. "Sure, what the hay." I watched the pink dress disappear, first beneath fluffy tissue paper and then inside a precious pink bag covered in even pinker, more precious hearts. All the while, I kept saying the name Charmine over and over again in my mind. *Charmine. Charmine. Charmine.* It sounded like charming without the "G." *How adorable is that?*

"Here you go," the clerk said. "She's going to love it!"

"I think so, too," I said with a grin. I mean, what woman didn't love expensive clothes? I signed the credit card slip, grabbed the pink, heart-covered gift bag and wandered dreamily out of the store.

Chapter Three

When I pulled up at my house, Tom's big, fat, silver SUV was already there, hogging up half the driveway. Which meant he was in *my* house. *My* space. *My home. Without my supervision!* I couldn't decide whether to be angry or perturbed. But then I remembered that I'd invited him over. So I decided I'd be just a little of both.

"Hey, Tom," I called out halfheartedly as I opened the front door.

He didn't answer. I set my purse on the kitchen counter and looked out the sliding glass doors into the backyard. Tom was straightening the lounge chairs around the fire pit. Why did he have to be so darn...*handy?* I slid open the door enough to stick my head out and yelled, "Hey! You ready to go?"

Tom turned his handsome blond head my way. "Sure. What happened out here? Your chairs were turned over."

"I dunno."

Tom pursed his lips and glanced around. "Must have been the wind."

"Sure. That's probably it." I clicked my short, unpolished nails on the glass door. "Come on. Aren't you anxious to meet Charmine?"

"Of course I am," Tom answered. "I'm just a little surprised that *you* are."

I frowned. "Why? I like kids."

Tom grinned. "Sure you do. I guess...I've never seen you around any."

"Not my fault," I said. "Nobody I know has any."

"You mean nobody you *knew*. I hope Vance and Milly know what they're getting into. Their lives as they knew them are now officially over."

I smirked at Tom. "*Now* who doesn't like kids?"

Tom wrapped his strong, cop arms around me and kissed me. "You and I are just a couple of old dogs, Val. We're both too set in our ways for kids."

I pulled back, bared my teeth and growled. "Grrr! Who you callin' an old dog, mister?"

Tom shook his head. "Geez! I hope you had your rabies shot."

"You better say something nice to me *right now,* or I'm gonna *bite* you!"

"Promises, promises," Tom whispered. He nuzzled my neck and used the tip of his tongue to tickle that place behind my ear that always drove me wild. Old dog or not, he knew a few tricks. A few really, really *good* tricks.

"Come on, let's go," I said, and pulled away from his embrace. I didn't really want him to stop, but we were already running late. "They're expecting us at 6:30, you know."

Tom pulled me tight to him again. "I know," he whispered in my ear. A shiver ran through me. "But you're gonna be doggone sorry."

I smirked and shook my head. "One thing you'll never learn, old dog, is how to tell a good joke."

Tom frowned, hung his head and pretended to pout. I patted him on the head.

"Don't worry, Tom. You more than make up for it by being house-broken."

WHEN WE PULLED UP IN front of Vance and Milly's place in Tom's SUV, the old dog let out a loud wolf whistle.

"I know, right?" I said. "Vance must be killing it with Kelly's Pub."

"I'd say," Tom said, shaking his head in awe at the Tudor-style mansion. "That house is huge. Looks to be what, five-thousand square feet?"

"Six-thousand, four-hundred," I said.

Tom shot me a look.

"What?" I said defensively. "Milly told me. She said Vance told her that his house was bigger than his restaurant."

Tom shrugged. "What's he need with all that room?"

"Apparently, he's got a growing family to house, remember? We should get going." I turned to climb out of the SUV, but Tom grabbed my hand.

His eyes locked onto mine. "You ever wish you had kids, Val?"

I shrugged. "Sure, for about five minutes. Once. But then I thought, what would I do with a kid? Most of the time, I can barely take care of myself."

Tom blew out a breath and stared absently past me toward Vance and Milly's mansion.

"How about you?" I asked.

"Never seemed like the right time," he said. Then his eyes locked on mine again. "Now, it doesn't matter, right? We're old enough to be grandparents."

He leaned over and tried to kiss me, but I was no longer in the mood. The thought of making out with grandpa was a real libido killer. "Keep your hands to yourself, *gramps*," I sneered, and climbed out of the SUV.

As we walked up the drive toward the humongous Tudor house, its massive, mahogany front door opened. Out poked a rear end in a yellow, polka-dotted dress. Then the rest of Milly appeared, followed by the baby stroller she was pulling. Tom and I exchanged excited grins.

"Milly with a baby," I said, almost whispering. I shook my head. "Who would have ever thought?"

Milly shut the door behind her, then leaned over and cooed into the stroller. Her beautiful blonde hair hung down, obscuring her face. She was so intent with her baby talk that she didn't notice us walk up.

"Hey, Milly," I said softly, so as not to frighten her or the baby.

She turned around, beamed at me and hugged me like a momma bear. "Oh my goodness! Val! Tom! It's so good to see you two! I want you to meet my Charmine! Isn't she precious?"

Milly lifted the thin baby blanket covering the carriage. I made a goofy face and stuck my head in for a peek. But instead of goo-gooing, I yelped with shock and surprise. Charmine's face was covered with fur! And her fuzzy ears were pointed! Either Charmine was a dog, or some weirdo in Hawaii had had an affair with Chewbacca.

"Geez, Milly! That's a dog!" I cried. I looked over at Tom, my eyes still doubled from the shock. He was no help. Unless you counted laughing hysterically at me as *help*, which *I, personally*, did not. I could barely hear Milly over his raucous hoots and haws.

"Well *of course* she's a dog," Milly said in a hushed tone, as if the pooch might be offended at discovering her canine heritage. She hastily threw the blanket back over the carriage. "What did you *think* she was, Val?"

"I...uh..."

I glanced over at Tom. He was beside himself with laughter, doubled over on the lawn like a puking drunk.

I turned back to Milly. "Well, the way you went on—"

"Oh! Is *that* for Charmine?" Milly squealed, cutting me off. She snatched the pink, heart-covered bag from my hand. "Oh! You *shouldn't* have!"

She was right. I shouldn't have. But it was a bit too late for that now. "Yeah...well," I fumbled. From the corner of my eye, I watched Tom fall on his knees in the grass, his crimson face contorted with laughter. Either that, or he was having a heart attack. I wasn't sure which one I preferred.

Milly pulled the frilly pink dress out of the bag and went ballistic with girly delight. "Oh, Val! It's beautiful! She'll look lovely in it. Oh! I know! It'll be perfect for her Barkmitzva!"

Tom snorted like an asthmatic hog.

"Barkmitzva?" I asked. "I didn't know Charmine was Jewish." I caught Tom's eye. He'd almost recovered, but that one sent him back down on his side, squirming in the grass like an epileptic lawn jockey.

"I'm not. *Vance* is," Milly explained. "So...I guess that makes Charmine Jewish, too. The Barkmitzva is this Saturday. Can you two make it?"

Tom snorted so loud Milly looked over her shoulder at him. He was on all fours. "Is he all right?" she asked.

"Too much sugar," I said. "But don't worry. He won't be getting anymore for a while. Let's go in."

"Should we just leave him like that?" she asked, glancing back at Tom as she turned the stroller around.

"Sure," I replied. "If he's not recovered in five minutes or so, I'll call a veterinarian."

"OH LOOK, SHE'S WAKING up!" Milly said.

Vance and Milly and Tom and I had paired off on two overstuffed couches facing each other in a living room bigger than my entire house. A massive, six-foot-square mahogany coffee table separated us. On it sat a collection of figurines of a caliber I'd never spotted on any of my yard-sale bargain hunts.

In style and scale, the room was reminiscent of a national-park lodge. A huge, stone fireplace stood in the center of one wall, and thick, wooden beams formed a ribcage design on the fourteen-foot-tall arched ceilings. Despite its gargantuan proportions, in the company of friends, the room felt cozy as we sat around drinking wine and swapping stories of Vance and Milly's honeymoon and our single days gone by.

For over half an hour, Charmine had slept through our boisterous conversation. I guess the growing girl really *did* need her sleep. But when Vance came back from the kitchen with a tray laden with chunks of cheese and sausage, the little pooch perked up like one of those balloons you shoot water into at the county fair.

"Oh! Look! Who's a good girl?" Milly cooed.

Charmine whined and stuck her furry little snout out of the stroller. Milly picked her up and set her on her lap. At first glance, Charmine didn't look to be much more than a ball of reddish-gold fur punctuated by three black dots—two for her eyes and one for her nose. But when she turned to face us on Milly's lap, I saw she had a white, heart-shaped patch of fur on her fuzzy little chest. Her bushy tail, thick as her head, curled and stood straight up, making it hard to tell which end was which.

Milly stroked Charmine's head while Vance tempted her with a tiny bit of sausage he'd bitten off and retrieved from his own tongue. When Charmine gobbled it up, Vance looked over at us, as proud of the pup as if she'd just graduated from Harvard.

"Isn't she smart?" Vance asked, his question more a statement of irrefutable fact. His smitten eyes never left Charmine. Instead, he grinned and nodded his head encouragingly while Milly cuddled the little dog. The scene was as endearing as it was ridiculous. I began to feel oddly voyeuristic, as if I'd snuck into a family love fest without buying the proper ticket for admission.

Tom squeezed my knee. We exchanged tight smiles. Vance bit off another tiny piece of sausage. Charmine snapped it up. It was all too...*intimate*. And, to be honest, *boring*.

"What kind of dog is she?" I asked, to break the awkwardness that perhaps only I had been feeling.

"What?" Milly asked. She looked up absently, as if she'd forgotten Tom and I were there. "Oh. We don't stand on pedigree here. But I think she's mostly Pomeranian."

"Where did you find her?" Tom asked.

Milly choked up as she spoke. "She was...living on the streets."

"Well, it *was* in Hawaii," Tom offered. "It couldn't have been *that* bad."

"She was scrounging around a dumpster," Vance said indignantly.

Milly's eyes doubled in size. She placed her hands over Charmine's pointy little ears.

"It was bad enough," she said.

"She was famished when we found her, wasn't she?" Vance said to Milly. "Poor baby. But it's all better now," Vance cooed to Charmine in baby talk.

"Well, it looks like she's found a wonderful home now," I said cheerfully. "And speaking of home...." I eyed Tom. He got the hint.

"Oh. Yes," Tom said, springing up from the couch. "We really should get going."

"But wait. You have to see this!" Milly said.

Our escape foiled for the moment, Tom and I stood in place and watched as Milly tugged the fancy pink dress on over Charmine's thick, golden coat. She tied the bow in the back and set the dog on the floor.

Charmine squeaked out a sound that could only be called a bark because it came from a dog. She squatted on the rug, and before Milly could say a word, three turds tumbled from Charmine's sphincter like brown Play-Doh.

"Oops! She's not quite housebroken," Milly laughed, as if the dog had done something unbearably cute.

"Apparently not," I said.

"Aww. It's just a little poo-poo," Vance gushed. "Good girl!"

I began to wonder if Charmine wasn't a dog, but an alien being who'd stolen Milly and Vance's brains—or evaporated their gray matter with a secret little ray gun.

I mean, really! Charmine's just a dog. What's the big deal?

"Our precious girl's adorable, isn't she?" Milly blathered.

"Yes. She's adorable," I said. "Congratulations, you two." I turned to Tom. "But we really must be going."

"Just one more thing," Milly said. She stood up and took my hand. "I was wondering, Val...would you mind staying with Charmine tomorrow? Just while I catch things up at work? I really hate to leave her alone all day."

I stiffened. Then I remembered I had a bona fide excuse. "I don't have any holiday time left," I said. "I used up all my days on my birthday trip, remember? That beach holiday I spent chasing lunatic fishermen and the inept pigs who wanted to throw me in jail?" I shot a glance at Tom. "No offense."

Tom grinned through one side of his mouth. "Good times."

Milly frowned and shook her head at me as if I were pathetic. "I *know* that, Val. I'm your *boss* after all. But, well...this is an *emergency*. I was thinking that you could maybe babysit Charmine instead of going in to work tomorrow? I'll work it out with Mr. Griffith. He won't mind. You know him. As long as the coffee gets made, he's good to go. And I'll pay you the same wages, so you won't miss out financially. I'll tell him you're taking unpaid leave."

I looked down at Charmine, then back at Milly. I bit my lip. I had no idea how to take care of a kid, much less a dog! "I dunno...."

"It's just *one day*, Val!" Milly said in a way that conveyed dismay at me not snapping up her amazing offer. "That's all I need to get the firm back on track. I promise. I'll make some calls and find someone else to watch her after that." Milly nuzzled her face with Charmine's, who had just licked her own poopy butt. *Yuck.*

I grimaced. Milly laughed.

"Come on, Val! Look at her! There ought to be a law against being so cute, right?" She kissed Charmine on the nose. "I couldn't bear the thought of leaving my doodle bug alone all day with some stranger."

"*I'm* a stranger," I argued. "I mean, Charmine doesn't know me."

Milly looked up, almost shocked. "No, you're not. You're *family*."

"That's right," Vance agreed. "Both of you are."

How could I argue with that? My reservations and objections had been worn away like a sandcastle at high tide. "Sure. Okay."

"Oh, thank you!" Vance and Milly practically sang a duet.

"Drop her by my place on your way to work," I said.

"Should I bring the stroller?" Milly asked.

"I don't think that'll be necessary. Oh. And you need to pick up coffee creamer on your way in. Mr. Griffith used it all up."

"Will do." Milly handed Charmine to Vance and reached out to give me a hug. "Thank you, Val."

"Sure. It'll be fun," I said, more to convince myself than anyone else.

"We better get going," Tom said. The four of us, plus Charmine, started the trek to the massive, carved-mahogany front door that probably cost more than my house.

"Tomorrow then!" Milly called out to Tom and me as we trudged down the driveway.

"Tomorrow," I muttered, and waved back.

"What's the matter, Val?" Tom teased and took my hand. "Does taking care of a dog for one day seem like too much of a commitment?"

"Ha ha. Very funny," I sneered. But Tom had nailed my problem on the head. I couldn't let him know it, though. "No," I lied. "I was just thinking about the lady I met today at that fancy baby boutique. I bet she never imagined that some mutt would be taking a dump in that hundred-and-fifty-dollar dress."

Tom whistled long and low. "A hundred and fifty... Never mind. Speaking of taking a dump, I need to—"

I stopped in my tracks and held my flattened palm up to Tom's face. "Stop right there, Tom Foreman. That's just way too much information."

Tom crinkled his nose quizzically, then laughed out loud. "Geez, Val! I just meant to say that you should make sure you have some baggies with you tomorrow." His voice shifted to baby talk. "For when you take precious little Charmine on her poo-poo walk."

I eyed him dubiously. "Yeah. *Sure* you did." I tried to laugh it off, but couldn't. Something had gnawed straight through my last funny bone.

I knew what it was. But I didn't want to admit it.

Not to Tom.

Not to Milly.

Not even to myself.

Chapter Four

I *hate dogs.*
There, I admitted it.

To be fair, it wasn't a gut-boiling hate, as in, "All dogs must *die, now!*" It was more like a long-simmering fearful distrust, as in, "I've got my eye on *you*, Mister Whiskers. Don't try anything stupid."

My less-than-cordial feelings about dogs had been set in stone the day I'd turned five years old. My adoptive parents, Lucille and Justas Jolly, hadn't thrown me a birthday party or anything fancy like that. There'd been no point. We'd lived out in the *rural* part of Greenville, Florida. And that was really saying something. Back then, Greenville didn't even have that highfalutin flashing yellow light where you turn off Highway 90 to get to the IGA grocery store. In other words, it was before "The Carter Incident." That was when Dallas Carter missed the turnoff, jumped the ditch and ran over a skunk with his monster truck. His back left tire had flung the squashed polecat clear up onto the roof of the IGA, where it, well, stunk to high heaven for nearly a month.

Anyway, my point was, there wasn't a lot going on in Greenville back then. And there weren't any other kids around for miles. So I'd spent my fifth birthday like I had my fourth. In my bathing suit, screeching and running through the garden sprinkler with my sister Annie while my dad, Justas, cranked away at an old, manual ice-cream churn. I remembered him adding handful after handful of rock salt to the watery ice sloshing and circling 'round and 'round the churn that

26

was shaped like a small, wooden barrel. I also recalled asking dad what flavor it was, but he'd just winked at me. He knew that I already knew. Dad had been making my favorite, like he always did on my birthday. Homemade vanilla with some Georgia peaches mixed in.

After Annie and I had whooped and hollered ourselves hoarse, the ice-cream was finally ready and Justas had yelled into the screen door for Lucille. She'd come out toting four bowls and spoons. We'd all gathered on the front porch to sing *Happy Birthday* to me. And, of course, to get our share of that incredible, mouth-wateringly delectable ice cream.

Being the birthday girl, dad had dolloped me out my bowlful first. I'd kissed him on the cheek, then run off with it like a wild animal through the yard. I'd snuck around the corner of the house and shoved a big spoonful of it into my mouth. Time had stood still as the vanilla and sugar and eggs melted into heaven on my tongue. Then I'd plopped myself down in the grass and dished out another mouthful.

That second spoonful had been almost between my lips when it happened.

I'd gotten pummeled head-over-heels by Buford, Dad's favorite hound dog. He'd knocked me backward into the grass, then licked my face clean with his nasty old dog tongue. I'd kicked and screamed in frustration. But Buford had paid no mind at all to my protestations. He'd finished me off and went to work on the sad remains of my bowl of ice cream, which was toppled over in the dirt.

Happy birthday to me.

That wasn't the first time that sneaky old hound had ambushed me. As I recalled, every time I'd ever had something good like a spoon full of peanut butter, a chicken wing, a piece of Bazooka bubble gum—whatever—that blasted Buford knocked me down like a bowling pin, licked my face half raw, and stole my treat right out of my hands...or mouth, depending on how far along I'd gotten in the process of eating it.

And I'd hated him for it.

As far as I could tell, the only thing that worthless hound had been good for was tormenting me. And that day, just like so many days prior, Buford had gone and ruined my fifth birthday. But he'd stolen more away from me than ice cream. That day in particular, Buford had taken away my love for dogs. *Any* kind of dogs. But *especially* rotten old hound-dogs.

They say early childhood programming is hard to undo. In all honesty, in the forty-five years since Buford killed my enthusiasm for canines, I'd never given a dog much of a chance to try and make amends. I'd avoided them and they'd avoided me. It had been a détente that had worked fairly well...*until now*.

As I lay in bed, recalling the past and dreading the day ahead, I tried to look on the bright side. I let out a big sigh. At least pet-sitting Charmine wouldn't require heels or pantyhose....

"Hey, you awake?" Tom asked. He rolled on his side and slipped an arm around my waist.

"Yes," I answered, leaving out the "since 3:00 a.m." part.

"You excited about spending the day with Charmine?" he teased.

"Sure," I lied.

"Well, you better hop to it. She'll be here in an hour."

"You go ahead," I muttered.

"What? No shower this morning?"

"What for?" I groused. "A dog doesn't care how I smell."

"I beg to differ," Tom said, and nuzzled my neck. "That's *all* a dog cares about."

I made a grouchy show of struggling against Tom's charms. I flipped over on one elbow to face him. "What do you mean?"

"A dog is nothing but a big nose," Tom said. As if to drive the point home, he rubbed his nose gently on mine. "For your information, they can smell over *a thousand times* better than *we* can."

"Oh really?" I smirked. "Can they smell *rejection?*"

Tom grinned wickedly. "Some breeds can. Some can't." He playfully bit my neck and growled.

"I guess you're one of those who can't," I snarled back.

"Good guess," he said, and wagged his blond eyebrows at me.

"Oh, all right. Go on, then," I giggled, and gave the dog a bone.

"HERE SHE IS!" MILLY squealed as I opened my front door to let her and Charmine in.

"I thought I said no stroller," I grumbled.

"Oh, come on, now. Charmine loves to ride in it." Milly shoved the baby stroller into my house. "I'm running late. Here's her bag with all her things."

Milly handed me a giant, pink baby bag. I grabbed it and nearly toppled over from the weight of it. "What have you got in here? A build-it-yourself doghouse?"

Milly laughed. "No. Just the necessities. Her special food, water, toys, stuff like that."

Geez! Dog sitting suddenly seemed a lot more complicated than I thought.

"What am I supposed to do again?"

"I wrote everything down on a list," Milly said, and blew a kiss toward Charmine. "It's all in the bag." Milly glanced up at me. "I'm running late, Val. I really gotta go. I still have to pick up the coffee creamer."

"But...."

Milly turned and walked out the door. I stood, open-mouthed, and watched her click down the driveway in her heels. As she climbed into her Beemer, she waved and yelled, "Call me if you need anything!"

I looked down at Charmine. She was sleeping peacefully in her stroller bed like a contented little ball of golden fur. I smiled. Maybe this wouldn't be so bad after all. I perked myself a cappuccino and went back to bed myself. Yes, this was going to be easy-peasy.

I had no idea what a rude awakening I was in for.

Chapter Five

"**G**oober! Get over here. You've got to help me!" I screeched into the phone.

"Who *is* this?" Goober asked, his voice tinged with suspicion.

"It's *me, Val*, you ding dong!"

"Oh. Sure, lure me in with flattery, would you?"

"Sorry. Look, I don't know what to do. A dog is tearing up my place!"

"What? When did you get a dog?"

"I didn't. I don't.... Look, I don't have time to explain. Get your butt over here!"

"Do I have a choice?"

"Why? Are you too busy?"

Goober sighed. "Okay, okay. Where is it now?"

"I've got it trapped in the bathroom."

"Trapped? Should I bring, like, a gun?"

"What? No...I mean...do you *have* a gun?"

"No."

"Then why the heck did you...aargh! Forget it. Just come over, okay?"

"I'll be there in fifteen."

I hung up the phone and looked around. My place was a shambles. An hour ago, Charmine had woken up and gone crazy. She'd jumped out of the stroller and snarled and snapped at me, then she'd gone on a rampage, tearing up my place like a Tasmanian devil on LSD.

I couldn't get near her, and, since I liked having all ten fingers, didn't really want to. So I'd set a trap. I'd thrown some doggy treats in the bathtub and hidden in my bedroom with my ear to the door. When I'd heard her nails clicking in my old, vintage tub, I'd skittered out of my bedroom and made a run for the bathroom door.

My hand was on the bathroom doorknob when Charmine's head popped up out of the tub like a deranged Whack-a-Mole. I'd screamed and she'd sprung up out of the tub, incisors bared, like a slow-motion scene from *The Matrix: Doggy Style*. I'd had just enough time to slam the door shut and escape with my life!

I'd had my share of childhood traumas. Apparently, so had the psychotic little dog from hell. It was only 9:30 and my entire house looked like a garage sale that had been ransacked by Godzilla. I knew I was never going to make it through the day on my own. I'd been in desperate need of reinforcements. I'd thought about calling Milly, but what could I say to her? *"Hi, Milly, uh...call the SWAT team. Your precious little 'doodle bug' is a raging nutcase!"*

So instead, I'd called the only person I knew who had experience dealing with bat-crap crazy on a daily basis. Goober. He lived with Winky, after all.

While I waited for Goober to get his scrawny butt over here, I straightened the cushions on the couch and picked up the cotton-candy tufts of pillow stuffing littering the place like forty years' worth of dust bunnies. How could one little dog make such a big mess?

Then I spied something under the couch that sent my blood boiling. The mangy little fuzz-ball had chewed the heel strap off one my favorite green sandals! *Dang it!* The strap's gnawed remains lay discarded on the floor like a mangled lizard. I bent over to retrieve the strap and nearly had an aneurism at what I discovered next.

That little crud muffin had chewed a hole in the side of my couch!

I belted out a two-minute medley of my favorite expletives. That dog and I were officially at war!

I needed a strategy. And, of course, I needed to pee. I took a step toward the hallway and stopped dead in my tracks. Hockey pucks! My fuzzy nemesis had already taken strategic control of the bathroom, cutting off my access route to indoor plumbing. This called for carefully calculated counter measures—the first one being an encore performance of my greatest swearing hits.

There was no way I was going to be defeated by a dog that weighed less than my belly fat! I stomped into the kitchen and yanked a metal saucepan out of the bottom cabinet. After a careful peek into the backyard to make sure the coast was clear, I pulled down my panties, squatted over the pot and took aim....

I WAS STILL WIPING up pee from the kitchen floor when Goober knocked on the door. I threw the paper towels in the garbage and pulled off my rubber gloves. When I flung open the door, I saw that Goober had come prepared for battle. He wore a hockey mask over his face, a long-sleeved t-shirt with gray elbow pads, and orange knee pads over his raggedy jeans. He held a length of rope in one hand. In the other, he gripped a handful of chicken bones.

"I didn't know witch doctors made house calls," I said.

Goober shrugged. "I was going more for voodoo priest, but I'll take it."

I crinkled my nose and stepped aside to let him in. "What's with the getup?"

"Always better to err on the side of caution," Goober said. "In matters such as these, it's advantageous to arrive over-prepared than under." He pulled his hockey mask up until it formed an odd-looking cap on his bald head.

"You've done something like this before?" I asked.

"Sort of. I babysat my sister's kids once."

"Close enough," I sighed, and shut the door behind him.

"So where is the dastardly beast? Still trapped in the toilet?" Goober ambled into the living room and sniffed around. "Woo doggy. Peed all over the place, huh?"

My face flushed with heat. "Yes. Sure did," I lied.

Goober put a finger to his lips to silence me. He craned an ear in the direction of the bathroom. I watched from the living room as he tiptoed down the hallway toward it. He leaned over and stuck a big ear on the bathroom door. After a moment of hearing nothing, he tapped his knuckles lightly on the door. Charmine let out a barrage of squeaky barks that sounded like someone stomping on a rubber duck.

"Dang. How *big* is that thing?"

"I dunno," I whispered. "Too much fur to tell, but I'd say well under ten pounds."

"Ten pounds?" Goober whistled and shook his head. "Fartknockers. It's always the little ones that are so vicious. Sneaky, quick little jerks, too." He walked back down the hallway and joined me in the living room.

"So what's the plan?" I asked.

"Plan?" Goober flopped onto my ruined couch. "I thought *you* had a plan."

"Crap, Goober! I don't know how to deal with a *dog!*"

"Then why the flippin' shizzle did you get one?"

"I *didn't!* It's *Milly's.* She asked me to pet sit for her."

Goober picked up a tuft of pillow stuffing next to a maimed pillow. "So this isn't some deranged wild animal that got loose in your house?"

"No."

"Well it sure tore up the place." Goober's eyes shifted from the tuft of stuffing to me. "What did you do to set it off?"

"What?" I protested. "Nothing! I swear!"

"There had to be some kind of trigger." Goober looked around again. "I mean, this place is a wreck!"

"Maybe Tom is right, Goober. He said dogs can smell emotions. Maybe it can smell my fear."

Goober laughed. "Don't tell me the mighty Valiant Stranger is afraid of dogs?"

I folded my arms over my chest and scowled.

Goober hitched up an eyebrow. "Well, that explains why you freaked out over our pet-cremation services."

I shook my head. "How does that...? Listen. Don't start. I don't need to be teased right now, Goober. I need *help*. I mean, *look* at this place!"

Goober's sarcastic face softened and he removed his hockey mask hat. "I didn't know Vance and Milly had a dog."

I sighed. "They didn't. She and Vance found it while they were in Hawaii. They brought it home with them."

Goober bit his lip and his face turned serious. "Hmmm." He smoothed his bushy moustache with his thumb and forefinger, then ran his hand over his bald head. "Hawaii, huh? Not good, Val."

"What do you mean, 'not good'?"

"I heard if you bring a native dog back from Hawaii, you'll be cursed by Peg-Leg forever. Unless you return said dog to the exact spot from which you absconded with it."

"Arrgh!" I cried out in exasperation. "That's *Pele's* curse, Goober! And it's for *lava rocks*, not dogs."

Goober shrugged. "Have it your way. But it looks like you've been cursed pretty well by it already."

I stared at the hole in my couch. "You have a point." I flopped into the easy chair opposite the couch. "What am I gonna do? Milly's supposed to pick the dog up at five-thirty. I can't just tell her to go fish her out of the toilet."

"Her?"

"The *dog!*" I yelled in frustration.

"I know!" Goober yelled back. "What I meant was, is the dog a 'her?' A female?"

"Yes."

Goober grinned. "Well, why didn't you say so in the first place?"

I eyed him, confused. "That makes a differ-ence?"

"Of course it does." Goober smiled and waggled the bushy eyebrows on his peanut-shaped head. "All the women love me. You should know that by now. I'm the quintessential Alpha male."

Goober got up off the couch and marched down the hallway. I flinched and held my breath when I heard him open the bathroom door. I looked around for something to defend myself. I grabbed my copy of *Love's Lusty Love.*

"Well, hello, little princess!" I heard Goober say. Charmine let out a yip. A moment later, he walked down the hallway with Charmine in his arms, licking his chin as if it had been recently dunked in beef stew. Knowing Goober, the possibility couldn't be ruled out.

"Isn't she the cutest?" Goober asked, grinning like a door-to-door salesman just to get my goat. "How could you hate such a loveable little ball of fluffiness?"

"You've got to be kidding me," I said dully.

Goober laughed. "She's harmless, Val. Being in a strange place probably just scared the crap out of her. But you don't have to worry about that now. There's no more crap left in her. It's all over your bathroom floor." Goober looked down at the pup. "You did that, didn't you, girlie!"

Charmine licked Goober's chin again. From a distance of about ten feet, she looked adorable. Maybe Goober was right. She'd just been scared when she woke up in that stroller all alone in a strange house. Maybe she'd just been acting out her fears while I'd snored away, oblivious in bed. Maybe I'd startled her by screaming in horror at the mess she'd made of my living room. Maybe I'd read her all wrong.

I walked up to Goober and raised a hand to pet Charmine. As soon as my fingers were within striking distance, she snarled and lunged for them. Her sharp little teeth snapped within a hair's breadth of my thumb. "What the hell!" I screeched.

"Whoa!" Goober said. He yanked Charmine away just in time to save my finger from amputation.

I beat a hasty, three-step retreat. "I don't get it," I said, shaking my head. "What's going on here?"

Charmine growled at me while Goober shrugged. "I'd say she smells fear, all right. I have to say, if this is the general reaction you get from dogs, it's no wonder you hate 'em."

"Geez, Goober! What am I gonna do?"

"Well, might I suggest you not make a huge investment in rawhide chew toys? And I can see now a career in international pet sitting is definitely out the window."

"Hardy-har-har." I sneered. "Dang it, Goober. This is a *disaster*. Could you do me a favor? Just stay here until Milly comes to pick up Charmine? Just hand Miss Monster there off to Milly and this nightmare will be over."

"Her name's Charmine? Aww. How cute!" Goober fawned over the little ball of fur in his arms. "Is that your name, little one?" he cooed. He looked up at me and his smile evaporated, replaced by a mocking, slant-eyed glare. "What's in it for me, dog hater?"

"Dinner and a beer?"

Goober grinned and sighed. "Ah. Back to working for food again. Well, at least this time I don't have to make a cardboard sign."

Chapter Six

Following the ransom protocol I saw in a crummy movie, I made Milly hand over the eighty-five bucks before Goober handed over Charmine. As I stuffed the cash into my pocket, I watched Milly go gaga over being reunited with her fluffy ball of fur and fangs.

"Oooooh! Who's my good girl?" Milly practically drooled as she made googly eyes at the sneaky little pillow shredder. Charmine should have gotten an Oscar for acting adorable.

With my sandals destroyed and my couch in tatters, I figured I'd ended the day about $815 in the hole. I bit my lip and decided to let it slide. At least I'd never have to see that mangy little home-wrecker again.

"Val?"

I blinked. Milly was staring at me. "Huh?" I asked, dazed and confused. I couldn't possibly have heard what I thought she'd just said.

"I *said*, I found a sitter," Milly repeated, "but she can't start until Thursday. Could you take care of Charmine again tomorrow?"

Oh, crap on a cracked-up crappy cracker! Panic shot through me like a bad oyster. I looked over at Goober. He nodded at me reassuringly. I forced my jaw open enough to mutter, "Sure."

"You're a doll!" Milly said. "Want to kiss Charmine goodbye?" She held the pup toward me. Its doggy smile started to morph into a menacing snarl.

"Uh...no, that's okay," I said, my eyes locked on Charmine's sharp little incisors. "I'll see her again soon enough."

Milly shrugged. "All right then." She put Charmine in the stroller and pushed it toward the front door. "Oh, boy!" she said to Charmine in baby talk. "We're off to go see daddy now! Say goodbye to Aunt Val and Uncle Goober!"

"Bye-bye," Goober said and smiled at me with one side of his mouth.

I waved a weak goodbye and shut the door behind Milly and her demented Pomeranian. As soon as the door clicked behind me, my whole body nearly melted with relief. Then I thought about tomorrow and it knotted up again.

"Goober!" I said, wild-eyed. "What have I done?"

Goober snorted. "A favor for a friend, Val. It's not the apocalypse, you know."

I sighed. "Geez. Are you sure? Look around!"

Goober surveyed my decimated living room, then patted me on the back. "You'll survive. So where's my beer?"

"Right." I forced a smile and padded toward the kitchen. "One beer coming up."

Goober followed me and plopped down on a barstool at the counter. I fished around in the fridge and pulled out a Fosters. "Enjoy it. It's the last one."

"What? Out of beer?" Goober cried. "Now *that's* the apocalypse."

I started to laugh, but it caught in my throat and hitched into a crying gasp. I turned my back to Goober to hide my face. As a ploy, I opened the freezer door and fumbled around for my bottle of Tanqueray. But my ruse didn't fool Goober.

"What's wrong, Val?"

I turned around and unscrewed the cap on the emerald-green bottle of gin. "Don't tell Tom."

Goober's bushy left eyebrow hitched up at the center. "Tell him *what?*"

"*That I hate dogs!*" I screeched. I started to reach for a glass, then thought, *what the hell.* I tipped the bottle of gin over my mouth and poured a shot straight into my open maw.

"Whoa!" Goober laughed. "And I thought *I* was hard core."

I frowned and wiped my chin. "I'm sorry. It's just that...you know how people feel about people who hate dogs."

"Whatever do you mean?" Goober teased and took a slug of beer. "Please. Enlighten me."

"You know *exactly* what I'm talking about. People think you're some kind of heartless psycho if you don't like dogs. I mean, dog haters are ranked two notches below serial killers!"

"I think that may be an exaggeration," Goober deadpanned. His head tilted to the right and his eyebrows met in the middle of his forehead. His mouth twisted to one side of his face. "Not much of one, but still...."

The front door opened. "I'm home!" Tom called out.

I slammed the cap on the bottle of gin and crammed it back in the freezer. "We're in here!" I called back. I shot a desperate look at Goober. "Not a word! I'm begging you!"

Goober grinned under his moustache. "Aww. You're so cute when you beg."

"WHAT HAPPENED TO THE couch?" Tom asked.

"Well, that's a funny story," Goober said, his words muffled by a mouthful of pizza.

I'd bought Goober's silence with beer and an extra-large pepperoni from Fat Jack's Pizza. While Tom changed out of his police uniform and showered, I'd made the call and had the pizza delivered, along with an emergency six-pack of beer.

"Yeah, a really funny story," I said. I smiled at Goober with every feature on my face except my eyes. They were too busy pleading.

"Oh yeah?" Tom asked. He looked over at me for an explanation.

I had nothing. So I stared harder at Goober. "*You* tell him, why don't you?"

"Well, you see, I was entertaining Val and Charmine with my knife-twirling act. You know, from my circus days."

I cringed. *Oh, crap!*

"Oh yeah," Tom said and leaned back on the couch. "Back when you performed down on Beach Drive. What did you call yourself?"

"Le fart-head," I said.

Goober scrunched his face in indignation. "If you're referring to my performance as a *fartiste*, I was modeling my *flatulist* act after my famous ancestor, Le Petomane. It's French."

"It *stinks*," I sneered.

Goober's eyebrows formed one hairy pyramid in the center of his forehead. "Not as much as something *else* that's going on here."

That shut me up.

"What do you mean?" Tom asked.

"Well, Charmine had a little accident," I blurted. "I had to clean it up."

"Oh," Tom said, not totally convinced. "I told you to get some baggies."

"Yes, well, you were right. I should have listened," I said too agreeably.

The unusualness of my subservient manner made Tom even more suspicious. He turned and studied me with his cop-trained, investigative eyes. "Well, other than that, how was your day with the little pooch, Val?"

"Really good," I lied.

Tom smiled oddly. "I see," was all he said.

AS GOOBER MADE HIS exit, I promised him more pizza and beer where that came from if he returned tomorrow. I left Tom in the living room and got ready for bed. After such a horrific day, I was craving some time to myself. But that just wasn't going to happen. When I got done in the bathroom, I headed to bed to read a little. *Alone.* But Tom had beaten me to the punch. When I walked in the bedroom, he was already nestled into the bed covers, reading a book.

I snatched *Love's Lusty Love* out of his hand.

"That's *my* novel!" I groused.

"Excuse me," Tom said, and showed me his open palms. "I didn't know it was off limits."

"Well...it's not." I put the novel on the nightstand and climbed into bed beside him. "It's just that, you know, I could really use—"

"What?" Tom asked, and smiled softly at me. "A kiss? A backrub?"

I sighed. All things considered, those sounded like reasonable alternatives. "Do I have to choose just one?"

"Nope." Tom kissed me, then gently rolled me over on my tummy. "You really enjoyed that little doggie today, didn't you?"

My body stiffened. "Sure. It was nice. The company, you know. But I'd hate to leave a dog like that alone all day. It's not fair."

Tom dug his thumbs into my shoulder blades. "Ugh," I groaned. It hurt so good.

"You're kind of tense tonight," he said as his hands moved to the base of my neck. The gentle pressure had me melting under his touch. "But what if you *weren't* gone all day?"

"What do you mean?" I managed between moans.

Tom kneaded my back. "What if you stayed home and worked? You're always talking about going back to writing again. You could quit your job with Milly at the accounting firm and stay home and write."

I flipped over to face Tom. "What's brought *this* on?"

Tom shrugged. "I dunno. I was just thinking."

"It's a nice idea. But who'd pay the bills?"

Tom kissed me on the nose. "Well, if we got rid of *my* place, we'd cut our expenses in half. We could definitely make it on my salary until your career got on its feet."

My brain started firing randomly like a nuclear reactor gone critical. *Dang! I could go back to writing! But I'd be dependent on Tom. I could do something interesting again! But Tom would be living here. I'd be free from pantyhose forever! But I'd lose my personal freedom. I'd have a financial safety net....*

Then a wicked sound like a needle scratching over a spinning vinyl record stopped my brain in its rutted tracks. *Hold on there just a minute, Val! Are you really gonna fall for that horse hockey for a* fourth *time? What kind of fool are you?*

I blinked hard and my mind came screeching back to my current plane of existence. I'd been so far away traversing the dead past and the imagined future that it was almost a surprise to find Tom lying there in bed beside me, smiling softly, his sea-green eyes twinkling at me.

"You're actually thinking about it," he said. His smile deepened until his dimples kicked in.

"Yes, I actually am."

And thank goodness you can't read my thoughts.

Chapter Seven

Five minutes after Tom left for work, the doorbell rang. I sighed with relief. Milly would be here in around ten minutes, so Goober was right on time.

I flung open the door. "Hey, Goob—"

I lowered my gaze about a foot. "Winky. What are *you* doing here?"

"Nice to see you, too, Val," Winky said, and ambled inside.

"I...uh...was expecting Goober."

"Yeah. He couldn't make it. Sends his gondolances."

"*Con*dolences," I corrected as I shut the door.

"*Con*dolences?" Winky scratched his ginger buzz-cut. "You sure about that?"

"Yep. Pretty sure."

"Huh." Winky cocked his freckled head. "I always wondered what some I-talian boat had to do with—"

"Winky!" I grumbled, cutting him off. "Why isn't *Goober* here?"

"Well, I figured you knowed already. Today's the all-day marathon of *Gilligan's Island* on TNT. You can't expect Goober to miss out on *that*."

"What? Why not?"

Winky shrugged and scratched the smiling beer mug on the faded t-shirt stretched tight across his belly. "Goober's uncle played that one part that one time. You know, the one where that one fella did, oh, what was it now?"

"Ugh! Forget it!"

"I thought you'd be glad to see me, seein's how you're a-feared of dogs and all."

"Goober *told* you?" I heard a sound outside and peeked out the window. "Dang it! Milly's here already. Hide!"

"Huh? What for? You 'shamed a' me or somethin'?"

I looked Winky up and down. Despite the fact that he was barefoot, dressed like he fell out of a dumpster and smelled like garlic mothballs, surprisingly, I wasn't ashamed of him. I just didn't trust his big mouth. "No...it's not that...."

Milly rapped on the door. "Just don't say anything stupid, okay?"

Winky nodded and twisted the key in an imaginary lock on his pooched-out lips.

I shook my head and opened the door. Milly came barging in with that blasted stroller like it was BOGO day at Walmart. I took a wary glance inside the stroller. To my inestimable relief, Charmine was fast asleep, just as she had been yesterday.

"Isn't she so cute?" Milly whispered. "Silly girl. The car ride puts her right to sleep." She took her eyes off precious Charmine long enough to notice Winky standing nearby. "Oh...hey, Winky. I didn't see your van outside."

"Mornin' Milly." Winky nodded and took a step toward the stroller. "Winnie dropped me off on her way to work." He looked down at Charmine. "So this here's the little monst—"

"Winky's going to help me around the house," I blurted, then shot Winky a hard look. "*Aren't* you, Winky?"

Winky blinked at me blankly. "Huh? Oh. Yeah. Her plumbin's all stopped up. Speakin' of plumbin', can I use your'n?"

"Ugh! Yes!" I said. "Just go do your business. But hurry!"

"What's the hurry?" Milly asked.

"I just...uh...want Winky to be here when Charmine wakes up. Uh...she's *so cute* when she wakes up from her little nappy poo," I cooed in baby talk, immediately loathing myself for it.

Milly eyed me with surprise. "I almost thought you didn't like Charmine." She elbowed me and grinned. "Turns out you're an old softie like me."

I plastered on a fake smile. "Old softie, that's me."

"I *like* me a softie," Winky said. "'Specially on the toilet."

Milly and I exchanged "I-don't-want-to-know" glances.

"I thought you were going to the bathroom," I hissed at Winky.

"All right, already! I'm on it," he said. He made a goofy face, lifted his elbows, kicked out a knee and exited the scene like a cartoon character.

"He is *so* weird," Milly said as she watched him exit, stage left. "Well, I've got to get to work. I'll just kiss Charmine—"

I yanked Milly by the arm. "No! Don't! You might...wake her up."

Milly grinned. "You *are* an old softie. Okay. See you after work. You three have a fun day!"

I eased the door closed behind Milly, tiptoed around the stroller and padded down the hallway. Winky was in the john belting out a Willy Nelson tune. "Be quiet and do your business!" I shushed.

Winky called back. "Which is it, Val? You want me to be quiet or do my business?"

I tried, unsuccessfully, not to roll my eyes. "Just do your business. And hurry up!"

While Winky was in the bathroom finishing *On the Road Again* and who knows what else, I watched Charmine from a safe distance, my stomach gnawing with dread. When she whined in her sleep, an electric bolt of panic shot through me. *I need protection from that mangy little throat ripper!* A thought struck me. I ran out to the garage and grabbed the laundry basket. I snuck up on tip-toes and carefully positioned the basket over the top of the stroller like a plastic cage....

"He he he he he he!" A sound like a deranged woodpecker startled me out of my skin. I jump six inches off the ground and whipped around to face Winky. He was red faced from laughing at me.

"Gaul-dang it, Val! You really *are* a-feared of dogs."

"I am *not!*" I protested too loudly. Charmine yawned and cracked open an eye. I slammed the basket over the stroller and jumped back a foot. "Get her out! *Now!*" I screeched.

"Geezy Pete, Val. Just where in tarnation you 'spect me to go?"

"Outside! Take her outside. *Now!*"

I scrambled to the glass sliding doors that led to the backyard and yanked one side open. "This way. Come on!"

"Yes, ma'am." Winky said and pushed the stroller across the living room like the proud, redneck inventor of the first upturned laundry basket on wheels. To my dismay, he stopped at the door's threshold and said, "Can I at least get us some water first?"

Charmine yipped. My spine straightened.

"Milly put special water in the stroller," I blurted. "Move it!"

"Oh," Winky said. He pulled a water bottle out of the holder in the stroller while my anxiety level shot through the roof. "Well wasn't that thoughty of her. I ain't tried this here kind a special water before."

"It's for the dog."

Charmine opened her eyes and looked around. She spotted me and her beady little eyes narrowed to slits.

"Then where's my water?" Winky whined.

"Arggh! I'll get you a bottle, okay? Just get out of here!" I scooted behind Winky and shoved him out the door with both hands, then slammed the sliding door shut, nearly catching Winky's heel in the process.

"Hey! Watch it!" Winky said through the glass.

"Sorry. But you haven't seen that little monster when she's conscious!"

Winky eyed Charmine's fancy water bottle, still in his hand. "Val, could you run my water through the percolator first?"

Charmine's little black nose poked out from under the laundry basket. She eyed me through a hole and snarled. My gut flopped.

"Percolator?" I asked. Then it hit me. "Oh. Sure. Cream and sugar, right?"

"Right-o," Winky beamed.

The sound of my voice must have set Charmine off. She started yapping her little head off like a rabid rubber duck.

"Well, look who's awake!" Winky said. He lifted the laundry basket up and bent over the stroller. Charmine leapt at Winky. He caught her in his arms.

"Watch out!" I cried in horror.

"For what? Too many kisses?" Winky asked, as Charmine covered his neck and face with friendly licks from her long, pink tongue.

I scowled. "Yes. That's it. For too many kisses."

WHEN I STUCK MY HAND out the sliding door to hand Winky his coffee, Charmine lunged at me. I managed to slam the sliding door shut just in time—right on my own big toe.

"Ooowww!" I howled.

As I hopped around and cursed up a blue streak, Winky watched my display through the glass door, doubled over with laughter. He spilled half his coffee, then followed Charmine's lead and started howling at me.

"Very funny," I grumbled. But I wasn't amused. I wasn't exactly mad, either. As I glared back at them through the glass, I felt like the odd man out—the kid not picked for kickball—the nerd stuck inside while all the cool kids played in the backyard without me.

I watched with envy as that little she-devil Charmine romped around with Winky like he was her new best pal. She hated my guts. Why?

Did I have doggie cooties or something?

I fixed myself a Tanqueray and tonic and pondered that thought, along with the unexpected proposal Tom had suggested last night. Did I want to restart my old career as an advertising writer? Or try my hand as a would-be novelist? Creating a snappy radio jingle *did* seem more appealing than making coffee and schlepping tax files at Griffith & Maas. Or maybe I could do something totally different. Like write a self-help book for people who hated dogs...

A rap at the back door made me look up. Winky was staring at me through pudgy-finger binoculars. I got off the couch and padded to the door.

"I'm starvin," he said through the glass. "And I done ate all the snacks."

He held an empty bag of bacon-flavored treats upside-down.

"Winky! Those were for Charmine."

Winky eyed the bag and shrugged. "Huh. You should 'a been more 'pacific."

I blew out a breath. "What do you want for lunch?"

Winky licked his freckled lips. I didn't even know lips could get freckles. "I sure could go for me a fish sandwich."

"Okay. Is there any food left for Charmine?"

"Yeah. I didn't like the kibble too much. Tasted like cat."

My nose crinkled. "How do you know...ugh...Never mind. You like tartar sauce on it, right?"

"Only on fish. Not on cat."

"Got it. Be back in a few."

Chapter Eight

I'd planned to take my sweet time during my lunch escape from Winky and Charmine, but the sky made me hurry home from the drive-thru instead. On the western horizon over the Gulf of Mexico, slate-blue clouds had begun to gather. As I watched them turn dark purple, I knew it was a sure-fire sign Mother Nature was getting ready to bless us with another tropical thunderstorm. Being the middle of May, we were definitely due for one. But as much as we needed the rain, on the drive back home I prayed it would hold off at least until tonight. I didn't want to think about what might happen if Charmine, the fuzzy little couch mauler, got loose inside my house again.

I pulled up in the driveway, then hit the switch on Maggie's rag top. I drummed my nails on the steering wheel and practiced a deep breathing relaxation technique as the convertible top slowly arched up, then over the seats. The can-opener whine of the motor ceased and the top collapsed onto the windshield frame like a worn-out floozy. I knew how it felt. The stress of dealing with Charmine had worn me to a frazzle, too.

I fastened the top's chrome latches into place and texted Winky. He met me at the side gate to the backyard, where I handed over the food, a safe distance from Charmine's snapping jaws.

"Hee hee!" Winky laughed as he snatched up the bags. "Look-it you, Val. Scared of a lil' ol' ball a fluff. What is Charmine, anyways. Some kind 'a miniature fox?"

"No. She's a miniature *Cujo.*"

I stomped off as Winky howled with laughter. I yanked open the front door and kicked off my sandals, sending them flying across the room. I plopped my butt down on a stool at the kitchen counter and tore open the fast-food bag. *Crap.* They'd forgotten my fries. As I nibbled sullenly on my cheeseburger, I watched the *Charmine & Winky Show* through the sliding glass doors. They were having a blast. It just wasn't fair!

Winky was perched on a barstool at the tiki hut, gobbling his lunch like he was in some kind of county-fair sandwich-eating contest. He devoured it in six bites while Charmine danced at his feet for scraps and fries. *My* fries. I didn't know if a dog should be eating that stuff or not, but what Milly didn't know wouldn't hurt her, I guess. Besides, that would have been the least of my lies to her about Charmine.

I scowled at myself. It wasn't like me to be envious. Or to lie to my best friend. I was about to feel bad when the universe sent me some comic relief. Winky slapped a hand to his forehead. Apparently, his vanilla shake had given him a brain freeze. I snorted with laughter.

Imagine that. Who knew Winky even had a brain to freeze?

I got up and padded over to the sliding glass door. "Put your garbage in the laundry basket and hand it over," I called out through the one-inch slit I'd opened up.

Winky grabbed the basket and tossed his wrappers in it. When he got to the door, he shook his head and chuckled. "I got news for you Val. This here basket ain't gonna fit through that there hole."

"I know!" I hissed. "Put the basket on the ground, then hold onto Charmine."

"All right, already. Hold your horses!" Winky said. "What's wrong with you, anyways?" Then he smiled. "Oh, yeah. Yore one a them weirdos that don't like dogs."

Winky laughed at his own joke while I scowled at him like a church lady at a harlot convention. One glimpse of my face sent his eyebrows up to his buzz cut. He snapped to attention and grabbed Charmine up in his arms.

"Coast is clear," he said.

I slung open the door, snatched the laundry basket and slammed the door shut again.

"Hey, Val?"

"What."

"Too bad you don't got no rod 'n' reel," Winky said as Charmine licked his lips. He nodded his head back toward the inlet to the Intracoastal Waterway. It marked the backyard property line of my little 1950's ranch house. "You got all this good fishin' water goin' to waste out here."

"I don't fish," I grumbled through the glass door. "You need anything else?"

"Gotta tinkle."

I shot him another church-lady scowl. He almost wilted.

"No problem. Me and Charmine can take care of ourselves in that department."

I sighed. "Super. Glad to hear it."

Winky picked up a stick and tossed it toward the fire pit. Charmine bounded off after it.

"I just don't get it," I mumbled to myself as I threw the fast-food wrappers in the kitchen trash bin. "Why doesn't that dog like me?" I headed out into the garage with the laundry basket. As I set it on top of the washing machine, I noticed a fishing rod leaning on the wall between the washer and some storage shelves. It wasn't *mine*, so it had to be *Tom's*.

My gut roiled. *Tom never said anything to me about putting a fishing rod out here.* More importantly, he'd never *asked if it was okay.* I yanked the rod and reel away from the wall. As I held it in my hands, a wave of confusing feelings swirled through my head. On the one hand, I was angry; He should have asked my permission! On the other hand, I was riddled with anxiety; He was creeping into my space, bit by bit! But then again, there was something oddly, yet deeply comforting about holding something of Tom's in my hand, knowing that he was near....

Clarity hit me between the eyes like a rubber bullet from a .357 Magnum.

Oh. My. Lord. This was the exact *same diabolical, schizophrenic, unsolvable conundrum that had plagued me through all my past relationships! Here I was, once again hurtling down a road that, three times already, had dead-ended in disaster and ruin.* It was the ultimate Catch 22.

Guys. You can't live with them...you can't live without them.

Flippin' Jehoshaphat! What was I going to do? I couldn't afford to let myself get swept down the drain again! I scowled at the fishing rod as if it were to blame for every bad relationship since Eve met Adam. I throttled it, carted it inside, and banged it against the glass door until I got Winky's attention. He came trotting up.

"Woo doggy!" he said. "Now that's what I'm talkin' about, Val! That's a Shimano Stella and a genu-wine Waterloo. And looky there. Already decked out with an all-purpose saltwater jig. Perfect!"

"Huh?" I grunted. Winky couldn't conjugate verbs, but he could brand-ID fishing equipment at twenty paces. *Guys!* I cracked open the door. "I think it's Tom's."

"He won't mind?"

"Not at all." *Finders keepers losers weepers.*

Winky beamed like it was the first day of hunting season. "Thanky, Val! Always wanted to try me one of these." He grabbed for it through the slit in the door just as Charmine came bounding toward us.

"Hurry!" I said.

Winky pulled. The rod made it through, but the reel got stuck. It wasn't going to budge, either, until I slid the door open another couple inches. But that wasn't gonna happen. Not with Charmine's little razor jaws on the other side, barking out another demented, squeeze-toy tirade.

"You want the reel, you're gonna have to get her away from me!" I groused.

"Boy, you got a bad case of the crabs today, Val," Winky said. He put a hand down to block Charmine and opened the door just enough to pull the reel through. As soon as it cleared, I slammed the door shut again.

Winky wrung his hand at the near miss. "Gaul-dang, Val! Why you so afraid of dogs, anyways? Goober never did say why."

"Does it matter?" I sneered. "And I told Goober not to tell anybody. So much for confidentiality."

"Way I heared it, you told him not to tell *Tom*. Well, I ain't Tom."

I shot Winky a stare that could melt lava. "No. You're not." *But you're a guy, so you're guilty by association.*

Winky stared back at me, an open, curious expression on his face. "So, why you hate God's poor little critters, Val?"

"Because *they* hate *me*, Winky!" I shrieked. "Just look at Charmine." The sight of her bared fangs caused me to instinctively cover my neck with my right hand. "She'd go for my jugular if she had the chance!"

Winky looked surprised. "Gaul-dang, Val. I didn't know you had you your very own *juggler*. I seen a guy juggle three chainsaws once at the county fair. Wat'n easy, either. Feller only had six fingers amongst both his given hands."

"Fascinating," I said, grinding my teeth. I looked down, then around. "Hey. Where's Charmine?"

Winky glanced to his left, then hitched a thumb in that direction. "She's over there digging a hole." He shrugged. "Dogs 'll be dogs, Val."

My fists clenched and my eyes turned to slits. "Yes, they most certainly *will*."

Chapter Nine

"Laverne, we've gotta think of something fast," I said into the phone as I flopped on the couch. "I found Tom's fishing rod in the garage."

"So?"

"He never asked me if he could keep it there."

I could almost hear the old woman gasp from her house next door. "Good lord, Val! This is getting worse by the day! Can you believe it? J.D. left his coffee cup in the sink this morning!"

"Unbelievable!" I commiserated. "It's not fair, Laverne. They move in and expect us to be their cooks, maids and housekeepers! We gotta figure out some way to keep these guys from weaseling in and taking over our lives. You got any ideas?"

"Well," Laverne hemmed and hawed. "I've been watching *Forensic Files*. Maybe we could poison 'em?"

"I was thinking of something a little less drastic."

"Oh."

"But let's keep that as Plan B."

"Right."

I glanced out the sliding glass doors and did a double-take. Charmine ran by carrying something's detached head in her sharp little jaws. Either that, or she'd morphed into a four-eyed monster. The way I felt about her, it really could have gone either way.

"I gotta go, Laverne. Keep thinking and I'll talk to you later."

I clicked off the phone and pressed my nose to the glass door. Charmine strutted over to Winky and dropped a fish head at his feet. Winky laughed, picked it up and tossed it across the yard. Charmine took off after it. As disgusting as *that* was, another look at Winky made me forgot all about it. That red-headed redneck was gutting fish in my tiki hut!

"Winky!" I called through a paper-thin opening in the door. He couldn't hear me. I slid the glass open another fraction of an inch. "Winky!"

He looked up and grinned. "Hey, Val-Pal! Caught me a mess a sheepshead! Lookee here!" He held up a stout, grey fish with bluish-black stripes. It was the size and shape of a dinner plate.

"Why are you cleaning fish in my hut?" I screeched. "You're getting scales and guts all over the place!"

Winky looked around at the mess as if he were surprised by it himself. "Huh. Oh well. Don't you worry none, Val," he hollered. "I know how to clean up after myself."

Yeah. Right. As if any man did.

I felt something cold and slimy land on my foot. I looked down to find a pair of dead eyes staring up at me. It was a bloody fish head.

"Aargh!" I jerked my foot away, then tried to kick the disgusting head back through the narrow slit in the door. Charmine seized the opportunity to snap at my toes like a starving gator in a cheap fur coat. Her little face was smeared with blood. Her once-fluffy pelt was matted with dirt and slime. She looked like some post-apocalyptic, zombie-Pom.

"Get away from me!" I squealed, and slammed the door shut.

"Ha ha! She really *don't* like you, does she?" Winky called out. He set his knife on the tiki hut counter and walked over. Charmine trotted happily by his feet.

"I *told* you she didn't! Just look at her, Winky! She's a mess! You're gonna have to bathe her before Milly gets here."

Winky shrugged and scratched his naked beer belly. "Not a problem. Gimme a washtub and some shampoo and I'll take care of it. Could I get a baggie, too? For my fish filets?"

I blew out a breath like an overheated steam valve. "Sure," I muttered to myself. "Always happy when I'm waiting on a man." I found a box of quart-sized baggies in the cupboard and handed him one through a narrow slit in the door as Charmine and I eyed each other warily.

"I might need me two," Winky said. "Oh, Val! You won't believe this! When I throwed them fish guts in the water, somethin' went to chompin' on em like a pile a them...what'cha call it...*per honor* fish."

"Piranhas?" I pushed another baggie through the slit in the door.

Winky grinned. "Yeah, that's the ones."

"Here's some paper towels to wipe down the tiki hut," I said, shoving them through the slit. "I don't want to find any fish guts out there later, stinking up the place."

"Yes ma'am," Winky saluted. He started to turn, then looked back at me. "Hey Val, what do you call a fish with no eye?"

"I dunno."

"A fsh."

I grinned despite myself. "Shut up and get to work. I'll fetch the shampoo."

"NOW DO LIKE I SAID, Winky. Don't let that darn dog get within six feet of me!"

Milly was walking up the driveway. Earlier that afternoon, after the dog's bath, I'd figured out Charmine's threshold of crazy. I realized that if I stayed around six feet away from her, she, for the most part, ignored me. Any closer and she started to go nutso.

"All right already, cool your jets," Winky said. "I got this."

The doorbell rang. "You answer the door," I instructed. "I'll stand over here by the hallway, out of the way."

"I tole you already I got it. Now git!"

Winky shooed me with one freckled hand and gripped Charmine tight with the other. I held my breath as Winky opened the door. Despite his best efforts, including a liberal dose of my Silky Strands hair conditioner, Winky had failed miserably at moonlighting as a canine hair stylist. Charmine looked as if she'd stuck a paw in an electrical outlet. Her coat was as round as a frizzy beach ball. I couldn't tell one end of her from the other, but at least she didn't smell like a dead fish.

"Hey Winky," Milly said as the door opened. "And there's my Charmine!" She stepped up and eagerly grabbed for her precious fur baby, but due to the frizz, she couldn't decide on the proper angle of approach. "What happened?" she asked.

"We gave her a bath," I said from my safe distance.

"A bath?" Milly asked. "Why?"

"Yes'm. It's all part of our complete pet-carin' service," Winky said proudly as he handed over Charmine. I grimaced as the tongue that had been carrying around dead fish heads all day now licked at Milly's open, smiling lips.

"Awww," Milly cooed and patted Charmine's head. "That's so sweet of you! Val, it makes me wish I could keep you on as her sitter."

"Yeah, too bad," I said. "But you found someone else. Right?" *For Pete's sake! You better have!*

"Yes. She starts tomorrow. It's a Friday. I figured it's better that way. The new sitter will just have Charmine the one day to start. To kind of get Charmine used to her, you know?"

I nodded. Milly nuzzled her precious pooch. "Then we'll have the whole weekend together, won't we, doodle-bug?" Charmine French-kissed Milly. I stifled a gag as Milly looked up at me. "That way, it's not too traumatic for her, you know?"

"Right," I said. "We wouldn't want poor, delicate little Charmine to be traumatized."

Milly tilted her head and smiled. "Thanks for understanding, Val. Here you go." She took a step toward me with the cash, Charmine in her arms.

"Stop!" I held up my hands. "Uh...you can give the money to Winky," I blurted.

Milly gave me a curious stare-down.

"Well, uh...you see...Val there's comin' down with a cold," Winky said. "Didn't want to give it to little Charmine, here."

Milly's face melted into a sweet smile. "Val. Sometimes you surprise me. I had no idea you loved animals so much."

I smiled and shrugged. "Who doesn't love dogs?"

Winky looked at me. "I thought you said—"

"Winky, take the cash!" I blurted.

"Here it is. Eighty-five dollars," Milly said. "Well, we're off to our castle!" Milly said, her attention fixated again on Charmine.

"And you're off to your prince charming," I added, doing my best not to sound sarcastic. But I wasn't happy about this whole Charmine business. Not one bit. That little ingrate in a fur suit was quickly turning all my buddies into syrupy-sweet saps.

"Toodles!" Milly said brightly, as if to prove my point. She gave Winky and me a silly finger wave, then took one of Charmine's paws and waved it at us. "Say bye-bye, Charmine!" She put her darling pooch in the stroller and pushed it out the door three seconds before I lost it. I closed the door behind me and leaned against it.

"Thank God that's over," I muttered. "I owe you for that 'cold' excuse, Winky. Thanks."

Winky smiled and shrugged one shoulder. "Weren't nothin'."

"Can I give you a ride up to Davie's Donuts? The first one's on me."

Winky grinned like a rotten Halloween pumpkin. "Sure thang. Hey! Did I tell you? Winnie's been 'sperimentin' on new donut flavors.

She called this mornin'. Said she's got one called the 'peanut-butter and bacon bomb.' I been chompin' at the bit all day to try it."

"That sounds amazing," I lied. "Let's go."

Chapter Ten

"This is hands-down the best thing I've ever eaten," I said to Winnie as she watched me anxiously through her red-framed eyeglasses. I scarfed another bite of the gooey, sweet-and-salty donut. "Who knew peanut butter and bacon went so well with vanilla custard?" I mumbled through another mouthful.

"Tol' ya." Winky said, elbowing me from the adjacent stool at the dining counter inside Davie's Donuts. He nodded proudly at his girlfriend Winnie, who ran the small, '50's-style donut shop when Davie was away. "She's my lil' donut darlin', ain't you?" Winky garbled through his own mouthful of Winnie's amazing donut concoction.

Winnie blushed. Her chubby face gleamed with an ear-to-ear grin that was in serious danger of splitting her head in two. "That does it!" she said. "*That's* the one I'm entering in the magazine contest."

"What contest?" I managed, just before circumstances beyond my self-control caused me to cram the remaining chunk of peanut-butter bomb into my eager mouth.

"The Desserts for Dollars competition in *Betty Cracker* magazine," Winnie said. She bent down and fished a magazine out from under the chrome-rimmed counter and opened it to a page she'd earmarked. Pictured on the contest page were enough cakes, pies and cookies to send all of Pinellas County straight into sugar comas.

"Wow," I said, and washed down the remnants of my donut with a slurp of coffee. That looks like some pretty tough competition."

Winnie frowned with uncertainty. "You don't think my donuts are good enough?"

"Oh, no!" I rebutted. "I didn't say that. That was the best thing I've eaten in like...*forever!* But to be honest, I've never heard of *Betty Cracker.*"

"It's new. Kind of like *Southern Living* meets *Guns and Ammo,*" Winnie explained.

"Yeah. If she wins, she'll get fifty grand and a lifetime supply of shotgun shells," Winky said.

"Well, I gotta tell you, Winnie, you've got my vote," I said. "Just one question."

Winnie leaned her plump torso over the counter. "What?"

"Can I have another one...to go?"

If Winnie were a balloon, she would have burst with pride. "Darn tootin'!" she said. "I'll bag one up for you now! Sure you just want *one?*"

"No. But if I eat more than that, I'll have to buy new jeans."

Winnie laughed. "I hear that."

I turned to Winky. "Thanks again for helping me out today."

"T'weren't nothin', Val. It's what friends do."

I smiled at my funny little friend. "Hey, I was gonna ask you. What's going on with your fishing tackle jewelry business?"

"Playin' Hooky, you mean? It's got kind a 'sporatical lately," Winky explained. "Seems like we done satisfied the need for fishin'-related ornamentation in Pinellas County."

"It isn't helping that Old Joe died, either," Winnie said sadly.

"He did?" I asked. "Was he a big customer?"

"Well...not directly, but yes," Winnie explained. "He owned the Bait and Tackle Shack next to Caddy's. He let us sell our stuff there."

"Oh yeah. I remember him," I said.

"Well, he up and died a couple of weeks ago, and the place has been boarded up ever since."

"We don't know what in tarnation is going on over there," Winky said. "Old Joe was our main distributor, you know. Until we find somebody to take on the line, we're kind 'a dead in the water." Winky cocked his head and smiled. "Hey, that was kind a ironical, wat'n it, Val?"

My lips twisted to the left. "You could say that."

"Here's your donut, Val," Winnie said, sliding a white paper bag across the counter toward me.

I picked it up. "This feels a bit heavy," I said to her.

She shrugged and grinned. "You know, I never did learn how to count to one."

I laughed. "All right. But if I split my jeans, it won't be the last you've seen of me."

Winky busted out laughing. "Good one, Val!"

I felt my face heat up. "Okay, maybe that was a poor choice of words," I said. "On that note, I'll take my leave."

As I walked toward the exit, a streak of giddiness shot through me. But it was no sugar rush. It was the childlike joy of *anticipation*. I had a bag of donuts, and the rest of the evening *to myself!* One thing was for sure; neither Tom *nor* my diet would be making an appearance tonight. I absently pushed opened the shop door. In my secret fantasy I was already in bed alone, in my sweatpants, snarfing down on those bacon and peanut-butter bombs, watching reruns of *Sex in the City*.

Oh, yeah. I opened the bag and took another peek at Winnie's miraculous new reason to be alive....

Whump!

Something thumped me hard on the back, knocking me off balance. Suddenly, the sidewalk was hurtling toward my face. I tumbled forward, landed on top of my purse, and gasped as the impact nearly knocked the wind out of me. My head hit the bag stuffed with peanut-butter bombs. The flimsy paper bag shielded my face from the sidewalk like an airbag, then burst open, sending custard and peanut butter exploding all over my face like a cream pie on a circus clown.

I scrambled to my knees and sucked in a bit of air. All of a sudden, something hot and rough swiped over my lips. *What the...?!!*

I squinted through the clotted custard covering my eyes. The sloppy jowls of a humongous dog came into focus. I screamed like a little girl.

"Aaaaghhh!"

"Gee, lady. You'd think you was bein' murderized or somethin'," said a man's voice from behind me. His accent screamed New Jersey jackass. "It's just a hound dog."

A hound dog! Ack! My worst nightmare come true!

"Could you please control your dog?" I screeched on the verge of hysteria. The mutt continued unabated to clean my face with its disgusting tongue. I tried to stand up, but my legs were too wobbly.

"All right, all right," the guy said. "Harvey, *stop*."

The dog ceased licking my face and sat back on its haunches. It licked its own chops for a change, while I wiped my eyes with remnants of the paper bag. My attacker was a rusty-red hound dog with droopy eyes and a six-inch snout that dripped with stringy saliva. *Gross!* I shivered in disgust at the thought that its grotesque tongue had been all over my face.

I craned my neck to the left to glare at the dog's insipid owner. But instead of giving him a piece of my mind, my mouth fell open and stayed there.

The guy was entirely covered in curly black hair—except for where he shaved it off. And, of course, the top of his head. He must have been proud of his abundant body hair. His attire—shorts and sleeveless t-shirt—seemed designed to display it to the max. The guy's face was almost round and as pasty-white as half-dried glue. His nose was sunburned red, and his neck and his face below his nose were being swallowed alive by a seven o'clock shadow. I figured in another hour or so, his upper lip would disappear behind a swath of greasy, black fur.

Somewhere near New Jersey, a village was missing its werewolf.

"I'm Jake Johnson. I'm new in town," he said as I scrambled to my feet. I searched the ground for my missing left sandal. The dog had knocked me clean out of it. I discovered it teetering on the concrete curb. I walked over and inched my foot into it.

"Said my name is Jake," the hairy man repeated. "And you are?"

"Mad as hell!" I bellowed, and continued marching to my car without looking back.

I SCREECHED OUT OF the parking lot of Davie's Donuts with Maggie's dual glass-packs blaring. I glanced at my face in the rear-view mirror. *Gawd!* I looked like I'd just popped a zit as big as my face. Thank goodness I was only a few blocks from home. With any luck, no one would see me.

But, of course, I didn't have any luck. In fact, I managed to make an old woman who lived down the street stumble backward in horror and drop her glass of iced tea. "Sorry!" I yelled, but as I pulled onto Bimini Circle, I wanted to scream myself. Tom's car was in the driveway.

Dad blast it! He wasn't supposed to come over tonight!

"Crapola!" I yelled to whoever was within earshot.

I pulled over to the side of the road and scrounged around for a napkin, paper towel, grocery receipt, candy-bar wrapper—*anything* to wipe the donut goop off my face. Nothing. Tom had cleaned out my car over the weekend. Just another example of my rotten luck.

I opened the glove compartment and scrounged around in it. My choices were my car registration slip, pages out of Maggie's owner's manual, or the business card of Ferrol Finkerman, a two-bit, ambulance-chasing attorney. He'd tried to sue me twice already. Once over a missing ring finger, and once over a botched toupee inspection.

Finally, for once that jerk will be of some use to humanity. I grabbed Finkerman's card and used it like a straight razor to shave away the biggest globs of custard clinging to my face and fling them to the curb.

When my face was fairly recognizable as human again, I licked my palms and rubbed them over my cheeks. I checked the results in the rear-view mirror.

Awesome. I look like a melted ice cream cake.

Why did crap like this always happen to me? If Tom wasn't here, it wouldn't matter. But he was, dang it! "Arrgh!" I was about to burst into tears of frustration when a thought hit me like a baseball bat to the noggin.

Wait a second! I could use this mess to my advantage. Tom thinks he can just drop by any old time he pleases, does he? Well then, he should expect the unexpected. He wants to move in with me? Well, I'll just give him a little taste of what he's in for!

I grinned like a demented clown and mashed the gas pedal. Maggie's twin glass-packs growled demonically. "Bring it on!" I yelled, and lurched into the driveway.

I cut the ignition, flung open the car door and marched up to the front door. *My* front door. To *my* house! *This was my castle, dang it! I shouldn't have to do anything I didn't want to in my own castle, right?* And at this exact moment, I was in absolutely no mood to share the throne!

I jammed the key in the lock. Before I could turn the knob, the door opened wide and there stood Tom, grinning at me. My mouth flew open in preparation of wiping the dimples off his boyish face, but when I looked down my train of thought derailed. I stumbled backward off the front porch, tripped over my own feet and landed flat on my butt on the walkway.

"Val?" Tom said. "Are you okay?"

I kicked a foot at him. "What are you doing with *that?*"

Tom looked down, then back up. He grinned sheepishly. "Oh. Uh...surprise!"

Nestled in Tom's arms was my canine nemesis, Charmine.

I wanted to scream, "Get that psycho witch out of here!" But I couldn't. Tom thought I loved dogs. *Crap!* I took a breath to calm myself, then asked, "Why did Milly bring her back?"

Tom cocked his head at me for a moment. "Oh! This isn't Charmine. But now that you mention it, he *does* look a lot like her."

I scrambled to my feet again for the second time in ten minutes. I brushed myself off and glared at Tom hard enough to bore holes through his thick skull. I spoke slowly through clenched teeth like a professional ventriloquist. "Tom. What. Is. That. Dog. Doing. Here?"

Tom's eyes shone as he spoke. "Isn't he a cutie? I found him wandering the street on my lunch hour today."

If Tom was waiting for me to say something cute, he had a long wait ahead of him. But it wasn't the dried-up custard on my face that had sealed my lips shut. It was lockjaw caused by blinding rage. I stared at the dog, then back at Tom. *This could not be happening!*

Tom nuzzled the little dog, then shot me another one of his boyish grins. "Val. You know, I was thinking about how much you said you enjoyed taking care of Charmine. Then I spotted this little fellow bumbling down the street. I thought, well, if nobody claimed him, we could keep him. You can work at home as a writer, and he can keep you company. He could be your *muse!* Come on, Val. What do you say?"

For the sake of all of humanity, I kept my mouth shut. If I'd said what I wanted to say, there was a very good probability it would've caused a rift in the time-space continuum, and we'd all have gone hurtling to our deaths inside a giant black hole.

Chapter Eleven

After carefully considering the peril I could have been placing on the entire universe, I settled on a one-syllable answer to Tom's question about keeping the dog. Though it was a small answer, I said it with big emphasis.

"No!" I screeched. The single syllable cracked like a dam holding back a raging river of unspoken obscenities.

"No *what?*" Tom asked. He was still standing in the doorway, blocking my access to *my* castle, completely unaware of the psychological power held over me by the four-legged beast in his arms.

I was dumbfounded by Tom's obtuseness. "No, you can't keep that *dog* here! We have no...no...no *dog food.*"

Tom grinned and tousled the fur shrouding the dog's face. "No problem. I picked up a bag of dog chow on my way over."

"But...but...but." I said, sounding like a stuttering chicken. "Why don't you just keep it at *your* place?" I inched my way cautiously to within three feet of the dog. It didn't lunge at me. Tom wasn't kidding. The dog really *wasn't* Charmine.

"You know I can't have a pet at my apartment, Val. Besides, the way you raved on and on about Charmine...I thought you'd *love* having a dog around the place."

"When did I rave?"

"You said Charmine was adorable."

"I wouldn't call that raving. Not technically."

"What are you saying? You don't like the dog?"

"Well, sure I do," I lied yet again. I clamped my eyes shut and scooted by them like a scared crab. Once inside the house, I opened my eyes and breathed a sigh of relief at not being bitten. "A dog is such a *responsibility*, Tom. Who's going to walk it? Feed it? Clean up the poop?"

Tom laughed and shut the door behind him. "We're not twelve years old, you know. We'll figure it out. Besides, it's only until we find the owner. I'm figuring a dog this nice *has* to be microchipped, right? Look at him. Isn't he the cutest thing you've ever seen?" Tom held the hair back from the dog's irritatingly cute face.

"Uh huh," I grumbled. "But...we both have to go to work in the morning. We can't leave it inside all day unattended. You *saw* what Charmine did to my...uh...I mean...how Milly didn't want to leave Charmine all alone by herself."

Tom grinned. "Already thought of that. I'm staying home from work tomorrow."

"But didn't you just say you can't have dogs at your place?"

Tom's eyes dulled and his enthusiasm skipped a beat. "I meant *here*. I'll stay home with the dog *here*."

Tom was on my last nerve. For a cop, he was being annoyingly clueless about my fears and objections. Besides, did I really *have no say in this at all? In my own home?* I glared at Tom, uncertain what to say to make him understand.

Tom cleared his throat. "Unless...what you're saying is, this *isn't* my home. Is that what you're saying, Val?"

"I...no...it's just that..." I flopped on the couch. "I'm not sure I'm ready for all this, Tom."

Tom sighed and pursed his lips. "You're not just talking about the dog, are you?"

I smiled sheepishly. "I mean, couldn't we just start with a houseplant...and you staying over maybe...every other weekend?"

Surprisingly, the crushed look on Tom's face nearly crushed me as well.

"Okay. I get it," he said, and took a step toward the front door. My mind raced with conflicting emotions. Still, I couldn't bring myself to say a word. If I caved now, I'd be doomed forever. Tom reached for the doorknob. I scooted forward on the couch.

"Tom," I whispered.

He turned around. A storm brewed in his sea-green eyes. "What?"

I looked up at him, then down at the little dog in his arms. *Dang it! Why did I always have to be the bad guy?* But I'd set my resolve. Nothing could change my mind. *Nothing!*

Then that blasted little mutt smiled at me. And winked! The dog wasn't cute. It was heart-meltingly adorable. *Dang it!* All of a sudden I felt like a heel.

"I...I'm sorry, Tom," I backtracked. "I was just so...*surprised*. That's a big thing to spring on me, you know." I sighed. "I mean, the *dog's* not big...it's the *surprise* that's big...I mean...well, you know what I mean."

Tom let me ramble, but his face shifted from disappointment to the kind of open-faced joy you only see on kids' faces at Christmas and the last day of school. I'd done it. I'd caved. And now I was a goner. There was no turning back.

"Of course the dog can stay here," I mumbled, loathing myself for my own betrayal. "*Overnight*. I mean.... *Both* of you can stay...I mean...."

Tom smiled, leaned over and kissed me on the lips to stop my babbling. The dog licked my hand and yipped excitedly.

"You taste like donuts and smell like bacon," Tom said.

"Yeah. I'm a cop and a dog's dream come true," I quipped.

But this was no laughing matter. One of us was majorly in the doghouse. And, whoever it was didn't have four legs.

I ONLY HAD TEN SECONDS to make it. I had to balance on the rub-
ber ball, climb the ladder and jump through the ring of fire into the kiddie
pool. Then I'd get a donut. I wagged my rear end and jumped on top of the
ball...whoooaa! Made it! I rolled the ball up to the ladder, jumped on it
and scaled it to the top.

"Good Val!" the dog with the whip said. "Now jump!"

I sprang off the top of the ladder, through the flaming ring and splat-
ted face-first into the shallow pool.

I shook myself off and looked up at my hairy-faced owner for approval.
But his tail wasn't wagging.

"Sorry, girl," he said, his muzzle dusted with powdered sugar. "We're
out of donuts. How about a dirty tube sock instead?"

I woke up in a cold sweat, plagued by that weird feeling you get after punching the "buy" button on a non-refundable airline ticket. I had
a sneaking suspicion I'd just done something I would live to regret.

Actually, I already regretted it. I'd planned to spend last night in
bed with a bag of donuts and Carlton. I'd gotten to the part in *Love's
Lusty Love* where it was do or die time. I should have gone to sleep last
night with a belly full of bacon custard and the satisfaction of knowing whether Carlton had set sail for Spain with Cecilia or planted a
bean farm in Bermuda with Barbara. But no. Instead, I'd been forced to
spend the evening sitting on the couch watching Tom toss an old sock
to the mangy little mutt he'd drug into my house. Uninvited, I might
add.

I mean, really? What was so riveting about watching a dog fetch a
sock? I'd pretended to enjoy their tug-of-war match. But honestly, even
if I'd drunk half a bottle of Tanqueray (which I, unfortunately, *did not*)
it wouldn't have made that insipid game any more entertaining. Maybe
dogs were like babies. Unless they were yours, you just didn't get it.

When Tom had finally called it a night and we'd mercifully headed
off to bed, I'd insisted that Tom lay an old blanket out in the garage
for the dog's bed. But as soon as Tom had left him alone in there, the

pooch had begun to whine. We'd both figured it would eventually get tired and quiet down, but it never did. In the end, Tom had gotten up to see about it. I didn't know how Tom managed it, but the whining had stopped. Exhausted, I'd fallen asleep before he'd come back to bed. When I'd woken up this morning, Tom wasn't under the covers with me.

I rubbed my eyes and stretched. Curious, I climbed out of bed and padded into the living room. Tom and the mutt were sprawled out on my couch like a couple of leftover party guests.

Great. I have no privacy and *no cappuccino in bed.*

To my mind, this was the worst of all possible worlds. It did not bode well. No indeed. For the first time in years, I didn't bother to make myself a cappuccino. And I didn't bother to wake Tom. Instead, I got dressed for work and snuck out the front door, spurred on by a burning desire that had nothing to do with the need for caffeine.

I'm gonna find that dog's owner if it was the last thing I ever do!

Chapter Twelve

When I got to Griffith & Maas, Milly's red Beemer was already in the lot. I stumbled in the door, cranky from lack of sleep, a shortage of caffeine, and the invasion of my home by two uninvited varmints of the male persuasion. I slammed my purse on my desk and made my way to the break room.

Even though it was my job to make the coffee every morning, I'd never actually dared to drink any of it. My double-espresso cappuccino at home had always been enough to fuel me until lunch. But today, I was desperate enough for a caffeine fix to give the nasty brew—and even the non-dairy powdered creamer—a try.

I filled the carafe with water, rubbed off a coffee filter from the stack, and heaped in four scoops of Cheery-O coffee, just the way old man Griffith had taught me. The smell of it as it perked was something of a cross between boiled peanuts and burnt rubber. I poured myself a cup, took a sip, and promptly spit it out into the sink.

"*Gross!*" I wiped my tongue with a napkin. No amount of creamer or sugar was going to make that cup of liquid tar taste *anywhere near* good. I poured it down the drain, fixed another cupful and headed down the hall to Milly's office.

"How can you and Mr. Griffith still be alive, drinking this stuff?" I asked. I clunked the cup onto her desk.

"Oh, you know the old saying, 'What doesn't kill us makes us stronger,'" Milly quipped. She picked up the cup and studied my face.

"You're even crabbier than usual this morning," she teased. "What's up with you?"

I was in desperate need of a caffeine injection and a new forwarding address for a four-legged mutt. But it appeared I'd have to make do with neither for the moment. "I didn't sleep too well last night," I said.

Milly smirked. "Man problems?"

A scowl stifled my fledgling yawn. "You could say that. Tom brought home a stray dog yesterday."

Milly's green eyes sparked to life. "Oh! A puppy! That's so wonderful, Val! What's it look like?"

"Why?" I grumbled. "Is Charmine missing?"

"Huh? No. Why would you ask that?"

I shrugged. "I dunno. Because I'm crabby. And because the dog actually looks a lot like Charmine."

Milly's eyes lit up. If she'd had a tail, she'd have been wagging it. "Really? Oh! Oh! We *have* to arrange a play date!"

"A play date?"

"Yes! Charmine's new in town. Your dog is, too. We can introduce them. You know, so they can both make new friends!"

My jaw clenched. "But my dog isn't staying."

Milly smiled coyly. "Are you *sure* about that?"

I was as sure about it as I was of anything. In other words, not at all. The thought of keeping the dog made me even crabbier, if that was possible. It also made me even more determined to send it back to where ever it belonged.

"We can't keep it, Milly. We need to find its rightful owner. Do you mind if I spend some time making up a 'found dog' flyer? And calling around to the animal shelters, in case someone reported it missing?"

"What about the tag on its collar?"

"It wasn't wearing one."

Milly choked as if she'd swallowed her tongue. "What? Unbelievable! The gall of some people!"

"Hold on, Milly," I said. "It might have fallen off or something. Tom's going to check at a vet's today to see if it's microchipped."

Milly climbed off her runaway high horse. "Oh. Okay. Well, in that case, sure. Go ahead and make the flyer. And the calls."

"Thanks."

Milly held up her mug. "I hope you find them. And thanks for the coffee." She took a sip. "Ahh. Perfect as always."

"Glad you like it." I turned to leave, but Milly stopped me.

"Val? I think it's sweet that you care so much about finding the dog's owner. I bet they miss it terribly."

"I know *I* would," I lied. I walked out of her office and shook my head. *Crap!* All this doggy business was turning me into a lying dog myself, and I didn't like it one bit.

WITH MILLY'S BLESSING and Mr. Griffith back at his home lounging around in retirement mothballs, I spent the morning calling local animal shelters and vets' offices trying to find out if anyone had reported a dog missing. I wasn't having any luck. But I had to admit, the folks who worked with animals were a friendly bunch. Every single one I spoke to had agreed to take my number and call me if someone asked about a missing Pom-mix. They even let me fax over flyers for them to post on their notice boards.

The genuine concern in their voices made me feel even worse about not loving dogs. Was I mentally disturbed? A psychopath? One step away from a serial killer? I had to know! The problem had plagued me like the heartbreak of psoriasis ever since I was a little girl. When I got a hold of an especially kind and chatty veterinary assistant, I thought I'd take a chance and pose the question, in a round-about kind of way, of course.

"Cindy, I was wondering," I began, "Could you tell me...I mean...you see...I have this *friend* who doesn't like dogs...."

The sharp inhale of breath on the other end of the line didn't bode well. I backpedaled. "What I *meant* was, dogs don't seem to like *her*."

"Oh. Well, that's a different story," the vet tech said.

"Not *all* dogs, mind you," I said. "Can you tell me why a dog would like *one* person, but not another?"

"Hmmm," Cindy the vet assistant said as she mulled over the question. "Well, it usually comes down to one of two things. Pack dominance or the smell of your scurf."

"Excuse me? The smell of my *what?*"

"Your scurf. The skin cells you slough off."

"Dogs can smell that?"

"Sure. You lose like, fifty-million cells a minute."

"You mean a *day?*"

"No. A minute. To a dog, we're like that kid in that *Peanuts* cartoon. You know, the one walking around in a dirt cloud? Only we all walk around in scurf clouds. Fifty-million cells a minute, falling off and swirling around us like our own private snowstorm. We can't see 'em, but dogs can detect 'em with their noses."

"They *smell* these dead cells?"

"Yeah. And dogs react to us based on how our scurf smells. That and, you know, your various lotions and potions. Plus the billions of bacteria munching away at all that stuff. And, of course, the bacteria's excreta."

"*Excreta!*" I looked down at my arms and freaked.

I'm losing a million skin cells a second! And bacteria are chewing on them and...pooping on me? Yuck!

"Did that answer your question?" the woman asked.

I shut my eyes and tried not to think about it. "Uh...yes. Thanks."

"Glad I could help."

Yeah. Help ruin my life!

I clicked off the phone and pouted angrily. *So that was my problem. My scurf stunk!*

"Any luck?" Milly asked from behind me. I whirled around.

"Uh...no. Not yet. But what do you think of this flyer?" I held up a piece of paper for her inspection.

"It's okay. But wouldn't it be better with a picture of the dog on it?"

"Sure. But I don't have one."

"No problem. I have pictures of Charmine."

I crinkled my nose at her. "How's that gonna help?"

"I thought you said the dog looks like Charmine."

"Oh. Duh! Sure, that could work. Do you have a good one?"

Milly smiled. "I think I can help you out."

She swiped over to the photo gallery on her cell phone and handed it to me. She looked over my shoulder and "oohed" and "awed" as I flipped through what appeared to be a never-ending collection of pictures of Milly and her pooch.

"Oh! Wait!" Milly said as I flipped to the next picture. "Go back one."

I did as instructed. Milly leaned over my shoulder. I grimaced and tried not to think about scurf. Or about how many of Milly's dead skin cells and pooping bacteria were dive-bombing my back and shoulders. I squirmed in my seat.

"I think she looks cutest from this angle, don't you?" Milly asked.

I studied the picture. It was a side view of Charmine looking a bit wide-eyed, as if caught off guard. Her sharp, white teeth were bared in such a way that her expression could arguably be interpreted as a friendly grin *or* as a menacing grimace. In other words, Charmine looked like an adorable—and potentially psycho—Pom-mix mutt.

"It's perfect," I said.

"Are you sure?" Milly asked. "I have plenty of others, but I just love that smile."

"Absolutely. Send me a text with the file and I'll download it."

"Okay, will do."

I WAS PRINTING OUT the flyers of the cute little fanged dog from hell when Tom called my cellphone.

"Hey," I said.

"Hey. How's it going?"

"Eh. You?"

"I went by the vet's office on Gulf Boulevard. The dog wasn't microchipped."

Crap! "Oh. That's too bad," I said, trying to sound sympathetic. "I haven't had any luck either. But I left word at all the shelters and put together some flyers. I'm planning on passing a few around when I go to lunch."

"Okay," Tom said hesitantly. "I'd say that I appreciate your efforts, Val. But I'm not so sure I do."

"What do you mean?"

"I dunno. I guess the little guy's growing on me. What do you think of the name Buster?"

Buster? As in sleep-buster? Bliss-buster? Buster of my nice little world without sock wars and poop patrol?

"Actually, Tom, Buster sounds like the perfect name." I knew it sounded crazy, but I would have sworn I heard Tom smiling through the phone.

"Okay, gotta go," he said, and clicked off.

Crap on a cracker! Time was running out! I had to find that dog's owner...and fast. I looked down at Charmine's maniacal little face on the flyers I'd made. I grabbed a flyer, stuck it in my stapler and pounded a few staples into her cute little mug.

"Take that, you mangy mutt," I grumbled. "Whose scurf stinks now?"

I BEGGED OFF MILLY'S lunch invitation to go to Ming-Ming's for sushi. The thought of a dog bumbling around my house, sniffing my scurf for the next twenty years had spoiled my appetite. Besides, if I heard Milly mention Charmine and that dang Barkmitzva one more time, well, I couldn't be held responsible for my actions.

On my lunch hour, I hopped in Maggie and cruised down Central Avenue, handing out flyers to anyone who would take one. I pulled into a parking spot at 6th Street and hit the pavement. Within half an hour, I'd gotten a good dozen or so shop owners to post pictures of the pooch in their storefront windows and community bulletin boards. Judging by the dent in my stack of flyers, I figured I'd handed out over a hundred. One for every blister on the back of my heels.

I hobbled back to my car, triumphant despite the pain. If it took blisters to get rid of Buster, I was willing to make the sacrifice. After, all, a girl's gotta do what a girl's gotta do.

Chapter Thirteen

On my way home from work, I stopped by my neighborhood grocery store. It was a small-scale Publix that catered to locals and tourists alike. It was more like a convenience store on steroids, with a penchant for beach floats and sunscreen. I told myself my mission for stopping was to pick up some blister pads and post a few more flyers. But as I hobbled my way across the parking lot, I knew deep down that there was more to my visit than just that.

I was stalling. For the first time in like *forever*, I didn't want to go home.

The thought of having to waste another stupid evening watching two old dogs fool around with a dirty sock made me want to hit the gas on Maggie and never look back. My lip twitched at the thought. I'd done it before. Ditched everything and ran off. Did I have it in me to do it again? Maybe. But there was a big difference this time.

It wasn't a human I was running from. Not entirely, at least.

Compared to my past relationships, everything had been relatively good between Tom and me until the dog issue had reared its ugly head. And, of course, Tom deciding he wanted to move in.

Arggh! Why did things always have to get so complicated?

I scowled and snatched a green shopping basket from a stack by the door, right next to a refrigerator case crammed with six-packs of beer and boxes of frozen pizzas. I guess those were the two food groups people couldn't do without whether they were on vacation or not. I was about to cram a couple of flyers in the basket when I spied a man wearing a crisp white shirt. In this beach town, an ironed shirt with sleeves could only mean one of two things. Either the guy was a store manager or he was a tourist fresh from the airport. No local resident of the male persuasion appeared to know such shirts existed.

My flyers in hand, I toddled after him toward the produce section, slowed down by my yowling blisters. When I turned a corner stacked with cases of cola and bags of chips, he was gone, proving my theory that waiters and store employees were actually leprechauns. How else could they magically disappear right when you needed them most?

I sighed and glanced around. Across the store, loitering by the cantaloupes, was a tall, skinny old woman dressed in sparkling gold lame. Laverne was wearing that gawd-awful pantsuit of hers again. She appeared to have just beamed down from a 1970s disco party. But she wasn't dancing, poor thing. From the expression on her face, it looked as if she'd just lost her favorite Bee Gees album.

I walked up and peeked in her shopping cart. All she had in there were three heads of garlic.

"Hey, Laverne. What's up? Having problems with vampires?"

Laverne looked up at me. Her pencil-thin eyebrows collided in confusion. "Vampires?"

"The garlic?"

"Gosh dang it! I thought garlic kept *dwarves* away." She snatched up the garlic heads and tossed them back into their bin by the onions. I was about to laugh, but thought better of it when Laverne burst into tears.

"Geez! What's wrong?" I asked.

"I can't take much more of this," she said. She sniffed back a tear. "I'm telling you, Val, it's just too much!"

I had a good idea what she was talking about. I touched her arm. "Hey. What say we go get a coffee? I've been dying for one all day."

Laverne sniffed again. "Can I get a Chai latte instead?"

"Huh?" Laverne wasn't usually so wishy-washy. "Of course! Geez, Laverne, J.D.'s really gotten your goat, hasn't he?"

Laverne focused her red eyes on me. "Val, you know I don't have a goat. It would ruin my garden."

"It's just a figure of speech."

"Oh."

I tugged her arm. "Come on," I said, and led her toward the corner coffee shop inside the store. I ordered our drinks at the counter as Laverne stood, silent and slump-shouldered, beside me.

"So what's going on?" I asked. I paid for the drinks and led Laverne to a booth.

"I don't want to go home," Laverne whimpered. She dabbed at her impressive mascara meltdown with a paper napkin.

I crinkled my nose. I hadn't seen Laverne this upset since she thought she'd cursed my life with her old sapphire ring. I didn't know what was going on with her and J.D., but one thing *was* for sure. I didn't like to see her cry.

"You know what?" I said, and took her hand. "I don't want to go home either. What say we pull a *Thelma and Louise* and just split this town?"

Laverne coughed out a laugh. "Don't tempt me."

I gave her a sympathetic smile. "So tell me. Why don't *you* wanna go home?"

"J.D.'s taking over the place," Laverne whined. "Do you have any idea what he did to me last night?"

Before I could stop it, my annoying brain flashed an image of the two of them having sex. *Dang it, brain!* I tried to look concerned instead of mortified. "No. What did he do?"

"He brought over a dang cuckoo clock he got in Germany." Laverne pouted and stared at me, as if that was all the explanation required.

I twisted my lips to the right. "So...you don't like cuckoo clocks?"

"I don't give a flip about 'em one way or the other!" Laverne snapped.

A woman sitting alone in the booth across from us gave us the evil eye. Either that, or she'd reached maximum capacity in her baby-blue polyester pants and was about to blow some serious elastic. Laverne bit her lip, leaned in and whispered. "Val, he wants to take down my pair-a-dice clock and hang that blasted thing instead."

"You mean the red acrylic clock? Where dice spell out the time of day?"

"Yes!" Laverne said, and slammed her palms on the table.

"The monster!"

Laverne's scowl softened a little. "Exactly. Thanks for getting it, Val. A girl's space is her sanctuary, right?"

"Absolutely. I'm right with you on that."

Laverne dried her tears with the napkin and tried to smile. "So, your turn. Why don't *you* want to go home?"

I let out a sigh that could extinguish birthday candles at forty paces. "I dunno, Laverne. It's just, you know...living with someone is for the birds."

Laverne nodded her horsey head. "Yeah. *Cuckoo* birds."

I snickered despite myself. "So is that what made you snap, Laverne?"

"Wadda you mean?"

"What did J.D. do to make you want to 'garlic' his ass? This couldn't just be about a cuckoo clock."

The lady in the booth shot us another dirty look. Laverne leaned in, her eyes angry slits. "JD *did his laundry* at my place yesterday."

"Laundry?" I hissed. "Oh, man. That's hard core!"

"Right? Men's dirty underpants all over the place. I thought I was done with all that horse hockey!" Laverne's jaw tightened, making the tendons in her neck stick out.

"I can do you one better. Tom wants us to get a dog."

Laverne nearly choked. "A dog? Dang, Val! That's worse than a whole houseful of dirty underpants!"

"I know, right? Can you imagine having to take care of a dog every day?"

Laverne shook her head. "Every single cotton pickin' day. You know, Val, it's those everyday things that get you in the end. And J.D.'s loaded with 'em."

"What do you mean?"

"Well, for one thing, he hums all the time. I mean *all the time!*"

My upper lip snarled involuntarily. "Gawd! That's gotta be annoying, Laverne. You know, now that you mention it, Tom taps his finger on his beer bottle. Tap, tap, tap. Always tapping! It drives me crazy!"

Laverne leaned back in her seat and crossed her arms. "I can top that." Her eyes darted left and right. "J.D. farts in his sleep," she divulged.

I shrugged. "So? Everybody does."

Laverne leaned forward. "I mean *a lot*, Val. Shuttle-craft blasts! I'm telling you, you wouldn't think a guy his size could hold all that gas."

"He can't," I quipped. "That's why he lets it go."

Laverne burst out in a laugh that would have made a cackling hen die of embarrassment. Her outburst was the last straw for the nosy woman in the booth across from us. She hauled herself up and waddled over to our table, her plump face ruddy from either frustration, or the effort it took to get herself out of that booth.

"Excuse me," she said. "But if those are the only problems you ladies have, you should count your blessings. I caught my husband playing 'hide the sausage' with another woman. Now I get to do my clothes at the laundromat."

"Ugh! The laundromat!" I said. "My condolences. That truly *is* the absolute worst!"

"I'd rather have no *car* than no washer and dryer," Laverne agreed.

"I know, right?" I said. "I mean, the people you meet in a *dumpster* are of a higher caliber than *laundromat* people."

The woman clad in polyester stared at me sourly.

"I mean...of course...present company accepted," I stuttered.

"Nice save," the woman deadpanned. "Anyway, here's my business card. I'm a realtor now. Yay. Lucky me. If you two really *do* decide to run away, you might as well get as much for your houses as the current market will bear."

She laid two cards on the table. "Yeah. You read it right. Name's Judy Bloomers. Another lovely parting gift from my ex-husband. And, sorry, but I just gotta ask. What's wrong with you two, anyway? Why don't you like dogs? *Everybody* likes dogs!"

Laverne and I both gulped and stared at the woman. She appeared to possess the strength and unpredictability that could lead to us getting our lights punched out. But to our relief, Judy just shook her head and walked away. After she'd reached a safe distance, I turned to Laverne.

"Geez! Does everybody know how I feel about dogs?"

"Everybody but Tom, apparently," Laverne said.

"You didn't seem too keen on the idea either. You hate dogs, too, don't you, Laverne?" I asked hopefully.

"No. Not usually, I mean," Laverne answered. "But that dang dog of Milly's is a little turd. I didn't want to say anything, but you've got to do something about her, Val. That overgrown mole rat's been digging up my garden. She's gotta be stopped before she kills my rose bushes!"

"Gee, I'm sorry, Laverne. I didn't know. But you don't have to worry about Charmine anymore. I'm done dog sitting for Milly. That's over for good, thank goodness."

Laverne cocked her head. "But...I just saw her in your backyard before I drove up here."

"Oh," I sighed. "That's not Charmine. It's the stray dog Tom found yesterday." I showed Laverne a flyer. "He wants us to keep it, but I promise, it won't be here long. I'm handing out these flyers to find the owner. The mangy little pooch should be gone in a day or two, tops."

Laverne cocked her head, confused. "Then why is Tom in the back-yard building a doghouse?"

My jaw nearly hit the table. "What?! You've got to be kidding me!"

"Nope."

Something inside me snapped. "That's *it*, Laverne. I declare...*war!* You and me against Tom and J.D. We can't let them take over our lives like this!"

"I'm in," Laverne said, setting her pointy jaw. "What are we gonna do?"

I opened my mouth, closed it, and slumped back in the booth. "I have no idea. But I'll think of something."

"Well, while you're thinking about that, you got any ideas on what I can cook for supper? J.D. doesn't go in for Skinny Dippers." Laverne shook her head. "I must have a hundred of them frozen dinners in the freezer...all going to waste."

"Well, if you want my opinion, I say if the man wants a home-cooked dinner, he should fix it himself."

Laverne looked horrified. "And mess up my kitchen? I can't have him ruining my Frank Sinatra skillet set!"

I drummed my fingers on the table until an idea popped up. "Well, there's always tuna casserole surprise."

Laverne's eyes brightened with curiosity. "So, what's the surprise?"

"Well, that's up to *you*."

Laverne stared at me blankly for a moment. Then a look crept over her face that made me shiver. Like Dr. Frankenstein himself, I was pretty darn sure I'd just created a monster.

Chapter Fourteen

As soon as I pulled into my driveway, a switch clicked over in my mind. *I forgot to buy blister pads. Great.* What good was a memory that only kicked in when it was too late? I shifted into park and realized not only had I forgotten the bandages. I'd forgotten to buy *anything.* And I'd forgotten to hand out the dad-gum flyers, too! This whole Tom-and-dog situation was scrambling my brain cells, and I really didn't have that many left I could afford to lose....

I cut the ignition, opened the car door and leaned over to grab my purse from the passenger-side floorboard. It had ricocheted into the far corner during an angry hairpin turn two blocks back. Maggie was about eight feet wide, so it was a struggle to reach it. I was bent in half with my chin rubbing against the red-leatherette passenger seat. Still, my flailing fingertips barely grazed the purse. One final grunt forward and I had the strap in my hand. As I scrabbled on hands and elbows to sit back up, something wet and dirty hit my back. From the corner of my eye, it appeared that someone had just bopped me with a dirty mop!

"What the...!"

I turned my head and got pummeled again. But this time the attacker didn't go away! I felt its hands circling my throat, tearing at my hair! I gripped my purse by the strap and took a wild swing at whoever was on top of me. My purse wacked the stuffing out of something, then spilled its guts all over the car and driveway. A lipstick landed in the ashtray, and the assault ceased. I swung around to face my attacker, hoping with all my might that my eyeliner pencil was stuck in his eye. To my dismay, there was no one there.

I looked right and left. No one! Was I going crazy? No, because whatever had hit me had left me covered in wet, muddy streaks! I looked up. Could I have just survived an aerial assault by a duck with diarrhea? No. I swung my legs out of the car, looked down and gasped. Sitting on the driveway was a dog. A dog covered from head to toe in mud. And thanks to his stupid antics, so was I.

"Dang it, Buster!"

Apparently, "dang it, Buster" in dog language meant "come jump on me." Before I could move, Buster sprang into my lap, wriggled all over me and licked my face like I was wearing Milkbone makeup.

"Arrghh!" I shooed him out of the car and looked in the rear-view mirror. It appeared as if I'd recently had a close brush with an exploding mud pie. "*Great.*" I climbed out of the car, slammed the door and marched over to the side gate. As I fumbled with the latch, Buster jumped up, scratched my leg, and slipped through a freshly dug hole under the gate.

Son of a biscuit eater! Things were definitely not looking good for Buster *or* Tom.

I stomped along the side of the house, trying to deep breathe my way out of an impending aneurism. As I turned the corner by the tiki hut, I saw the bare, muscular back of Tom. Swinging a hammer. In the sunshine. His golden skin glistened with sweat.

My infuriation skipped a beat, and I stumbled on my warpath.

Dad blast it! For a Southern gal like me, handyman skills were the unbeatable ace in the redneck game of love. In fact, back in Greenville, fixing somebody's porch was a bona fide display of serious courtship. A man who knew his way around power tools was hotter to me than Brad Pitt in an EasyBake Oven.

The sight of Tom hefting a hammer got me going faster than a shot of sex pheromones. It took all the strength I had to keep my bad mood intact. But I *did* have one thing working in my favor. Laverne had been right. Tom was building a doghouse. I set my jaw to self-righteous and stomped over to Tom.

"Is that for you or the *dog?*" I asked, and pointed at the doghouse.

Tom turned around and looked me up and down. I'd just lost a mud-wrestling match with Buster, but Tom didn't say a word about it. He knew better. Instead, he grinned sheepishly and said, "Well, Val, I guess that's up to you."

"*Why don't I find this amusing?*" I muttered to myself as I watched Tom and the dog having a ball, horsing around in the living room. I pulled the tuna casserole surprise out of the oven. The surprise tonight was smoked oysters. I knew Tom hated them. Phase one of my passive-aggressive campaign to lure him away from my house was underway. I sneered at him and the dog and took a step toward the counter. My bare foot landed in something that made me not want to look down.

"Tom!" I screeched. "He's done it again!" I lifted my toes from the puddle of pee on the kitchen floor. "You have to watch him better. I won't have the house smelling like a kennel. Or a public urinal!"

"Sorry, Val," Tom said. "It won't happen again."

"*Sure* it won't," I scowled. "Could you please take him outside while I set the table?"

"Yeah. I'll clean that up."

"No. I'll do it. Just keep your eye on Buster. Please don't let him get filthy again."

"Yes, ma'am." He opened the sliding door. "Come on, Buster."

"And don't let him wriggle through the hole at the gate. And whatever you do, don't let him get into Laverne's yard!"

Tom saluted. "Anything else?" he asked sourly.

"Not that I can think of."

"Okay then." He shook his head and slid the door shut.

My stomach churned. I watched the two goofing off in the backyard and felt like a crabby old kill-joy. I hated feeling that way! But *someone* had to set the rules. I didn't *want* to be the one who did, but what choice did I have? That dog was ruining my house! And Tom didn't seem to be doing much about it...or lifting a finger to help find the owner. That left *me* to be the adult in the situation. Never a very good idea.

I tapped on the sliding door and motioned to Tom to come inside.

"What's for dinner?" Tom asked as he and Buster tromped back through the door.

"It's a surprise," I answered, and set the noodle casserole on a trivet in the center of the table. I dished a pile of it onto Tom's plate. He eyed it suspiciously.

"What's the grey lumps?" he asked.

"Your favorite. Smoked oysters."

"I hate smoked oysters."

I feigned surprise. "Oh. Sorry. Well, just eat around them."

While Tom picked at his food, Buster set up camp just far enough away from the table that he could make eye contact with us. He didn't whimper or make a sound, but there was no mistaking it. He was begging, all right. Every forkful on its way to my mouth was watched with razor-sharp focus and pleading eyes. After a few mouthfuls I felt like a gluttonous shrew stuffing herself while her children starved.

I couldn't take it anymore. I "accidently" dropped a forkful on the floor. It disappeared in a flash beneath a fuzzy vacuum cleaner with four legs.

"Well, at least *Buster* appreciates my cooking," I said. "That's *one* point in his favor."

Tom looked up from his plate. "I know you haven't warmed up to the dog yet, Val. But I think it's because you two got off on the wrong foot. Why don't you try playing with him? I tell you what. I'll wash the dishes while you two—"

"Tom! The dog practically *attacked* me. He's half wild! He needs proper training. He needs to go to obedience school."

Tom laughed in a way that made me want to stuff a smoked oyster down his throat.

"Buster doesn't need obedience school," he said. "I figure a dog only needs to learn six tricks to make it in this world. And Buster already knows four of them."

"What are you talking about?"

Tom stood up. Buster came running over to him. "Sit," Tom said. Buster sat.

"Speak," Tom said. Buster barked.

"Roll over," Tom commanded. Buster fell onto his side.

"That doesn't count," I said. "He didn't roll."

Tom rolled his eyes. "Okay then, let's call that one 'play dead.'"

"That's four," I said. "What are the other two?"

"Housebreaking and staying," Tom said.

"Oh. I thought you were going to say 'begging.' He's definitely got that down pat."

Tom smiled. "So, what do you say, Val? If I can teach Buster to do his business outside and not run away, can he stay?"

I looked down at Buster and his begging eyes, then back up at Tom. I felt as if I were being double-teamed. *Two against one. Not fair!* Still, I'd be a jerk not to let Buster stay at least until someone called and claimed him. "Okay," I sighed.

Tom grinned and leaned over and kissed my forehead. "Thank you!"

"But only until his owner comes, Tom. And you need to take full responsibility for him. I don't know *anything* about taking care of a dog."

Tom cocked his head, confused. "But you babysat Charmine."

Oh crap.

Tom's phone rang. I nearly jumped out of my seat. "Hey!" I said. "You better get that. It might be important!"

I scrambled out of my chair, grabbed some dishes and hustled into the kitchen. Tom answered his phone, but mostly listened to whoever was on the other end of the line. With only the occasional "yes," and "uh-huh," I had no idea what was going on. I was washing up the last dishes when he finished his call.

"Yes, okay," Tom said over the phone. "If you're sure. You know you can count on me. Bye." Tom hung up.

"Who was it?" I asked.

Tom bit his lip. "My boss. Seems the governor's called some emergency meeting. He wants me to drive to...uh...Tallahassee."

"Oh. When?"

"I have to leave tomorrow morning."

"What?" I nearly choked. "Why?"

"It's complicated," Tom said, and bit his lip again. "You see, my boss needs to brief me before this political thing. He wants me to deliver this speech."

"Sounds like a big deal."

Tom shrugged. "Yeah."

"I guess *not going* isn't an option, then?"

"No." Tom's eyes widened. "Oh crap, Val! I hate to leave you alone with Buster like this."

Me, too. "I'll manage," I said through pursed lips.

Tom hugged me. "I know you will. You always do. Who knows? Maybe by the time I get back you two will have hit it off."

"Maybe," I muttered. "But if his owner shows up...."

Tom nodded. "Of course."

"You'll miss the Barkmitzva."

"The what?" Tom asked, his head cocked to the side.

"I knew you'd laughed yourself into brain damage that night we were at Vance's. The *Barkmitzva*. Milly's party for Charmine on Saturday?"

"Oh, yeah." Tom smirked. "Well, life is full of little sacrifices."

"Ha ha," I said. I looked over at Buster. He lifted a leg and christened my couch. "Dang it, Tom!"

"Oops." Tom cringed.

"Whether he stays or not, you have to buy me a new couch."

Tom hugged me tight and kissed me on the nose. "Deal."

"And bring me back some Minneola tangelos from Indian River."

"Deal."

"A *big* sack. A twenty-pounder."

"Yes, ma'am," Tom smirked.

"And be nice to me, or I'll call my mom and tell her you're in the neighborhood."

Tom's eyebrows shot up. "You are a cruel-hearted woman, Val Fremden."

"You said it yourself. Life is full of sacrifices."

Chapter Fifteen

"Don't forget my tangelos," I said as I kissed Tom goodbye.
"I won't. Be nice to Buster, okay?"

I frowned. "I will. I'm not into animal cruelty, you know."

Tom smiled apologetically. "I know. And I also know that you didn't sign up for this whole dog thing. Sorry for bringing Buster home without checking with you first. And thanks for giving him a chance."

The right corner of my mouth hitched upward. "Seems I'm a sucker for old dogs with no place else to go."

Tom grinned and turned the key in the ignition. "Thank God for that." Unexpectedly, he turned the ignition off. He stared at me as he bit his lip.

"Everything okay?" I asked.

"You know, I was going to wait until I got back, but I changed my mind." Tom leaned over and opened the glove compartment. He retrieved a small, gift-wrapped box and handed it to me. "Open it."

I grinned. "Really?"

"Yes. Go on, open it before I change my mind."

I tore open the paper and lifted the lid on the small, white box. Inside was a pair of gorgeous, diamond-stud earrings.

"Oh Tom! They're beautiful! But...why?"

"Do I have to have a reason?"

"No, but...."

"Let's just say because I love you. And to make up for the engagement ring disaster. And because you've been so great about the dog."

"I don't know what to say," I fumbled.

"Well, that would be a first." Tom shot me a boyish grin complete with dimples. I laughed, leaned in the car and kissed him. He kissed me back.

As he fired up the engine and backed out of the driveway, I waved, then watched him and his SUV until they disappeared down the street. After the engine faded, I heard Buster whining through the living room window.

It was going to be a long weekend.

I SET THE EARRINGS on the counter and poured Buster his breakfast. He gobbled down the brown kibble like there was no tomorrow.

"Hungry, huh?" I asked. He looked up and whined. So I poured some more. He scarfed that down, too.

I figured I should feed Buster about as much as Milly had written in her instructions for Charmine. But then again, males always seemed to be able to eat more than females without gaining an ounce. Another injustice I was going to talk to God about later. I searched around for the list Milly had brought over the other day, but couldn't find it. So I decided to call the guy who'd been in charge that day.

It took a strip search of my house to find my cellphone. It had hidden itself on the nightstand in my bedroom under my copy of *Love's Lusty Love*. I grabbed it and punched a familiar number.

"Hey Goober. How much food should a dog eat?"

"Who is this?"

"Cut the crap. It's me. Val."

"I thought you were done with dog sitting."

"So did I. But Tom brought home a stray. The little mutt is eating me out of house and home."

"Huh. How big is the dog?"

"I dunno. Maybe eight pounds?"

"How much have you fed him?"

I shrugged. "Three...maybe four cups of kibble?"

"I see. What's today?"

"Huh? Saturday. Why?"

"Well, don't give him any more food until Wednesday. And make sure he's outside when he explodes."

I nearly gasped. "*Explodes?*"

"Val, you've fed that dog half his body weight in food. That stuff's gotta go somewhere. And I mean that literally."

"Crap!"

"Exactly."

"Ugh. Thanks, Goober." I hung up the phone and padded back to the kitchen. What awaited me there made me take the dog's name in vain.

"Buster!"

One of the kitchen barstools was knocked over. The open bag of kibble that once sat on the counter was now strewn all over the floor, along with bits of chewed cardboard. I followed the short trail of clues to Buster, who was contentedly sleeping off his feeding frenzy in the rays of sun beaming through the sliding glass doors. Next to his snout was the remains of a small, white box.

"Oh, no!" I screeched. "My earrings! You didn't!"

I counted to eight million and then redialed the phone. "Goober?"

"Who is this?"

"It's *me* again!"

"Huh. Exploded already? That was fast."

"No!" I said. "It's something else. The dog...ate my earrings. What should I do?"

"Depends on how much they're worth to you."

"Why?"

"Because there are only two ways I know to get 'em back. Surgery or poop patrol."

My nose crinkled. "Poop patrol?"

"Yep. You gotta follow the dog's every movement. Or, should I say *bowel* movement. Then you've gotta search through his poop."

I looked over at Buster's swollen belly. "How much does surgery cost?"

"WHAT'S PROPER ATTIRE for a Barkmitzva?" I asked Milly.

"Oh, just something you'd wear to church."

Seeing as how I hadn't been to church since the current year started with a one and not a two, that wasn't helpful. "Okay. See you soon."

I clicked off the phone and searched through my sundresses, trying to find one that would show dog hair the least. I found a brown-and-green patterned sleeveless A-line with a cute leather belt that matched my green sandals. Only one problem. Those sandals were in the trash, chewed to death by Charmine. I hung the green belt back on its hook and found a blue one. It didn't really go with the dress, but matched my blue sandals. I shrugged. Who was I trying to impress, anyway? Dogs didn't give a crap about fashion...did they?

I looked down at Buster. He was lying at the threshold of the bedroom door, watching me intently, still recovering from the scolding I'd laid on him.

"What do you think?" I asked, and held the dress up to my torso.

Buster whined and put his paws over his eyes.

"Everybody's a critic," I sneered, and unzipped the dress. "You ever been to a Barkmitzva?"

Buster yipped. I wasn't sure if that was a 'yes' or 'no,' but at least his bark didn't sound like a run-over rubber duck. I finished dressing and did my makeup, then tied a red kerchief around Buster's neck. I thought he looked pretty dapper as I toted him in the laundry basket out to the car. I set the basket on the driveway, fumbled for my keys and opened the car door. Before I could bend over to pick up the basket, Buster leapt out of it and onto the passenger seat.

"Looks like you like to travel," I said. I set the basket on floorboard. "Get in the basket."

Buster looked up at me as if to say, "You're kidding, right?"

"Okay," I said. "Have it your way. Behave yourself and you can stay on the seat."

Buster yipped. I slid into the driver's seat. The sky looked clear, so I left the top down, turned the ignition key and backed into the street. As we cruised down Gulf Boulevard in Shabby Maggie, I discovered that Buster and I had something in common. We both enjoyed the salty sea breeze on our faces, and watching the sunburned tourists stumble by in attire that, worn anywhere else, would probably have gotten them arrested.

When we arrived at Milly's mansion, I realized Buster and I had *another* thing in common. Both of us had hair as tangled as a bowl of spaghetti in a tornado.

By the time I managed to brush all the snarls out of my hair, it was frizzy enough to win first prize in a Rosanna Danna look-alike competition. With no other option at hand, I used the same brush on Buster. He seemed to enjoy it, and thanked me with a lick on the hand. It wasn't my diamond earrings back, but it *was* a goodwill gesture.

"Hey Buster. I never asked, but are you by any chance Jewish?"

Buster poked his chin sideways and barked. I took it as a "no."

"Me either. But I suppose to a dog, God is God, right?" Buster yipped out what I was pretty sure was a "yes." I smiled. "Okay, then. Glad we got that settled. Here we go."

I scooped up Buster and carried him to the massive mahogany door. After ringing the bell, I whispered into Buster's fuzzy little ear, "Remember what I said, now. Play nice!"

Milly answered our knock.

"Hi, Val!" She said. Then her eyes locked on Buster and my existence was forgotten. "Oh my! Is this the little cutie? How adorable!" She reached both hands out to pick up Buster. He growled out a warning. She flinched and took a step back.

I was as shocked and surprised as Milly. Then a tinge of pride swelled inside me. *Now you know how it feels, Miss Milly Halbert-Pantski! Buster likes me, not you!*

I smirked. "Be careful. He's a little...*protective* of me."

Milly took another step back. "I can see that. Well, come on in."

I stepped inside and set Buster down. He shot out of my arms like a fuzzy cannonball. In a split second, he joined the pack of other small dogs busy sniffing each other's rear ends by the stone fireplace. Thank goodness humans didn't greet each other like that. At least none that I knew of....

I glanced around the opulent Tudor palace, then warily took my place among the handful of snooty, pucker-lipped, sour-faced women gathered around the punch bowl. Every last one of them appeared to have kissed somebody's butt to get where they were. So maybe we weren't so different from dogs after all. Marrying a wallet might have assured these women a nice house and fancy clothes. But I'd rather take my chances roaming the streets *without* the leash.

"My Hildegard came from champion sire Albert Weissington," said a lady holding a trembling white Chihuahua that looked like a naked mole rat having a nervous breakdown.

Pedigree-shaming? Really? "How nice," I said haughtily. "Buster, of course, hails from the House of Squalor."

"Is that a Chanel scarf he's wearing?" another woman asked. "My little Tiffany adores her designer things."

I looked at the Dollar Store kerchief on Buster. "D.S.K.," I replied.

"Oh! Who's that?" the woman asked.

"A very up-and-coming new designer," I said, looking around for Milly. Where did all these women come from? I needed a familiar face.

I was beginning to feel like a plucked chicken trying to swim in a lake full of geese. I turned and sighed with relief when I saw my friend coming up behind me.

"Val gave Charmine her beautiful dress," Milly said.

"Oh," the women said as one chorus. Something in their tone suggested my presence had been legitimized.

"Wherever did you find it?" asked the lady with the naked rat-dog.

"The new baby boutique on Central Avenue," I said.

"But it's direct from Paris fashion week," Milly blurted, as if that made it all right.

I wasn't sure where Milly had been going with that comment. The dress label *had* read, "From Paris." But I wondered if somehow my answer...or maybe *I myself*...wasn't good enough for this crowd. I looked around for the only other friendly face in the room. Buster. When I spotted him in the doggie pack, my face grew hot with embarrassment for both him *and* me.

Mixed in the crowd with Charmine in her hundred-and-fifty-dollar dress was a Yorkie in a jewel-studded yamaka and a pug in what I hoped was a fake diamond tiara. A spaniel wore a fancy leather collar with a silk bow tie. A Pekinese had on a pearl choker. *Geez!* Buster was the only dog not wearing designer bling. He also didn't have a manicure. Or even a professional trim. But then again, neither did *I*....

I was...*a bad doggy mother!*

"Have you been to the new doggy day spa on Ninth?" a lady with a tight, shiny face and swollen, rubbery lips asked.

"I...uh...."

"Grrr!" "Yap!"

The pack of munchkin dogs had erupted into chaos. I turned my head and saw Buster humping the pug. "Buster!" I yelled. He stopped, looked at me, then took off after a pink, fuzzy blur of fur. I curtseyed to the ladies. Their faces were frozen. Whether it was from horror or botched plastic surgery was anyone's guess.

"If you'll excuse me," I said.

I walked calmly out of Milly's huge living room in the direction Buster had gone, my heels clicking on the polished hardwood floor. Once I was out of sight, I bolted down the hallway. Every one of the dozen-or-so doors along the hallway were shut except one. I pushed it open and peered inside. There, in the corner of a posh guest room, I found Buster and Charmine in a compromising position.

"Buster! Charmine! You should be ashamed of yourselves," I whispered. The two stopped for a moment and looked up at me. I shook my head. "You can dress 'em up all you want, but you can't take the trailer trash out of a pair of mutts. Break it up or I'm calling the cops."

The copulating couple returned to their business at hand. But when I took a step forward and clapped my hands, they both took off past me out the door.

I was halfway down the hall after them when I heard the first shriek. By the time I got to the living room, it sounded as if I were crashing some kind of posh ladies' cussing convention.

"Look what that %%$#& dog has done!" screamed rat-dog woman.

"Well, I &#@$% never!" shrieked rubber lips.

I looked in the direction their gel-nails were pointing and my mouth fell open. Buster was standing in the middle of the Barkmitzva cake, munching away like a plow through a snowdrift. Milly tried to grab him. He leapt off the table into a collection of crystal water bowls set out on the floor for the dogs. They clattered like wind chimes as they scattered across the floor.

Dripping with soggy white frosting like a melting snowman, Buster leapt over a crystal bowl and stopped dead in the middle of the circle of ladies that had surrounded him. He yipped once, then shook out his coat. Everyone within a six-foot radius was splattered from head to toe in a shower of sticky, white mess. I could scarcely believe it. For once in my life, I wasn't one of the unfortunate bystanders!

"Buster!" I yelled. "Bad dog! Come!"

Buster looked up at me. He yipped once, then did that charming smile-and-wink thing he'd done the day we'd met. Like some magical dog in a fairytale, his wink instantly transformed my horror to giddiness. I suddenly had to fight not to burst out laughing. I knelt down and pursed my grinning lips. Buster ran up and leapt into my arms. I stood and surveyed the room full of ruined hairdos and sour faces.

Being a lady from the South, I thought it a prudent moment to beg our leave.

"I'm so sorry about all this, Milly," I said as she stared at me, dumbfounded. She'd escaped being splattered, but I was pretty certain my name would be as soon as I left. "If you'll excuse us, we'll be going."

I grabbed my purse off a couch and turned toward the door. An unstoppable grin burst across my lips as I yanked open the huge mahogany door, stepped outside and let it shut behind me. I didn't look back. I couldn't. I would have fallen on the ground laughing. A dozen highfalutin' ladies had just been taken down by a pair of lowfalutin' mutts.

I hugged the sticky little dog to my chest.

"You were a bad, bad boy, Buster," I said. "And you just made your redneck momma proud."

Chapter Sixteen

After peeling myself out of my sticky dress and tossing it into the washing machine, I spied an aquarium-sized fishing net hanging on the wall. I'd found it when I'd cleaned out the house last year. Instead of tossing it, I'd hung it on a little hook over the washing machine "just in case." Just in case of *what*, I didn't know. Maybe just in case one day I turned out to be a hoarder like my father, Tony Goldrich.

As I pondered that scary thought, an idea hit me. I grabbed the little net off the hook. I'm not a hoarder. I saved that net for a purpose. And today, it will finally come in handy.

After changing into a jean skirt and sleeveless top, I fixed myself a drink and let Buster out in the backyard. I sprayed him down with the garden hose. He seemed to enjoy his shower, and danced around in the spray, trying to bite the tube of water coming at him. Afterward, he shook himself out and his golden mane glistened in the sunlight.

But I was worried. When I'd wet down Buster's fur, I could see the outline of his body. After all that kibble this morning, then half a Bark-mitzva cake, Buster's swollen belly looked like it was about to burst. Something had to give, and I needed to be there when it did.

I grabbed the little net and trailed behind Buster as he snooped and sniffed his way around the backyard. First he toddled around the tiki hut, then the fire pit, then along the picket fence between my yard and Laverne's. Finally, he began to circle around a patch of grass.

"All right, here we go," I said. "Showtime." Buster squatted on his haunches and pooped out a respectable load. I caught it up in the little net. "Good boy!" I cheered.

"Dang. Wish I'd thought of that."

I looked in the direction of the voice. Laverne was standing at the fence wearing a tailored pink blouse and a pair of crisp, white shorts that came almost to her knees. I barely recognized her. Something was off. Way off. Then it hit me. Laverne looked...dignified!

"Uh...what did you say?" I asked.

"Wish I'd thought of that," Laverne repeated, her red lips pursed with frustration.

"Huh? Wish you'd thought of what, Laverne?"

She nodded toward the net full of dog turds. "For the tuna 'surprise.'"

"What? This? Ugh! Laverne! No! It's for...uh...something else."

Laverne's bug-eyes got even buggier. "What then?" she asked. "A booby trap? Sabotage?"

Dang. I really *had* created a monster. "No, Laverne. Buster ate my diamond earrings. I'm trying to...you know...recover them."

It took Laverne a moment, but she finally figured it out. When she did, she looked disappointed. "Well, could you do me a favor? Keep him out of my yard? Just look at the mess he's made!"

Laverne stepped sideways and waved a thin, spotted hand dramatically across the vista of her yard, like Vanna White revealing the answer to a puzzle on Wheel of Fortune. I took a gander over the short fence. To my shock, her yard was pockmarked with holes. And Buster was a digger, just like Charmine.

"Geez. Sorry, Laverne. I had no idea it was that bad. I'll do my best to keep an eye on him from now on."

Laverne sighed. "Have you figured out any more ways to give J.D. and Tom the heave ho? I tell you, the tuna surprise thing isn't working.

J.D.'s got a cast-iron stomach. I think he would eat anything—including dog crap—just so long as he didn't have to cook it."

"No," I confessed. "Not really." I studied the holes in her backyard. Something didn't seem right about them, but I couldn't put my finger on it. "I guess we could cut the guys up into pieces and bury them in your yard. The holes are already dug."

"What kind of knives would we need?" Laverne asked.

I couldn't tell if she was joking or not. But I didn't have time to think about it. Something else vied for my attention. Buster had come running up to me with a bone in his mouth.

"Where did you get that?" I asked him.

"He came from over there," Laverne said. "Your other neighbor's place."

"You mean the vacant house next door?"

"Dag-nabbit, Val! That's it!" Laverne practically shouted.

"What's 'it'?"

"We could buy that old dump and let the guys live in it! I think I could swing half of it if you could."

I looked at her like she was nuts. "I don't have that kind of money, Laverne."

"I thought you got an inheritance. We'd only need about fifteen grand apiece. I bought my place for $37,500, and it was in pristine condition."

"Laverne that was what? Twenty years ago?"

"Yeah. So? What are they now, double?"

"Try ten times more expensive. Haven't you bought anything since 1985?"

"No. Not much, anyway. Why should I? I brought everything I needed with me from Vegas."

Considering her house was a mausoleum to Elvis, The Rat Pack, and Siegfried and Roy, she wasn't kidding. "I don't think we can swing it," I said.

"Dang it," Laverne muttered and adjusted the crotch on her white shorts. "I guess it's just as well. They say the place is haunted, anyway."

"Haunted? What are you talking about?"

"I thought you knew, Val. Why do you think it's been vacant all these years? Somebody blew up in there the year before I moved here. I think that's why I got my place so cheap. Well, that and the fact that your parents had turned your place into a garbage dump." Laverne bit her lower lip. "No offense."

I shook my head. "Wait a minute. Someone 'blew up' in there?"

"Something like that. Sporadic helium combination, as I recall."

"Huh?"

Laverne nodded and looked behind me. "Looks like Buster's making another deposit. Let me know if you're not gonna use all of it."

I forced a smile at the strangely undignified, dignified old lady. "Sure. Gotta go."

I ran over and kept a close eye on Buster. As the second round of poop fell into the net with the first batch, I tried not to think about what I had to do next.

I WAS PANNING THROUGH poop when the phone rang.

"Hello?" a man's voice said. "I'm calling about the dog in the flyer?"

My heart flinched. "Yes?"

"I think it might be my dog, Pat."

"What makes you think that?" I asked as I sifted through the last turd. Crap. No diamonds yet.

"Well, because the dog in the flyer looks like Pat?"

"Oh."

"Can I come over and see the dog? I'm really anxious to get Pat back."

"You mean...right now? Today?"

"Yes. I can get in my car and leave now."

"Well..." Crap! I can't let Buster go now. Not until he lets go of the goods! Plus, he looks like a swollen toad. "Um...I'm afraid today isn't a good day."

"What do you mean?"

"Well, um....I took the dog to a Barkmitzva and um...now they're all under quarantine."

"Quarantine?"

"Yeah. There were a lot of dogs there. One had a severe case of Jew...ish...en...vitosis."

"I've never heard of that."

"It's very rare. And I think he might have caught it."

"Did you say 'he'?"

"Uh...yes."

"Oh. My dog Pat's a girl."

"So Buster's not your dog," I said, strangely relieved. "Wrong anatomy."

"Too bad. Well, if you don't find anyone to take him, I will."

That's odd. "Yeah. Sure. You'll be the first person I call."

"Okay then, thanks. Hope your dog gets well soon."

"Thanks. I hope you find your Pat."

I clicked off the phone. Buster ran up, wagging his tail. As I petted him, he dropped another bone at my feet. I didn't know where he was getting them, and thanks to Laverne's story about the person blowing up next door, I wasn't at all sure I wanted to find out.

Chapter Seventeen

By late afternoon, Buster's considerable efforts had yet to pan out for diamonds. So far, he'd yielded a nickel, a button, a rubber band and my missing hair scrunchie. Yuck! I took the pooch for a walk around the neighborhood, hoping to help move things along. I'm not sure it helped, but I *did* discover one thing.

Buster had an issue with skateboards.

He and I were almost back to my place when a scrawny, red-headed kid with purple headphones over his ears nearly ran us down with one. I jumped off the sidewalk to get out of his way, but Buster stood his ground. I tugged on the leash, but Buster took a snapping lunge at the kid's ankle that nearly jerked me off my feet. I had no idea he was so powerful! The kid whizzed by in a blur of Metallica and Teen Spirit, not bothering to slow down. After he rolled past us, he looked back long enough to yell, "Mangy rug rat!"

I could have said the same about him.

"What a jerk!" I said to Buster as I watched the kid disappear down the street. Buster yipped in agreement.

I patted his head and turned back toward my house. A chill ran down my spine. I could have sworn I saw the front door on the vacant house next door close. *Were my eyes playing tricks on me? Had I imagined it?* I felt a little weirded out about the place ever since Laverne said it was haunted.

Haunted? Naw. That's not a real thing. Is it? No matter how I tried, I just couldn't get Laverne's conversation out of my mind. *Can people really just blow up?*

I couldn't stand it anymore. Enquiring minds needed to know. I let Buster out into the backyard and called Judy Bloomers to find out what she knew about the vacant house next door.

"Hello, Judy?"

"Who are you again?" she asked.

"One of the ladies you met at the coffee shop at Publix yesterday."

"Oh yeah. The dog haters."

"Look, I don't hate...ugh. Listen. I was wondering if you could tell me anything about 1333 Bimini Circle."

"You interested in buying it?"

"Maybe," I lied.

"Hold on a second."

I listened as Judy punched some keys on a computer. Then I heard her gasp. "You said 1333 Bimini Circle, right?"

"Yes."

"Just my luck," she sneered. "That place has been vacant for over two decades. I finally get a client who's interested, and it went off the market last week. Dad blast it!"

"It sold? Really? Who bought it?"

"I can't tell. It should be in public records in the next few days. Why?"

"Well, I live next door."

"Oh my word! You're the *Thelma and Louise* gals, right? If you're ready to sell, I could move your houses in a heartbeat!"

"Then why did it take so long for the one next door to sell?"

"Well, you know, as a realtor I'm not obligated to divulge this...but seeing's how you're such a good client and all, between you and me, the place has a bit of a shady history."

I bit my lip. "What do you mean?"

"Well, the old lady who owned it died under suspicious circumstances. Everyone says her *son* killed her. Set her on fire. Human barbecue. He went to prison for murder, you know."

"What? That's horrible!" I gasped. "But...Laverne said she thought the lady had died of something like...a sporatic helium combination?"

I listened while Judy laughed for a full minute. I wondered if her polyester pants were up to the challenge of all that wiggling belly flab.

"Thanks, I needed that," she said, still giggling. "I think your friend meant 'spontaneous human combustion.'"

"What?"

"Yeah. That's what the son claimed as his defense during the trial. Said he came home to find his mother Mabel burned to cinders by some freak act of nature. There wasn't anything left of her but a charred foot, as I recall. But just like that old house itself, nobody bought it."

"Until now. The house, I mean."

"Right."

"I'm curious, Judy. How long did he get?"

"From what I heard, he was sentenced to around twenty years."

A movement outside made me glance at the sliding glass door. Buster was scratching to be let in. In his mouth was a bone that looked suspiciously as if it could have come from someone's barbecued mother.

"Thanks, Judy. I gotta go," I said, and clicked off the phone.

I STARED IN HORROR at the bone in Buster's jaws. The house next door had been vacant for two decades. The son had gotten twenty years in prison. It was all too much of a coincidence to be...well...a coincidence.

OMG! Do I have a murderer living next door?

I reached for the handle on the sliding glass door to let Buster in. Suddenly, his ears perked up. He dropped the bone and ran off to the right, toward the once-abandoned house. Is that where he'd found the bone? I jerked open the door and ran after him.

"Leave that alone, Buster!" I screeched.

"I can do what I want. It's a free country," a man's voice yelled back at me.

Shock and surprise double-teamed me and caused me to trip over my own bare feet. I recovered without eating a dirt sandwich, then stood on tiptoe and peeked around like a meerkat, trying to ascertain the source of the voice. Living on the water, noises bounced and echoed, making it hard to be sure. It sounded as if the voice had come from the house next door. Was that possible? After decades of neglect, the yard was so overgrown, I couldn't make out anything beyond the unkempt bushes bulging through the sagging, chain-link fence.

I looked down at Buster and squealed. He was trying to wriggle his swollen belly through the hole he'd excavated under the chain link fence. I dove to my knees and grabbed him by his hind legs and pulled him back into my yard.

"Naughty boy!" I scolded. I reached over and grabbed a potted plant with my free hand. I dropped it like a plug into the hole. Buster took the opportunity to lick my face with the same tongue that might have just been chewing someone's final, boney remains.

"Aargh! You're disgusting, you know that?"

"What did *I* do?" the same man's voice asked.

It *had* come from next door. I yelled back through the hedges, "Sorry. I wasn't talking to you."

As I scrambled to my feet with Buster squirming in my arms, the tangled jungle of overgrown bushes began rustling like something out of *Jurassic Park*. Suddenly, they separated, and a creature peered at me with eyes as black as the hair covering most of its face. I gasped. The guy could've been mistaken for the missing link if it weren't for three things. One, he was carrying a shovel. Two, he was wearing a red

Speedo. And three, he had a three-foot-long iguana draped around his neck like a Neanderthal kerchief.

My mouth fell open and I blinked hard. I couldn't believe my eyes. It wasn't the shovel or the Speedo or the lizard that knocked me for a loop. It was something else entirely. We stared at each other for a moment. *No. It couldn't be...could it?*

It was the jerk from Davie's Donuts.

"Oh. It's you," I said, bristling. "I didn't recognize you without the hound dog."

He laughed dryly. "I didn't recognize you without the custard facial."

So that's how it's gonna be, huh? I shot him a dirty look. "What's with the iguana cape?"

Ape man petted the iguana's head. "I like to think he adds to my allure," he said in a way that left me wondering if he was joking or not.

"Well, given what you've got to work with, it certainly couldn't hurt," I sneered.

He eyed me up and down, but said nothing. Buster licked my face again. I clenched my jaw in disgust. All of a sudden I remembered something. *I could be talking to a murderer!* My sarcastic bravado evaporated. But this was no time to show weakness. I could collapse once I'd gotten myself safely back into my house....

"Y...you the...n...new owner?" I stuttered, taking a blind step backward.

The hairy guy stroked the iguana's tail, but kept his black eyes locked on mine. "No."

I let out a sigh of relief. My buckling knees straightened. "Oh. So, what are you doing over there?"

"Surveying the property."

"In a Speedo?"

"Last time I checked, it's not illegal." He looked me up and down and licked his lips, giving me a case of the willies.

My own mouth had gone dry. I wanted to say, "Well, it should be," but thought better of it. "Okay," was the best I could come up with for a snappy alternative.

"After all, it's *my* place," he said, and grinned at me like that guy in *Silence of the Lambs*.

"But...." My heart skipped a beat. I took another step back and nearly tripped. I lost my grip on Buster. He leapt out of my arms. "I...I thought...you said you *weren't*...the new owner."

"I'm not, technically," he said. "Not *new*. You see, I've owned this place for over twenty years. It was tied up in some legal disputes, but I took care of that recently."

A chill ran down my spine despite the heat. I wondered who he'd "taken care of" recently, and if Buster was now bringing me body parts as evidence. *Aaarggh!* I took yet another step back, trying to calculate how many more I would need to reach my back door. I tried to smile, but my face was locked in place, my eyebrows frozen somewhere up near my hairline.

"Well...uh...in that case...welcome to the...uh...jungle," I stuttered, trying to sound casual.

The hair-covered bald guy glanced from side to side at the overgrown plants surrounding him. "That's funny," he said. But he didn't laugh. Instead, he stepped back into the bushes and disappeared.

I stood there for a few moments, too stunned to move. I caught a whiff of charcoal lighter. Then, dark gray smoke began billowing from above the bushes in ape man's backyard. I turned and fled into my house, Buster hot on my heels.

Chapter Eighteen

"Goober, you've got to come spend the night with me. Tom's out of town!"

"I didn't know you cared," Goober sneered.

"Argh!" If I wasn't already scared out of my wits, I'd have lost them right then and there. "Goober! It's not...That's not...ugh! It's my neighbor. I think he's *a murderer!*"

Goober's tone shifted from sarcasm to mild interest. "Why? What's he done?"

"He's in the backyard. Barbequing. In a Speedo!"

"Val, if that made a person a murderer, half of Florida would be incarcerated by now."

"No! I mean...that's just.... Listen, I'll explain later. Can you come over or not?"

"I'll check my schedule."

I waited on the line and listened as Goober shuffled through some papers.

"You're in luck. I had a cancellation."

"Gee. Lucky me."

"But Winky has to come, too."

"Argh! Why?"

"He's got a cold."

"So?"

"Winnie's paying me five dollars a day to keep him from calling her every three minutes."

"Argh! I'll pay you twenty to leave him there."

"Tempting. But I've already made my deal with the devil."

I ground my teeth for a moment. "Ugh. Okay. Both of you can come over." *What the hell. My couch is already ruined, anyway.*

"Thanks, Val. You're all heart."

Great. Goober was on his way over with Winky, and the freckled little redneck had a cold. *Gawd! Just what I needed.* Men were such babies when they were sick. I didn't know which had me worried most; Winky with a cold, or my psycho neighbor grilling gawd-knows-what next door.

To top it off, Buster still hadn't let go of my diamonds.

"Sorry. No lunch for you. Dr. Goober's orders," I said to the reddish-gold ball of fur that looked like Charmine, but, thankfully, didn't have her vicious vendetta against me. "Besides, you didn't do your job, Buster. I was talking to a *murderer* a few minutes ago and you just stood there looking cute. You're supposed to be protecting me!"

Buster didn't seem phased at all by his dereliction of duty. Instead, he positioned himself at my feet and drilled me with his beggar eyes every time I took a bite of leftover tuna casserole. When I called him on it by staring back at him, he let out a yip, then jumped up on his hind legs and twirled around.

I laughed. "Maybe Tom's right. You *do* know a few tricks." I picked a smoked oyster out of the noodles with my fingertips and suspended it over Buster's head. He twirled around again and then put his paws together and pumped them up and down like a kid left alone with a foaming soap dispenser. I giggled and dropped the oyster. It never hit the floor. Buster snapped it up mid-air, licked his chops and danced around for more.

I was dangling a second smoked oyster when an unpleasant thought occurred to me. Considering the current unfinished business at hand, feeding smoked oysters to Buster was probably not one of my better ideas.

"Let's go, boy." I stood up and lured Buster toward the back door with the oyster. "Let's go make mama some earrings."

Buster yipped and danced around me until I opened the back door. I flung the oyster out into the yard. He leapt into the air and snatched it before it hit the ground.

"Geez. What are you? Some kind of circus performing pooch?"

Buster yipped again, as if to say "yes," then began circling in the grass. I knew what that meant. I snatched the aquarium net leaning against the wall just outside the backdoor. I was trailing behind Buster, about to nab some doggie Tootsie Rolls, when I heard Laverne yell.

"Dad blame, egg-sucking son of a hockey puck!"

I looked over at her. She was on her knees, a spade in her hand, shoveling dirt into a hole.

"You okay over there?" I asked.

"Val, that dog of yours is still tearing up my yard!"

"Sorry Laverne." I walked over to her. "How do you know it's Buster? It could be a possum or something."

As if on cue, Buster ran under the fence and started helping Laverne excavate. She looked up at me, her left eyebrow an inch higher than her right.

"Buster! No!" I yelled. Buster yipped, licked Laverne's face, and wiggled back under the fence. I grabbed him up in my arms. "Sorry, Laverne. I'm doing my best to keep an eye on him until we find his owner. I promise he won't do it again."

"He better not, or I'll bean him with my shovel!" Laverne pursed her lips. "I got enough man problems as it is, Val. That dog of yours has just about killed my prize-winning Princess Margaret rose bush." She looked mournfully at the wilted rosebush. "Thank goodness some rain is on the way to wash the dirt back in."

I looked out to the west where Laverne had nodded. The bruised sky over the Gulf of Mexico portended a nasty-looking thunderstorm on its way. My cellphone pinged. It was Tom.

"Sorry!" I said to Laverne again. "Listen, I've got to get this." I grimaced apologetically, let go of Buster and the net, and stuck a potted plant in the hole under her fence. I fished around in my back pocket and, for once, I managed to click on the phone before it went to voice mail.

"Hey, Tom."

"Hey!" he said cheerily. "How are things going?"

"Fantastic."

"Is Buster eating okay?"

Buster began circling again. "No problem there." I found the net in the grass and angled it under Buster's haunches.

"Good." Tom switched to his sexy voice. "So, are you wearing your new earrings?"

"Uh...of course," I lied.

"Take a picture. I want to see you in them."

Crap! "Uh...I can't right now, Tom."

"Why not?"

"Uh...I'm outside...Buster's uh...doing his business."

"His what?"

"I'll send you a picture of that, too. Listen. Someone's at the door, Tom. Gotta go. Bye!"

I clicked off the phone before I got myself in even *more* trouble. *Geez!* The world was squeezing in on me. I looked to the left toward Laverne's place. She was mad as a three-fingered banjo picker. I looked to the right at the unkempt bushes concealing the new psycho killer next door. Then I looked down at Buster. His back haunches were still crouched over the net.

"Come on, boy! Drop the goods. I got a hot cop looking for those diamonds."

As if on command, Buster released a few more nuggets like a fuzzy Pez dispenser. I scooped them up in the net. "Good boy!" I walked over to the garden hose, turned it on full blast and pulverized the contents of the aquarium net. The turds disintegrated, leaving nothing but a bottle cap and a chewed match stick. I slumped back on my heels.

Geezy Pete! Is this what my life has come to? Sifting through dog poop, dodging an angry Vegas showgirl, and hoping two dim-witted derelicts can save me from a murderous Sasquatch in a red banana hammock?

"Why don't I take a picture of *that* for you, Tom," I muttered.

Funny. Why was it Tom was never around when I needed him? I mean, Goober and Winky were more reliable than *he* was! The doorbell rang. *Awesome. I was livin' the dream.*

"Come on, Buster," I said, and headed toward the house. But he kicked up some grass and took off around the tiki hut. "Buster!" I yelled. The doorbell rang again. I gave up my chase and sprinted through the sliding glass doors, across the living room and to the front door. I opened it to find Goober looking a little worse for wear, and Winky looking a little green around the gills. Still, my gut unclenched. I was relieved to no longer be alone with the nutcase running loose next door.

"Hey guys," I said. "Thanks for coming." I looked past their shoulders. "I half expected Jorge to come along for the ride. What's he up to?"

"On a date." Goober said.

"A *date?*" I asked, incredulous.

"A *hot* date," Winky rasped. "Paid us two dollars apiece to clear out."

Goober fingered a few bills in his shirt pocket. "Well aren't we just a pair of good Samaritans today," he said to Winky.

"Yeah. Killing two bird-brains with one stone," I sneered.

"So, what's with the net, Einstein?" Goober asked.

I looked down, surprised to find I still had the poop net in my hand. "It's for the dog."

Winky coughed. "No offense, Val, but ain't no kind a dog gonna fit in that."

I sighed. "It's not exactly the dog I'm trying to catch with it." I lowered my eyes. "He ate my diamond earrings this morning."

Winky scratched his buzz cut above his left ear. "Well, how you think yore...?" A knowing smile crossed his freckled, red-nosed face. "Oh. I get it."

Goober twitched his bushy moustache. "Lovely. So is that why you called us over? To scrape through dog scat?"

"Not exactly."

"So, what's the deal, then? You a'feared of this new dog, too?" Winky asked.

"No," I said, realizing the fact for the first time myself.

"Then what's going on?" Goober asked.

"Well, two things," I said, and shut the front door behind them.

"So?" Goober asked.

"I need a picture of me in the earrings. For Tom."

"Ever heard of a selfie?" Winky sneered.

"Yes. But, if you recall, the earrings aren't exactly *available* at the moment."

"Oh yeah," Winky said, and collapsed onto the couch in a heap of wrinkled, thrift-store clothes. "You could always get you a fake pair at the Dollar Store."

The thought must have amused Goober. He grinned. "So, where is the little diamond thief?"

"In the backyard." I yelled over my shoulder out the open back sliders. "Buster! Come here, boy!"

The fuzzy golden ball of fluff came bounding in. He pranced around Goober, then jumped on top of Winky. He sat up on the couch and grinned as he petted the squirming pup. "This little feller's happier'n a dog with two tails."

"Good thing he's only got *one*," I said, and held up the net. "Because I've only got one of *these*."

The guys laughed. Suddenly, the air crackled with blue energy. The hair on my arms stood on end. A second later, thunder boomed like a cannon shot, rattling the windows. Buster yelped and leapt out of Winky's arms. He shot under the couch like a furry missile.

Winky put a stubby finger to his chin. "Huh. Just like my cousin Fred."

"He's afraid of lightning?" I asked.

"Nope," Winky said, shaking his head. "He's always hiding under the couch."

Goober and I exchanged glances.

"Storm's coming," Goober said. "What say we order pizza and battened down the beer hatches?"

"Sounds like a plan," I agreed.

"And take that poor old dog out on the poop deck a'fore the rain hits," Winky said. "Maybe Mother Nature'll scare the diamonds out of him."

"Leave poor Buster alone," I said.

Goober smiled at me and wagged his bushy eyebrows. "Don't tell me you actually *like* the little pooch."

"He's okay," I shrugged. "But I'll like him even more when he gives me back my earrings."

Goober grinned. "Well, *that's* a change of heart. What brought all this about?"

"I dunno. I guess he likes my scurf."

"My granny always liked scarves," Winky said.

"I said *scurf*. My dead skin cells. I think Buster likes them."

Goober and Winky looked at me as if I'd just confessed to eating turds and whey.

I ground my teeth. "Anyway, you're not here to help with the dog. You're here because of my creepy next-door neighbor."

Winky shot upright on the couch. "Ah woo! I'm tellin' Laverne!"

"Argh! I'm not talking about *Laverne*. I'm talking about the new guy who just moved in next door."

The guys stared at mc blankly.

"Who?" Goober asked.

Rain began to pelt down on the roof.

"Let me call Fat Jack's Pizza," I said. "And then I'll tell you all about it."

Chapter Nineteen

"**...A**nd they never found a trace of her...except for a charred foot," I said, then bit into a slice of pepperoni pizza.

Goober, Winky and I were sitting cross-legged in a circle like campers around a fire—only the woods was my living room and the fire pit was an empty pizza box. Winky stared, wide eyed, as I relayed the harrowing tale of the murderous man next door and his unfortunate mother.

"Gaul dang it, Val," Winky gulped. His forgotten pizza hovered next to his mouth like a greasy UFO. "Then what happened?"

"He went to jail for twenty years. He just got out last week."

"*That's* the guy living next door?" Goober asked. He whistled and smoothed his moustache with his thumb and forefinger. "Are you *sure?*"

"Who else could it be?" I asked. "They say his father was a were-wolf!"

Goober sneered. "Come *on*, Val."

"Not like a *real* werewolf. He was one of those hairy people that pretends to be one. You know, for the *circus*."

"A freak show carny!" Winky said, his eyes as big as boiled eggs. "Like my cousin Whitey, 'The Man with No Brain.'"

Goober grinned out of the side of his mouth. "Obviously a close relative."

I tried not to smirk, but failed. "Look. You have to see him to believe it, guys. I swear, the man is as hairy as a chimpanzee. I'm talking
missing-chromosome hairy!"

Goober shrugged, unimpressed. "That still doesn't prove he's a
murderer, Val. Besides, how do you know how hairy he is? You couldn't
have gotten that good a look at him through all those bushes."

"That wasn't my first sighting. I ran into him the other day at
Davie's Donuts. He had a hound dog with him."

"You mean *that* guy?" Winky interrupted. He took a moment to
shift the cough drop in his mouth to one side. "She ain't lyin', Goober!
When he come through the door, I tole Winnie to call the *National
Enquirer!*"

"Okay," Goober said dryly. "We've established the guy's hairy. So
what? Lots of people suffer from hypertrichosis."

"Hyper tricky what?" Winky asked.

"Hypertrichosis. Overgrowth of body hair."

"How do you know what it's called?" I asked.

"My circus days, remember?"

I groaned. "Okay, Mister *Fartiste*, then how do you explain the fact
he was carrying a shovel? And that his hound dog was nowhere to be
found? And then Buster starts digging up bones? I'm telling you now, I
think the guy's barbequing bodies in his backyard!"

"Well, I mean, who hasn't?" Goober argued. "Meat of any sort, Val,
came from a body."

"Yeah," Winky said. "Or he could be crematin' pets, like we used
to."

"A valuable public service, I might add," Goober said, and took another slug of beer.

"Guys, you don't get it. The bone that Buster dragged up. I think it
might have been...*human*."

Goober spewed his beer. Winky farted.

"Human?" Goober gasped. "That's a whole different situation."

"Right," I agreed. "When I talked to him, he told me that he 'took care of somebody.' That's how he got the house!"

Goober whistled again.

"I need another beer," Winky hacked, holding his throat. Judging by his expression, he'd swallowed his cough drop whole.

"Sorry, Winky. That was the last one."

"What else you got?" he choked.

"Gin. Or red wine."

"Wine," he wheezed.

I got up and poured him a wineglass full, then thought better of it and poured the booze into a paper cup. I handed it to Winky, who was still cross-legged on the floor. He took a gulp and finally got the cough drop down his throat.

"You okay?" I asked, and sat back down on the floor beside the pizza box.

"Yep." Winky raised the paper cup in a toast. "To the winos that I knows," he said and grinned.

I burst out laughing.

"It wasn't *that* funny," Goober said.

"No. Look!" I said, and pointed at Winky's mouth. The red wine had stained the cough-drop residue coating Winky's teeth, turning them blackish-blue. Every time he opened his mouth, it looked like he had a mouthful of rotten choppers. The absurdity of it was too much for my frazzled nerves. I burst out laughing again and couldn't stop.

"What?" Winky asked, and hitched up one side of his mouth.

Goober laughed and I lost it all over again.

Winky's eyes danced between me and Goober, trying to figure out what the hell was going on. Every time he asked, "What?" he flashed his ugly teeth, and Goober and I cracked up again. After the third or fourth "What?" Goober and I were on our sides rolling around on the floor, squealing and holding our splitting sides.

I was just about to pee my pants when Buster saved me from certain incontinence. He jumped on top of me, then used me like a spring-board to leap toward the back door. When I looked over and saw him circling the threshold, the thought of Buster taking a dump on my floor sobered me right up. "Uh oh," I said, and scrambled to my feet. "Looks like he's gotta go. Dang! It's raining cats and dogs."

"I'll let him out," Goober said, and ran a hand over his bald head. "I don't have a hairdo to consider."

"Thanks," I said. "Don't forget to take the net. And be careful! Buster's an escape artist. If he gets loose in that psycho guy's yard and poops, I'll never get my earrings back!"

"I know one way to avoid that," Goober said.

"Really? What?" I asked.

"Ever heard of a leash?"

"Oh." My face grew hot. "There's one in the garage."

While Goober left to fetch the leash, Winky see-sawed himself up to standing.

"Escape artist, huh?" Winky asked.

"Yeah. He's already dug under the fences to both neighbors' yards," I explained. "I don't know what to do about it, either. I'm out of potted plants to cover the holes. And Buster keeps digging up Laverne's garden. Boy, she's none too happy about it, either."

"My cousin Sharleen had a cat like that," Winky said. "One time it tried to cross over a swimmin' pool by sneakin' along a clothesline like a tightrope walker. Notice I said '*one time*.'"

I was still eyeing Winky funny when Goober came back in the room. As he fastened the leash on Buster's collar, he transformed from a hard case to a soft-sided baby-talker.

"Who's the dirty digger?" he cooed at Buster. "Hmmm? Is it you? Come on, little one. We'll see who the *real* escape artist is."

"Watch it," Winky warned. "I heard a dogs scaling chain link fences a'fore."

"Thanks for the helpful hint," Goober said.

"The point is, keep an eye on Buster at all times, okay?" I warned. "He's sneaky."

Goober nodded. "Aye aye, Captain Curmudgeon." He slid open the back door and disappeared into the night.

"What's a cur-muh-gin?" Winky asked.

I opened my mouth to answer, but was cut short by a horrible, high-pitched howl. It shot out from somewhere in the darkness, and echoed through the open back door. The hair on the back of my neck stood up. Winky and I exchanged wide-eyed stares.

"Goober!" we hollered simultaneously. We were scrambling toward the back door when the lights went out, plunging us into total darkness.

"Lord help us!" Winky cried out.

My heart throbbed in my throat. I cautiously inched my head out the back door and whispered, "Goober?"

A hand grabbed my shoulder. I nearly peed my pants. "Winky!" I screamed and whirled around. "You nearly scared me to death!"

"What's going on?" he whined.

Another hideous, mournful howl reverberated in the blackness, sending shivers down my spine. As best I could tell, the howl had come from the right, in the direction of my psycho next-door neighbor's place. I strained to make out shapes in the inky night air, but it was too dark. For a split second, a sudden flash of lightning lit the backyard like a black-and-white photo. During the millisecond snapshot, in the overgrown hedges lining the chain-link fence, I thought I saw someone swing a shovel or a shotgun. A sickening sound like cracking bones split the air, followed by an inhuman scream, then the boom of thunder.

Winky and I stood frozen in place like two tongues on a flagpole. I could barely breathe.

Out of the blackness, a dim figure emerged. It was running right for us! Before Winky and I could swallow our spit, Goober slammed into us, sending us tumbling like three bowling pins across the living room floor.

Goober scrambled to his feet first. "Don't go out there!" he yelled. He slammed the sliding door shut and set the lock. "Hurry!" he ordered. "Lock all the doors and windows!"

Winky and I scattered like crack heads in a police raid. We climbed over beds and bathtubs and dressers until we'd secured every last window latch. Then we stumbled back to the living room to find Goober collapsed in the easy chair, his face slack.

"What happened?" Winky asked.

Another blood-curdling howl pierced the night sky. Then someone—or some*thing*—started banging on my front door!

Winky and I fell to our knees on either side of Goober in the easy chair. We stared at the door, too petrified to speak. Suddenly, the banging stopped and the doorknob slowly began to twist. Terrified, I grabbed Goober's arm.

The doorknob shook violently. Winky whimpered. I bit my lip to keep from screaming.

The doorknob went still. All was quiet for a moment. Then the scratching began. Slow at first, then faster and faster, as if something were trying to rip the door to shreds.

I looked at Goober and realized my nails were biting into his arm. I loosened my grip, but he didn't move. He just stared straight ahead at the door. I glanced around for Winky, but he'd disappeared. I was about to swallow my tongue when the scratching suddenly stopped.

"Winky?" I whispered. I started to get up, but a thump at the door sent me back to my knees.

The banging at the door started up again. It was faster and more furious this time. It kept going until the whole frame shook. I was certain that at any moment, the door would splinter and we'd all be eaten alive by the monster on the other side!

But the door held. The banging stopped. An eerie silence took its place.

"Is it gone?" Winky whispered from under the couch.

"I think so," I whispered back.

I looked up at Goober. He was still sitting motionless in the chair. Buster's leash was clutched in his hand, but Buster wasn't at the other end of it. The only thing that remained was his collar, and it had been chewed to bits.

Chapter Twenty

Last night, once the horrifying banging and scratching on my front door had ended and Goober, Winky and I had regained full use of our limbs, Goober had crept over to the back door and opened it wide enough to allow a few molecules of air to pass through. While he'd stood guard with a rolling pin and Winky with a spatula, I'd called out into the black night for Buster. Over and over I'd called, but the poor pooch hadn't come back. Sometime after 3:00 a.m., our crazy adrenaline highs had worn off and we'd collapsed, exhausted, into unconsciousness.

I WOKE UP ON THE LIVING room floor, my back slumped against the wall. Goober was leaning against me, his peanut head on my shoulder, his long fingers still wrapped around the rolling pin. It was comforting to know he was still on guard and at the ready, in case we were attacked by the sudden urge to make a batch of sugar cookies.

Somewhere nearby, Winky was sawing logs. I glanced around and spied him under the couch. An empty Nyquil bottle lay on its side on the floor near his pudgy left hand. I shook my head softly.

I hope God isn't watching this.

I moved my shoulders. My neck cracked loud enough to echo off the kitchen cabinets. I rubbed my shoulder and gently nudged Goober. He jerked to attention, cleared his throat and blinked.

"You okay?" I asked.

"Yeah. You?"

"Yeah." I mustered the courage to ask the question I had been too afraid to pose last night. "What do you think happened to Buster?"

Goober looked down at the floor. "I dunno, Val. Even back in the day...you know...camping in the woods with all those other homeless guys. Nothing like this ever happened. Last night was *unreal.*"

"What do you mean, *unreal?*"

Goober sucked in a breath and blew it out. "It's hard to explain, Val. I was just, you know, waiting for Buster to do his thing. I had the net ready and everything. Then, all of a sudden, the lights went out. I couldn't see a thing. Buster started tugging on the leash, kind of like when you get a good nibble fishing. Then there was this howl. Then one hard yank. The leash went slack."

"Then what happened?"

Goober looked away. "That's when I heard that freaking cracking noise. Like something munching bones. I couldn't see *anything*, Val. *Nothing.*" He turned to face me, more serious than I'd ever seen him before. "I panicked, okay? I ran for the house. I'm sorry, Val."

"It's okay, Goober," I said, and touched his arm. "Don't get me wrong. I'm not blaming you. I'm just trying to figure out what happened. You did the best you could, I'm sure. And I'm glad you're safe. Believe it or not, you're more important to me than Buster."

Goober's lip twitched under his moustache. "Easy to say when you hate dogs."

"I didn't hate Buster. I told you that already."

Goober smiled weakly, then frowned.

"You don't think he's *dead*, do you, Goober?"

Goober's bloodshot eyes looked down. "I don't know, Val."

"From what you just told me, it doesn't sound good."

"No. It doesn't," Goober agreed. "It was almost like...I dunno...like something grabbed him and *ate* him."

I blanched. "Geez, Goober! What could have done *that?*"

Goober hitched an eyebrow. "In Florida? Lots of things."

I sighed. "I hope you're wrong. If Buster *is* still alive, we've got to find him. *Today.* Tom will be back tomorrow."

"And you need the earrings."

"Well, yes. And Buster, too. Tom's pretty attached to him."

Goober studied me. "Tom. Right."

"*What?*" I asked.

"Nothing. I'll get up. Take a look around. See if I can find him. Or what's left of him."

I elbowed Goober in the ribs. "Don't joke. It's not funny!"

Winky rolled over and coughed. His face was covered in ginger stubble and dried snot. He opened a crusty, red eye and muttered, "Do I smell coffee?"

"Oh no, Goober," I said. "Winky's cold has gotten worse. He's delirious."

"Naw," Goober replied. "He always looks like that in the morning. Put on a pot of coffee and he'll spring back to life."

"Back to life...." I muttered Goober's words, thought about Buster, and nearly burst into tears.

Goober twitched his moustache to try and amuse me. It didn't work. "Val, you remember those freeze-dried shrimp things you used to could order from the back of comic books?" he asked.

"Huh?" I asked.

Goober scrambled to his feet. He held a hand out for me. I grabbed it and hauled myself up.

"I think so," I said. "What were they called? Sea monsters?"

"Sea *monkeys*," Winky corrected as he scooted out from under the couch. "And they wasn't no shrimps, neither. They was gen-u-ine monkeys of the sea. That one in the picture had a crown and everything."

I shot a glance at Goober.

"You can't win this one," he muttered under his breath.

"So why on earth did you bring up sea monkeys?" I asked.

Goober hitched a thumb in Winky's direction. "Well, Winky's kind of like a sea monkey. Only instead of water, you have to add coffee. He springs to life, but he never quite lives up to the hype on the package."

I offered the best smile I could, given the circumstances. "Thanks for the warning...and for trying to cheer me up. I'll get the coffee going for King of the Sea."

I grabbed a coffee filter and ran some water into the carafe. When I switched on the machine, I realized that sometime during the night, the electricity had come back on.

"Coffee should be ready in a minute or two, Winky," I said. "Why don't you go get yourself a shower?"

"All right," Winky said, and brushed himself off. "Val, you really should dust under your couch more often."

I MADE TOAST AND SCRAMBLED eggs for us while Winky showered. Goober went outside to poke around in the yard to see what he could find, now that it was daylight. I set aside a few clumps of eggs in a saucer for Buster, then remembered he wasn't here. My eyes stung. A lump welled in the back of my throat. I scraped the eggs back into the skillet as Winky bumbled out of the hall wearing nothing but a towel wrapped around his middle. I sniffed back a tear.

"Dang, Val. Hope I ain't gone and give you my dad-burned cold."

"Oh. Yeah. No. It's—"

The front door flew open. Goober's bald head jutted inside like a mustachioed tortoise. "Hey you two! Come take a look at this!"

Winky and I sprinted over to the front door. We looked down at the spot where Goober was pointing. Something had scratched the heck out of the bottom half of the door.

"What the hell did that?" I asked.

"Gaul-dang it! I know what it was!" Winky said, and hitched the towel further up over his freckled beer belly.

"What?" I asked.

"I seen somethin' about this on TV, y'all. I bet it was one a them there polter-geezer things."

I rolled my eyes. "Poltergeist. And there's no such thing."

"Huh." Winky scratched his buzz cut. "Min-ature swamp monster?"

"No."

"Well, how about a tiny little—"

"Look, Winky! There's no such thing as monsters!"

Winky pouted and pulled his towel tighter. "Sure there is, Val. And where there's monsters, there's little baby 'uns, too. Hey! Maybe that guy next door really *is* a gen-u-ine werewolf."

"Or perhaps a skunk ape in a witness protection program," Goober sneered.

"Nope," Winky said. "Can't be that. Skunk apes don't scratch up stuff. They usually just throw rocks or break off tree limbs."

My upper lip twitched. "How do you know that?" I asked, immediately regretting it.

"My Cousin Jim Bob's a certified bigfoot tracker," Winky said.

"I'd say he was certified all right," I muttered.

Winky nodded proudly. "Yep."

"Well, whatever it is, it appears to possess a respectable set of claws," Goober said.

"But why are all the scratch marks so low?" I asked.

"Maybe he was on its hands and knees. Drunk," Winky offered. "I mean, it *was* Saturday night and all."

I sighed. "Let's have some breakfast and figure out what to do next. I think I have an idea."

I WAS DRYING THE BREAKFAST dishes when a sudden move-ment out the kitchen window caught my eye. I peered through the pane. Winky was standing atop my neighbor's chain-link fence, half naked, wind-milling his arms like a whirligig to keep from toppling over.

I yelled through the window pane. "Get down from there!"

Winky looked my way, then obliged me by tumbling backward. He hit the ground flat on his back. "Geez!" I hollered. I flung my dishtow-el aside and ran out the back door. The fall had knocked the wind out of the pudgy redneck. He was sitting up barking like an asthmatic seal. I knelt beside him and whacked him on the back until he caught his breath.

"What in the world do you think you were doing?" I asked.

"Reco...recon...," Winky gasped. "Spyin'!" he finally got out. "That nut job neighbor a yore's has got holes dug all over the yard, Val. And little tombstones, too."

"*Come on*, Winky," I said. "You must have knocked what sense you've got clean out of you."

"I ain't kiddin'. It's like that scary movie. You know. *Pet Seminary.*"

"Cemetery."

"Whatever. Somethin' ain't right, Val. It just ain't right."

"Somethin' ain't right, all right," I said, shaking my head. But to be honest, I wasn't sure *what*. Was I supposed to believe Winky? Under the influence of Nyquil, no less? I had enough on my hands trying to find Buster without having to babysit a hopped-up redneck who thought he could fly.

Fly....

A thought hit me like a spit wad between the eyes. *Flyers! I have a box full of flyers in the trunk!*

"Listen, Winky," I said, helping him to his feet. "I'm hoping Buster just ran off because of the storm. Before we stir up a hornet's nest with my crazy neighbor, I think we should explore the other possibilities."

"I reckon yore right," Winky said. "Like my Aunt Daisy always says, 'Ain't no use ticking off a wackadoodle a'fore you used your *own* noodle.'"

"Yes, a classic adage from the backwoods," Goober's voice rang out behind me.

I turned around. That rat! He'd been five feet away, stretched out in a lounge chair the whole time. "What are you doing, Goober?" I asked.

"Thinking," Goober said. "Clearly *someone* has to."

I shot him a sneer. "Think you could make yourself useful and go door-to-door handing out my missing-dog flyers?"

"Negatory," Goober said, and re-crossed his long legs. "Winky's gonna to have to do it."

"Why?" I grumbled.

Goober sat up and smoothed his bushy moustache. "Remember a few months back, when I went through the neighborhood handing out those flyers for our pet cremation services?"

How could I forget? I haven't been able to look my neighbors in the face since. "Yeah."

"Well, let's just say that it's possible I might have burned a couple of bridges along the way."

My jaw tightened. "Great. Well, do you think you might be able to trouble yourself to keep an eye on Winky for me? I think he might have a concussion."

"I got no such thang," Winky argued. "Winnie made me get tested for that a'fore we hooked up."

I rolled my eyes so hard I could feel them nearly get stuck. "Come with me, Winky," I said, and marched in the back door. I loaded Winky up with a basketful of water, cough drops and flyers and pointed him down the sidewalk. If he ended up alienating as many neighbors as Goober had, at least this time I knew a realtor to call if I needed to leave town quick.

Judy Bloomers. The thought of her made me reach for my phone. I needed to get as much information on the guy next door as I could, and pronto. Her line rang ten times, but Judy didn't pick up. I left a message for her to call me back and returned to the backyard. Last night's thunderstorm had made a mess of things. I straightened the lawn chairs and started picking up sticks and palm leaves strewn about the lawn. All the while, Goober watched me, stretched out in a lounge chair.

"Any bright ideas?" I asked grumpily as I pulled a palm frond out from under his feet.

"Nothing has yet sprung to mind."

I looked over at Laverne's place and saw two fresh holes in her garden. I winced. When I'd sent Winky on his way, I'd noticed Laverne's car wasn't in her driveway. Neither was J.D.'s white Mercedes. "How about helping me fill the holes in Laverne's yard?" I asked Goober.

"Manual labor? No can do. I'm on vacation."

"Vacation? From what? You haven't had a job since 1985."

"1987."

"Come on, Goober. Help me out."

Goober sat up and sighed. "I've already checked your entire yard, Val. There's no trace of Buster."

"Well, you could cruise the neighborhood for him."

Goober smoothed his moustache. "Cruising. Well, that sounds like something I could handle." Goober stood up and held out his hand. "But I'm gonna need money for gas."

"Of course. I wouldn't have thought any different."

Chapter Twenty-One

The spade hit something that made a hollow, tinny sound as I shoveled dirt into the fresh hole around Laverne's prize rosebush. Worried it might be one of my missing earrings, I dug deeper and sifted the dirt. A bone about five inches long emerged. Hunks of bloody meat still clung to it.

"Arghh!" I screamed and fell backward onto my butt. *What the hell is going on here?*

I looked over into my yard for Goober. Then I remembered I'd sent him off to cruise the neighborhood for Buster. My neck hair bristled. If Tom were here, he'd have known what to do. But he wasn't. Panic shot through me.

I'm all alone—and a killer is lurking somewhere nearby! Maybe looking at me right now...

I scooped the bloody hunk of flesh onto the spade, flung it back in the hole and gave it the world's most hasty burial. As I scrambled to my feet, a low, angry-sounding growl emanated from the direction of my psycho neighbor's overgrown hedges. I stifled a screech and leapt over Laverne's picket fence as graceful as a deer, then tripped over my garden hose and barrel-rolled through the grass all the way up to the backdoor.

I had my hand on the door handle when my cellphone rang, startling me out of what was left of my wits. I yanked open the door, whipped around inside, slammed it shut and locked it tight. My legs wobbled as I spoke into the phone.

"Hello?"

"Hey Val, what's up?"

"Winnie!" I noticed the spade in my hand and flung it away as if it were the smoking gun that could put me away for good. It skittered across the living room floor. "I...uh...nothing. What's up with you?"

"I was just calling to talk to Winky. He's not answering his phone."

"Oh. I sent him to hand out flyers around the neighborhood. He probably forgot to take it with him."

"That doesn't surprise me," Winnie laughed. "Thanks so much for watching after him the last couple of days. He was driving me crazy. I have to get my peanut-butter bacon bomb recipe just right before I send it off to the contest."

I studied the dirt trail left by the spade. "Oh. Right. How's that going?"

"I made another batch this morning with a pinch more salt. It was the best yet. The contest entry deadline is tomorrow. I just want to try one more thing before I mail off my recipe. I may need to pull an all-nighter. I hate to ask, but can you handle Winky for me for one more night? Goober said he's got PTWS."

"Huh?"

"Post Traumatic Winky Syndrome. He's been saddled with Winky for three days."

Spending the night with Winky sounded better than being alone with a monster hiding in the bushes. Relief washed over me. I really *must* have been scared witless. "Well...okay. Sure. I really want you to win."

"Thank you so much!" Winnie exclaimed. "I couldn't have done this without you and Goober keeping Winky out of my hair. I owe you. What can I do to repay you?"

"Well, I can think of something. How about a dozen peanut butter bacon bombs? Throw in free delivery and you're debt is paid in full."

"Ha ha! Okay, it's a deal. I'll drop them by tomorrow when I pick up Winky."

"Great. I'll keep an eye on him until then."

I hung up and noticed Goober walking up the driveway. I opened the door. "Any luck?"

"Nope. I circled around the neighborhood twice. I even checked the roadkill. Just a squirrel and a possum. But I almost flattened some jerk on a skateboard."

"Red-headed kid with purple headphones?"

"Yeah."

"Buster and I had a run-in with him yesterday. The kid practically ran us over. You don't think *he'd* have done anything to Buster, do you?"

"Who knows?" Goober shrugged. "He didn't look the serial killer type. But then again, who does? Speaking of closet psychos, where's Winky?"

"Still handing out flyers."

"Good." Goober put a finger to his chin. "What say you and I do a little brainstorming while we still can?"

"What do you mean?"

"Grab a notepad and pen. And a couple of beers. Let's figure out a list of possible scenarios of what happened to your pooch."

"Do you think Buster ran away, or someone took him?"

"Well, that's what we need to figure out," Goober said. "And, just so you know, I always think better with a belly full of tacos."

I WAS PULLING UP IN my driveway with a twenty-pound sack of tacos and a case of beer when I saw Winky huffing it down the street toward my house. He waved and then headed up the walkway that lead to the front door of my psycho next door neighbor's house.

I nearly drove into the ditch. "No! Winky! Not there!"

He didn't hear me. I slammed on the brakes, shoved the car in park, scrambled out and ran toward him. I rounded a line of unkempt shrubs just in time to hear him ring the doorbell. I cringed. I was too late. I crouched behind a bush and peeked around it. Winky was standing at the door holding a flyer in one hand, scratching his butt with the other.

No one answered the door. "Winky!" I whispered, then nearly fainted when he mashed the doorbell again. "Winky!" I whispered louder.

"Huh?" Winky turned to look in my direction. I saw the doorknob start to jiggle. I tucked my head back behind the bush and braced myself for an Olympic sprint. I heard the door creak open. Against all good sense and reason, I couldn't resist a peek. I stuck an eyeball around the bush. The door opened wider to reveal the hairy ape-guy standing at the threshold wearing a chef's apron. He was wielding a bloody meat cleaver.

"Good lord a mighty!" Winky hollered. Then, before I could blink, Winky flashed by me, nearly knocking me over. As he whizzed by, he caught sight of me hiding in the bushes and shot out a hillbilly scream that nearly pierced my eardrums. I shook my echoing head, then switched gears and scrambled off behind him, the two of us fleeing on foot like two kids just who'd pulled the school fire alarm.

I caught up with Winky at the front door. He was yanking on the knob like it was a stingy vending machine. I unlocked it and we tumbled into the house.

"What's up with you two?" Goober asked as we stood, doubled over, trying to catch our breath. "You look like you've seen a ghost."

"A dang...swamp monster's more...like it," Winky wheezed.

Goober looked to me to provide some sanity in the situation, but I didn't have much left to offer.

"Winky...rang bigfoot's doorbell," I panted. "He came...at him...with a cleaver!"

"My, my," Goober said, scratching his chin. "The plot thickens. This definitely calls for some serious taco eating and beer drinking."

I shot Goober an incredulous look. "Are you insane?"

"No. The brain requires protein to process complex problems," Goober said. "Like solving the mystery of the missing mutt?"

"Fine," I hissed. "But someone has to go outside and get the tacos out of the car."

Goober stared at Winky and me. "What's the problem?"

"I'm not going out there!" Winky bellowed.

"Me either," I said.

"Sissies," Goober said. "As usual, I have to do everything."

A FEW BEERS LATER AND Winky was back to his usual self. I wasn't sure if that was a good thing or not.

"*Nobody* said they'd seen Buster?" I asked him.

"Not a single, solitary soul, Val," Winky said, then crammed half a taco into his maw.

I shook my head and looked at Goober. "What do you think that means?"

"Hard to say. The leash was mangled, Val. Something could have grabbed him...for, like...*dinner*."

Winky started to open his mouth.

"Don't you dare say werewolf," I warned him.

Winky poked his chin up. "I wasn't gonna. I was gonna say 'gator.' Could'a even been a shark. If'n Buster fell in the water, I mean. When I throwed them fish guts off your seawall it was a regular feedin' frenzy out there."

I gulped. I hadn't thought about that. "Okay," I said, and wrote on the notepad. "That's one theory. But let's say he *didn't* get eaten by a gator or a shark. What else could have happened to him?"

"Alien abduction," Winky offered.

I popped him on the arm. "I'm serious!"

"Well, he's right, in a way," Goober said. "Somebody could have taken him."

"But who?" I asked. I shot Winky a dirty look. "Don't say aliens."

Winky switched gears and employed his open mouth to insert another taco.

"Well, there are quite a few suspects, if you think about it," Goober said.

"You're right," I agreed. "Laverne was pretty ticked off over Buster digging in her yard. I think she was kidding, but she *did* threaten to get rid of Buster if he did it again. And he *did*. Last night."

"Is that why you were filling in those holes?" Goober asked.

"Yes. And...there's something else. I found a hunk of dead animal in one of them."

"Oh my lawd!" Winky said, and eyed his taco suspiciously.

"She and J.D. were both gone this morning," Goober said. "They could have been getting rid of his body."

"Or just droppin' him off in front a Walmarts," Winky offered.

I shook my head. "I can't believe Laverne would do such a thing." But I wrote it down in the notebook anyway.

"What about J.D.?" Goober asked.

"He does have ties to criminal types," I said, shrugging. "You know, it was his nephew who broke into my house last year looking for that dead finger." A light-bulb went off in my head. "Oh my gosh! His nephew knows where I live!"

"Hmmm," Winky said. "Come to think of it, he does look a little haggardly lately."

"Who?" I asked.

"J.D."

"Well, he *is* shacked up with Laverne now," Goober said.

The two guys exchanged glances and snickered.

"What?" I asked. "I don't get what's so funny."

"Well," Winky said, "That's a lot a work in the sack for J.D., you know."

My eyes turned to slits. "Moving on. There's also that bratty kid on the skateboard."

"Long shot," Goober said. "What would be his motivation?"

"I dunno. Just because he's a jerk?"

"Possibly," Winky said. "My Uncle Elmer was a jerk."

I sighed. "Or there's the weird guy who called about Buster from the flyer. He said he'd take Buster, even though it wasn't his dog."

"He doesn't know where you live," Goober said.

"True. But Tom says that's easy enough to find out from somebody's phone number."

"Okay," Goober agreed. "But if Buster was loose wandering the streets, any random person could have picked him up. Just like Tom did."

"Buster wouldn't go with them," I argued. "He'd miss us."

"Really?" Goober asked, one eyebrow lifted. "How long have you and Tom had him? Two days?"

"Two and a half." I looked out at the empty doghouse. "I've got to get that dog back."

"For the diamonds," Goober said.

"Forget the earrings," I said. "Tom will be pissed...and heartbroken. He trusted me to take care of Buster...and look what happened."

"What happened?" Winky asked, as if he'd just joined the conversation.

"We're still trying to figure that out," Goober said. "Have another beer."

"Don't mind if I do," Winky said, and grabbed another from the case.

"That only leaves one other suspect," I said. "Somebody's gonna have to go check out the guy's place next door."

"Doggie Dahmer's?" Goober said. "No way!"

"I ain't goin' back over there," Winky bellowed. "I didn't believe you at first, Val. But you wasn't 'zageratin'. That guy's meaner'n my Aunt Vera. And she done been banned from public toilets in three counties."

I opened my mouth. "Don't ask," Goober blurted. I shut my mouth.

"Besides, he done seen me," Winky said. "He'll know the fig is up."

"Jig," I corrected.

Winky looked at me cockeyed. "Who's Jig?"

I turned to the only half-sober guy in the room. "That leaves you, Goober."

"Yeah. Let the poor intellectual do your dirty work," Goober griped. He sighed with resignation. "I guess I owe it to you. I *was* the one who lost him, after all. So, what's the plan?"

"I don't exactly have one," I said. "Just snoop around his house, I guess. See what you can find out. You know, check out his backyard for suspicious...*activities*. But we'll need a cover story for you. In case you're...uh...*spotted*."

"Taco delivery," Winky offered, and slid the last taco into his mouth.

"We don't have any tacos," I said, and held up the empty bag.

"All right then," Winky mumbled through his full mouth. "Health inspector."

"It's a house, not a restaurant," I argued.

"I've got it," Goober said. "Cable guy. It makes sense. He's just moving in. He'll want cable. I mean, what kind of psycho doesn't have a TV?"

I shrugged. "Could work. But what about a uniform?"

"I have a jumpsuit in my trunk for just such occasions," Goober said.

I looked at him funny.

"Don't ask," he said.

"I wasn't going to."

Chapter Twenty-Two

We waited until dusk to set our plan in motion. Dressed in a tan, threadbare, one-piece jumpsuit, Goober looked like a delivery man who had taken a wrong turn ten years ago and just kept going. He was teetering on the middle rung of a six-foot ladder. The ladder itself was straddling the chain-link fence between me and my nutso neighbor.

"Be careful, Goober," I whispered as I handed him a flashlight. "Winky says there's graves back there."

Goober's eyebrows raised an inch. "You're just telling me this *now?*"

I cringed. "I didn't want to worry you. Come back alive and there's half a bottle of Jack and a Zagnut bar waiting for you."

Goober paused in mid-step. His moustache twitched as he weighed his options. "Okay," he shrugged, and continued his climb until he'd reached the rung that was even with the top of the fence. He looked back at me and Winky. "Don't forget to turn the ladder around, in case I need to make a quick getaway."

"We're on it," Winky said, and gave him a freckled thumb's up.

Goober poked a huge, orange-tennis-shoed foot around in the bushes, trying to part the branches. "Geronimo," he said, and jumped into the wild tangle of hedges. The string of muttered cursing that followed had Winky and I exchanging muffled giggles. We hauled the ladder up over the fence and turned it around in my yard. We were about to reinsert it into the bushes when a strange, guttural grunt stopped us in our tracks.

"Was that a human bein'?" Winky whispered.

"I don't—"

Suddenly, the bushes across the fence came alive with crackling and rustling. We whipped our heads to the right and saw an orange sneaker and a long, tan pant leg poke out of hedges and bob up and down like the world's worst chicken impersonation. A second later, the rest of Goober appeared, his facial expression making the world's second-worst chicken impersonation.

"Where's the freakin' ladder?" Goober yelled. Winky and I stood there frozen, the ladder in our hands, looking like two petrified idiots trying to change a light-bulb.

"Argh! Get outta my way!" Goober yelled and grabbed the top of the fence with both hands. He swung a long leg over. His shoelace got tangled on a branch and he fell, face first, onto my side of the fence. Unfazed, he scrabbled himself back together like a half-squashed grasshopper and took off toward my back door.

Winky and I stared at each other, still frozen in place by moronic shock. A snorting growl from the crackling bushes thawed us out quick. We dropped the ladder and ran like the last two humans in a zombie apocalypse.

I made it through the sliding glass door after Goober. Winky scrabbled in right after me. He slid the door shut and slammed the lock in place.

"What happened?" I asked Goober between gasps for air. He was rifling through my kitchen cabinets. "Are you okay?"

"He didn't have a TV," Goober said, and slammed a cabinet door. "He had a Doberman."

A loud, deep rumble emanated from outside. The three of us jerked like a trio of Mexican jumping beans.

"It was just thunder," I said, and sighed with relief.

A loud bang on the front door turned us back into jumping beans.
"What was that?" I asked.

"How should *I* know?" Goober sneered. He opened another cabinet door. "Call the psychic hotline. Maybe *they* can tell you. And also help *me* find your Jack Daniels."

I shot Goober a dirty look and tiptoed over to the front window. I pulled down a slat, peeked through blinds and nearly squealed like a pig.

"It's him!" I choked.

"Who?" Winky asked.

"The psycho from next door!"

"Holy flippin' jalapeños!" Winky screeched. "Don't answer it!" He dove across the living room and started stuffing his body underneath the couch.

"I wasn't planning to," I hissed. I grabbed the flyswatter from the coffee table and plastered my back against the wall by the front door.

Ape man banged on the door again.

"Just like last night," Goober said. He'd abandoned his search for Jack Daniels and had begun throttling my poor living room lamp to death. "Don't make a sound!" he warned.

Winky farted loud enough to rattle the windows. We held our breath, for obvious reasons.

The banging stopped.

Despite the deadly olfactory assault like a week-old bag of rotten cabbage, we remained silent and held our positions. After about a minute, Winky whispered, "Sorry, fellers."

I rubbed my burning eyes. "What happened over there, Goober? Did the guy see you or something?"

"I'll tell you all about it. But first I want to see the Jack and the Zagnut bar."

I HANDED GOOBER THE candy bar and poured him a shot of Jack. Goober swallowed it down and slammed the shot glass on the kitchen counter. Winky and I waited with bated breath for Goober to spill his guts. He motioned for another pour. I obliged.

"It's kind of a blur," he wheezed. "I only got a quick glance through the bushes. The guy was doing some kind of weird ritual thing. The Doberman had a sack over its head. It was tied to a post. In some kind of a harness. It looked to me like some kind of voodoo sacrifice or something."

"Sacrifice?" I squealed. "Geez, Goober! What are we gonna do?"

"I have an idea," Goober said, and reached for the bottle of whiskey.

"What?" I asked.

He poured another shot. "Nothing. I say, let's do nothing."

"Nothing?" I protested.

Goober unwrapped his Zagnut bar. "Unless somebody's got a better idea?"

It was clear from the blank expressions on our faces, none of us had squat.

"I guess that's all we *can* do right now," I agreed reluctantly. "Tom will be back tomorrow. He'll know what to do."

"I don't like this one bit," Winky said. "I ain't waitin' around for that weirdo to slit my throat. We need to organize us a watch."

"A watch?" I asked.

"Yep. Help me move the couch."

Goober and I followed Winky's lead and helped push the couch across the living room until it was positioned in front of the sliding-glass doors, facing the backyard. Exhausted from lack of sleep, we flopped on the couch, me in the middle of an idiot sandwich. The plan was to take turns keeping watch out the back door. As if written into a bad horror script, Mother Nature decided to put on another thunderous fireworks display that night. Each time lightning streaked across the sky, it lit up the night in a blue-white flash, like an old-time flash bulb. And each time the thunder clapped, the dog next door let out a bone-chilling howl.

"That poor dog!" I said. "Shouldn't we call the police or something?"

"No!" Winky and Goober hissed simultaneously. I shrunk back in my cushion.

"If it's still howling, it's still alive," Goober said.

He had a point. I wondered if Buster was still alive, too. "I'll take first watch," I said.

"Fine with me," Goober said.

"Me, too," Winky said. "And don't you worry none, Val. We'll find Buster tomorrow. Prolly just chased a gopher into a hole." Having said his piece, he tipped his head on the back of the couch and started snoring. *Unbelievable!*

A crack of lightning lit up the backyard and boomed. Winky didn't budge. Another cracked a second later. I thought I saw something moving along the fence line in Laverne's backyard.

I elbowed Goober in the ribs. "Did you see that?"

"Ouch," he grumbled. "See what?"

"Something's walking around in Laverne's backyard."

"It's probably Laverne, Sherlock."

"No. Whatever it is, it's not much higher than the fence."

Goober sat up to attention. "The Doberman, you think?"

"I dunno. Where's the flashlight?"

"Winky's using it for a neck roll."

I yanked the flashlight out from under Winky's head. "What's goin' on?" he grumbled as he regained semi-consciousness.

"Val thinks she's seen the creature making those holes in Laverne's yard," Goober explained.

"Is it the hairy ape man?" Winky asked.

"No. Too short."

"Aha!" Winky said. "I tole you all they was miniature monsters out there, but you wouldn't listen!"

"We gotta find out what it is," I said. "Maybe it's Buster. This could be our only chance. Guys, go in the garage and get the rubber garbage can. I'll find the trash bags."

"We gonna pretend we're garbage collectors?" Winky asked.

"No," I said. "We're gonna capture it."

"Capture it?" Goober asked. "Are you crazy, Val?"

"What if it's some kind a chooper kabre or somethin'?" Winky squealed. "It'll kill us all!"

"Chupacabra," I said. "And *they* don't exist either."

I hope.

Chapter Twenty-Three

"**I** still prefer the original plan," Goober said. "Doing nothing."

"Not an option," I said. "We have to find out what's out there digging those holes in Laverne's yard."

"And by 'we' you mean 'you,'" Goober replied.

"Whatever," I said. "You guys ready to roll?"

"Couldn't we at least wait 'til it stops rainin' and lightnin'?" Winky whined.

"No. It may be too late then."

"Gaul-dang it," Winky whispered.

The three of us were gathered at the back door, holding our positions like the world's most poorly trained SWAT team. Goober was armed with a spatula and a garbage can. Winky had the rolling pin and a garbage bag. I had a garbage bag, too, and the poop net I'd found lying in a corner on the living room floor.

"I done tol' you once, Val," Winky said, looking down at it. "You're gonna need a bigger net than that to catch that varmint."

I blew out a breath. "I told you before. I'm just taking it outside, okay? It's not part of the plan."

"So what per-zackly *is* the plan?" Winky asked.

"We're going to catch whatever it is in the trash can," I said. "Winky, you and I are going to herd it toward Goober. Goober's going to trap it in the can and slap the lid on it."

"You didn't say anything about a lid," Goober said.

I unclenched my jaw enough to say, "Go get it."

Goober set the can down and sauntered off toward the garage.

"So you mean to tell me you aim to capture it?" Winky asked.

"Yeah."

"Then what?"

Good question. I hadn't thought that far ahead. "Uh...we'll uh...call...animal control," I improvised.

"Got me a cousin who's a critter gitter."

"Maybe we could call him," I said.

"Naw. His truck's broke down. Besides, he lives in Alabama. But I know this other feller..."

"Okay, got the lid," Goober said, returning from the garage. "Ready when you are, commandeerer-in-chief."

"All right, then," I said. "Slide open the door, Goober, and let's roll."

"TURN ON THE FLASHLIGHT, Val," Goober muttered. "I can't see a dang thing."

"Me either," Winky said.

It took the pouring rain three seconds to soak through my clothes and wash my bangs into my eyes. "I don't want to use the flashlight unless I have to," I said. "The battery's nearly dead. And we don't want to scare the thing away."

"*We* don't want to scare *it?*" Goober sneered.

A crunching sound echoed in the darkness. It came from the direction of Laverne's yard.

"Shhh!" I hissed. "Did you hear that?"

"Sounds like a pack a wild armadillas," Winky said.

"Hush! Follow my lead."

I crept toward the white picket fence. It glowed palely in the faint moonlight like an endless row of ghostly, pointed teeth. I stopped. Goober ran into the back of me.

"Ungh," he grunted. "Geez. Say something next time you stop."

"Grnngh!"

"Something besides that," he hissed.

"That wasn't me," I said. "Winky, hush!"

"I didn't say a gaul-dang thing!"

The hair on the back of my neck stood up. I turned to the guys and whispered, "I think the sound came from just over the fence. Okay, on the count of three, jump over the fence with me. Ready? One. Two. Three!"

I jumped over the fence. Winky and Goober stayed put.

"Really?" I hissed. I tugged Goober on the arm. "Get over here!" He reluctantly stepped over the fence. "You, too, Winky!"

"Okay, already," Winky grumbled. "Don't get your bloomers in a wad."

"For the millionth time, would you hush?" I whispered.

"How come I'm the only one who can't say—"

"Grnngh. Ugh."

It was that strange sound again. This time, closer.

"What *is* that?" Goober whispered.

"I dunno. It sounded like it came from over there." I pointed to a dark corner of the yard. I could barely make out my own hand in the darkness. "Can you guys see anything?"

"I can hear it digging," Winky whispered. "Foller me."

We tiptoed across the grass between Laverne's rosebushes, Winky in the lead. As I stepped cautiously behind Goober, something grabbed me from behind. Its claws dug into my arm. I screamed.

"Aaargh!"

As I struggled to break free of its grasp, something short and dark and breathing heavily ran past me in the dark. I screamed again.

"Aargh! Help! Over here, guys!" I shone the dim flashlight on my attacker. It was Princess Margaret, the rosebush. I yanked my sleeve free just as Goober and Winky bumped into me. "It went that way!" I

screeched, and pointed the flashlight in the direction I'd seen the creature run. "I think it was a panther!"

"A panther?" Goober choked.

I pushed my sopping bangs from my eyes. "Yes. Hurry! It's getting
away!"

Goober yanked Winky's arm and the pair sprinted off. A second
later, I heard a struggle, then a thump, another grunt, and finally, the
click of the garbage lid locking into place.

"We done it!" Winky yelled from somewhere in the darkness. I
took a few cautious steps toward the sound of his voice, shining the
anemic flashlight as I went. When I arrived at the scene, Winky and
Goober had a hold of either side of the trash can, toting it toward me.
Whatever was inside was snarling and thrashing around. The rubber
bin was jerking and swaying like an off-balanced lump of clay on a pot-
tery wheel.

"What is it? I asked. Then, to my horror, Goober stumbled over a
garden gnome.

As he fell face-forward in the pouring rain, the dimly-lit scene un-
folded in slow-motion. Goober's right foot lurched forward. He lost
his grip on the trash can. It fell and bounced once on the ground. The
lid popped off and flipped through the air like a tossed pizza dough.
Winky lost his grip and the garbage bin lunged forward. It skidded on
its side in the grass, the open end headed right for me. Inside the bin,
two glowing red eyes glared back at me.

I screamed, stepped back, and fell ass-backward onto the ground.
The flashlight flew out of my hand. As the lamp hit the ground, the
jolt must have improved the battery connection, because suddenly the
flashlight shot out a blinding beam right into the can. I watched,
dumbfounded, as a short, black creature with a silvery mane came
crawling out.

"Oh my gawd!" I cried out.

"Goober! Slap the lid back on!" Winky hollered.

Goober came charging out of the darkness, holding the garbage lid like a shield.

"No! Don't!" I shouted. "Let it go!"

Goober screeched to a halt. The three of us stood in the deluge and watched, silently, as the creature emerged from the garbage can and straightened out its three-and-a-half foot frame. Laverne's mysterious garden digger was J.D. Fellows himself.

"WHAT WERE YOU DOING out there?" I asked J.D. as I poured a round of whiskey for the guys, gin for me. We'd toweled off our wet clothes and were huddled, inquisition style, around my kitchen counter. We stared down J.D., who was perched like a towel-headed criminal on one of my kitchen barstools.

"I could ask you the same thing," groused the diminutive attorney. He was pissed, and downed his shot of whiskey in one gulp. I poured him another.

"Laverne's been complaining about something tearing up her rose-bushes," I explained. "We were just...you know...keeping an eye out. Trying to help."

"Cut the crap, Val," Winky said. He spun J.D. around on his barstool. "Buster's missin', buster!" Winky stopped for a second to smile and nod at his own eloquence, then got back to business. "Val done found evidential body parts in yore yard. And now we done caught you red handed buryin' more. What is you, J.D.? Some kind a animal murderer?"

J.D. looked down at the empty shot glass in his hand. "I don't know what you're talking about," he muttered.

"Then how do you explain this?" Goober held up a garbage bag containing an animal carcass. We'd found it in the yard beside a freshly dug hole around Laverne's rosebushes. Thanks to our ambush, J.D. hadn't had time to finish his task. Goober slammed the bag on the counter in front of J.D. I bit my lip and fought back the Southern urge to grab the bottle of spray bleach under the sink.

"J.D., we're just trying to get to the bottom of this," I said, trying to calm the three men's testosterone-fueled pissing match. "You have to admit, the case against you doesn't look good." I rubbed the scratches on my arm inflicted by Princess Margaret, the rose-thorn monster.

"I really don't have to answer you guys," J.D said woodenly. "This isn't *Judge Judy*."

"I know," I said. "But...geez, J.D. I really wish you would."

"Show him the evidence," Winky said. "Open the bag."

As Goober reached for the bag, J.D. threw up his hands.

"All right," he said. "Pour me another shot, would you, Val?"

"Sure."

I did as he asked, and J.D. began presenting his argument before a jury of very unlikely peers.

He cleared his throat. "Let me begin by saying, having attended the Thanksgiving feast at Laverne's, I'm sure you are all aware of my lovely girlfriend's...um...*culinary talents*."

We all exchanged grimaces and nods.

"Well, what for *you* was a one-off occasion, is for *me* an everyday logistical problem."

"What do you mean?" I asked.

"Laverne's cooking," he said. "It's inedible. Agreed?"

"That's putting it nicely," I said.

"Yep," Winky said.

"No doubt," Goober concurred.

"So we are all in agreement here," J.D. said. "Therefore, you can certainly understand that actually *eating* the food she cooks is not an option. So, I've had to come up with...uh...*other arrangements*."

"But Laverne told me you eat everything she puts in front of you," I argued.

J.D. reached inside his waistband and pulled out a Ziplock bag. "Exhibit A. My 'second stomach.'"

"Huh?" Winky asked.

"Let me demonstrate," J.D. said. He unzipped the baggie and positioned it on his thigh with the open end up. "When she's not looking, I drop what food I can into my lap, see? And stuff it into the bag."

"Why?" Winky asked.

"Because I'd like to live long enough to enjoy my retirement," J.D. answered impatiently.

"I still don't get it," Winky said.

J.D. threw up his hands again. "Look! Here's the long and short of it."

"The *short* of it! Good 'un, J.D.!" Winky said.

I cringed. Well, at least Winky would never be accused of being politically correct. To his credit, J.D. ignored Winky's remarks and continued with only the slightest pause.

"I don't want to hurt her feelings," J.D. said, "but Laverne's cooking could kill a buzzard. I can't throw the stuff away. She'd find it in the garbage can. And lord knows, we've already killed enough possums with it. So I started throwing it in the water. But then dead fish started floating up. So I was left with only one option. I started burying her deadly dinners in the backyard after she went to bed."

"Oh. I get it," Winky said. "I had a cousin once who—"

"I knew something weird was going on!" I said, cutting Winky off at the pass. "I couldn't put my finger on it until now. Laverne kept blaming Buster, but *dogs don't try to cover up the holes they dig.*" Convinced of his innocence, I poured J.D. another shot. But Winky and Goober still had a few more questions they wanted answered before they were going to let him off the hook.

"So, you didn't kill Buster?" Winky asked, scratching his head.

"Kill? No!" J.D. said. "I wouldn't do such a thing."

"But you killed *this*," Goober said, and held up the garbage bag.

"Let me tell you something," J.D. said. "The chicken in that bag died in vain, that's true. But *I* wasn't the one who killed it."

"It's still bloody, though," I said. "Just like the piece of meat I found earlier."

J.D. sighed. "I made the mistake of telling Laverne I liked my meat rare," he said. "So tonight, she served me a half-raw chicken."

"Ugh," I said involuntarily. My gut boiled at the thought.

"I told you her food was deadly," J.D. said. "I had to defend myself."

"We understand," I said. "Don't we, guys."

They nodded.

"Well, I better be getting back," J.D. said, and climbed off the barstool.

I walked with him to the door. "No hard feelings, I hope?"

"No. You keep *my* secret, Val, and I'll keep *yours*."

"Deal," I said, and opened the front door. "Wait a minute. What's *my* secret?"

"That you hate dogs," J.D. said matter-of-factly. He walked out and closed the door behind him.

"Geez! Does *everybody* know?" I asked.

"Not everybody, or it wouldn't be a secret," Goober smirked. "Tom doesn't know. Not yet, anyway. But when he gets back and finds Buster gone, well...."

"That J.D.'s a strange feller," Winky said. "Reminds me of my nephew, Dexter."

I rolled my tired eyes. "At least we know that J.D. isn't a killer." I looked at the guys wistfully. "And there's still hope Buster's alive, right?"

"He's got to be out there somewheres," Winky said.

"I just hope he's not lonely. Or scared," I said.

Goober snorted. "Or giving someone indigestion."

Chapter Twenty-Four

I woke up Monday morning with thoughts buzzing around my brain like flies around a crap casserole. Last night, the guys and I had solved the mystery of the holes in Laverne's yard. But as I rubbed the sleep from my eyes, I wondered if the potentially lethal food Laverne had served J.D. was *intentional*. Was it possible she was trying to get him out of her house by poisoning him? She'd mentioned something about seeing that on TV. But then again, her cooking *was* the kind of stuff that started urban legends....

I sat up in bed and yawned. For the moment, that was one mystery that would have to remain unsolved. The first order of business for the day was to make a cappuccino.

I heard a snuffled snore from the living room. *Wait a minute. No. The first order of business is to get rid of Winky and Goober. Tom will be coming home this evening.*

I sucked in a breath.

Tom will be here tonight! The first order of business is to find Buster. But in order to do that, I need to not have any other business....

*Okay. The first order of business is to call in sick....*after *I make a cappuccino.*

My flapping ducks settled in a row in my mind. I crawled out of bed, put on my ratty bathrobe and crept into the living room. As I slipped past the living room, I saw Goober's long arms and legs sprawled out all over the sofa like a besotted orangutan. Winky was wedged underneath the couch like the loser of a drunken idiot's bet. I shook my head at the ridiculous pair, perked my cappuccino, and snuck back to my bedroom before I woke the goofballs.

Back under the bed covers, I took a sip of cappuccino and checked my phone. There was a text from Tom saying he missed me, along with a picture of him sitting next to his boss at one of those hotel convention dinners. From the looks of it, he'd ordered the rubber chicken breast. I texted him back, "I miss you, too. Can't wait to see you!"

It was my first white lie of the day. Not that I didn't miss Tom. That part was true. But I could wait to see him until after I'd found Buster—or at least knew what had happened to him. If I didn't find Buster before Tom got home...well...I didn't know what I was going to do.

I clicked on Milly's number and texted her, "Can't make it today. Buster sick. Okay?"

Before I could set the phone down, she pinged back. "I understand. Take all the time you need."

Huh. Either Milly was the most thoughtful boss in the world, or she was still steaming mad about the Barkmitzva disaster. I guess I'd find out tomorrow. I finished my cappuccino and got up to search for my favorite jeans. With all the commotion over the last few days, I hadn't had time to do laundry. I found them crumpled in the dirty clothes hamper, wrinkled to hell. I wriggled into them anyway. They were so tight I knew all the wrinkles would scrunch out.

The realization that I knew this made me question myself. Am I that big a slob? I sighed and looked through my closet for a blouse. I guess it really didn't matter how I looked. I had no one to impress this morning. Not even myself.

I WAS POURING WINKY a cup of coffee when the doorbell rang. "That must be Winnie," I said. I put the carafe back in the coffee machine and padded toward the door.

Winky burst out laughing.

I whipped around. "What?"

"Looks like you got yourself a panny-tumor," Winky said.

"A what?"

Winky pointed to the back of my shin. "Winnie gets 'em all the time. Either that, or you forgot to flush."

I looked at the back of my left leg. An odd bulge protruded from inside my jeans, halfway down my thigh.

"What the?" I looked up at Winky. He was grinning at me through one side of his freckled face.

"Answer the door," I groused, and sprinted back to my bedroom. I yanked down my jeans. Wedged inside the pant leg was a pair of wadded-up panties—a relic from the last time I'd worn them.

Panny tumor...panty tumor! Oh, Lord! I really am *a slob!*

I shook my head, knowing I'd never live this one down. Then I braced myself to be teased within an inch of my Southern graciousness. I marched back to the kitchen prepared to do battle. But Winky's attention was no longer on me. He had his eye on Winnie...and her bag full of peanut-butter bacon bombs.

"Keep your mitts off those," Winnie scolded Winkie, and slapped his hand. "Those are for Val."

"Are those the bombs?" I asked.

"Sure are," Winnie said. "A baker's dozen."

"Awesome!" I took one out of the bag and bit into it as Winky looked on with envy. "Oooh, these are soooo good!" I teased.

"Thanks," Winnie said. "Keep your fingers crossed. I sent the entry in this morning."

"Well, if you don't win, it would be a crime against bacon," I joked. "When will you know?"

"Coupla weeks," Winnie said. "I saw Goober's car outside. Where is he?"

"In the shower."

"Not anymore," Goober said, emerging from the hallway. He was wearing a fresh t-shirt but the same dirty cargo shorts. But hey, who was *I* to judge?

"I was just telling Winnie these donuts are to die for," I said to Goober. "If Winky had any sense, he would marry her and snap her up!"

Winnie giggled, but Winky didn't look too keen on the idea.

"I dunno," he said, still pouting. His eyes shifted left and right. "I been tricked by bacon before."

"Huh?" I grunted.

Goober closed his eyes and shook his head softly. "Don't ask."

WITH WINKY SAFELY BACK in Winnie's care, it was one stooge down, one to go. I was about to give Goober the boot when my phone rang.

"Hi. I'm calling about the dog in the flyer?"

"Uh...yes?"

"Is it still available?"

"What do you mean, is it still *available?*"

"Oh. I mean, has anyone claimed it yet? Uh...you see...uh...my dog is missing. He's got all four limbs, right?"

I put my hand over the speaker and looked over at Goober. "Someone's calling about Buster. There's something really odd about him....and his voice sounds familiar."

Goober grabbed the phone. "Hello. Could you describe the dog? Yeah. Uh huh. Uh huh. You don't say. Huh. That sounds like a pretty good deal, actually."

What was Goober doing? Negotiating? For a dog I didn't have?

I shot Goober a dirty look. He got the message.

"But not this time," he said. "See you around." Goober clicked off and handed me back my cellphone.

"Well?" I asked.

"Oh. It was Capone. You remember, the guy who tried to scam you for fifty bucks over that guitar guy's missing finger?"

"How could I forget?" I said, suddenly irritated. "I know who Capone is, Goober. Why was he calling about Buster?"

Goober shrugged. "Says he knows a guy who'll pay twenty bucks a head for decent lookin' pooches."

"What? Why? What does he do with them?"

"How the hell should I know? Maybe he re-sells 'em online. Maybe they go to research labs. I didn't ask."

"Animal research? What happens to—"

The tune *Dixie Land* blared out from underneath the couch, cutting me off. It was Winky's signature ringtone. He'd forgotten his phone again.

"Should I answer it?" I asked Goober as I scrounged for it on my hands and knees.

"Sure. He might be calling to tell himself he lost his phone."

I laughed. "Wouldn't surprise me one bit." I clicked on the phone. "Winky? Is that you?"

"I'm calling for Wallace J. Winchly," the man said.

"Who?"

"Wallace J. Winchly."

"You've got the wrong number."

"Uh...he goes by Winky, as you, apparently, are aware."

My shoulders straightened. I knew that voice, too! "What do you want, Finkerman?"

"Val Fremden?"

"Yes," I sighed. "What's Winky done?"

"Nothing, unfortunately."

"Then why are you calling him?"

"I've been hired to dispose of...I mean *distribute* the worldly belongings of one Joseph Bateman. Of Old Joe's Bait & Tackle?"

"His last name was Bateman?"

"Huh? Oh. Yes. Well, it appears your friend left some merchandise in his shop. He needs to reclaim it or it will be disposed of."

"Really. Well I'll be sure and let him know."

"Thank you. He needs to respond by next Friday or he forfeits his opportunity."

"Why?" I sneered. "Is that when you start serving your next jail sentence?"

"You wish."

"Yes, I certainly do," I hissed, and clicked off the phone.

"Who was that?" Goober asked.

"Just another unwelcome blast from the past."

Chapter Twenty-Five

"I don't understand. I told my butler to have it fully serviced before he drove me here," Goober deadpanned. He climbed out of the dead hulk of his rusty, baby-blue, 1985 Chevy Chevette. "I'm going to have to have a serious talk with my entire house staff."

"Let me drive you home," I offered.

"Nah. I'm in no hurry. Just drop me by Davie's Donuts. Maybe Winky can come take a look at Maybelline."

"Maybelline?" I snorted.

"Hey. You call your car Maggie. Mine's Maybelline. Don't be a hypocrite."

I sighed. "Okay. I'll take you to Davie's. I've got to give Winky back his phone anyway. Here. Take it." I handed the phone to Goober. "I also need to tell him about Finkerman."

We hopped in Shabby Maggie and I hit the gas. Davie's was just a few minutes ride away.

"So what are you doing with yourself these days?" I asked Goober, not particularly curious about the answer. I glanced over at him. He'd stuck his right arm out the side of the car and was surfing air waves as we sped along. His eyes were focused straight ahead.

"I was helping Winnie and Winky out with the jewelry stuff," he said. "But that's kind of dried up. The price of scrap metal has plummeted, so it's hardly worth recycling cans anymore."

"Goober, what are you? Fifty? Why don't you get a *real* job?"

"You mean like *you?*"

"Hey, I have a *real* job."

"Val, if it weren't for Milly, you'd be playing a kazoo on a corner for tip money. Face it, you're as unemployable as me."

"I really don't see the need to insult someone who's doing you a favor," I sneered as I pulled into the parking lot at Davie's. "Oh my lord!"

"What?"

"Look! Over there! It's him!"

"Who?"

"Ape man! My psycho neighbor! And he's heading right for the front door of the donut shop!"

"In a bipedal fashion, too," Goober observed. "Impressive."

I slammed into a parking place. "Call Winky!"

"Why?"

I grabbed the phone from Goober's hand and started punching buttons. "Ape guy can recognize him. He ran Winky off with a cleaver, remember? We need to warn him!"

I saw Winnie's number in contacts and punched it.

Winky answered. "Hello? Is this me?"

"What?"

"Winnie said I was calling her on her phone. But I'm here, so I don't figure—"

"Winky! Shut up and listen. Ape man is about to walk in the donut shop!"

Winky's eyes doubled in size. "Whoa! You think this is someone from the future? Callin' to warn me? Like in that *Terminator* movie?"

"Argh! It's *me,* you dingbat. Val! I don't have time to explain. Just get out of there. We're outside in the parking lot!"

"How do I know this ain't a trap?" Winky asked. "Maybe *you're* that ape-man feller waitin' outside to get me."

"Don't you recognize my voice?" I asked.

"Huh. Well, he could be holdin' you hostage. Or impersonatin' your voice."

Ape man was at the door, his hand on the handle. I took a deep breath. "Winky. Look out the door. What do you see?"

I heard a hillbilly holler. A second later, the side door flew open. Winky came running at us for all he was worth. He dove into the backseat. I hit the gas.

"Gaul-dang it, Val!" Winky bellowed. "That was a close call! You should give a feller more warnin', you know? 'Specially since y'all know what's gonna happen in the future an' all!"

Goober and I exchanged glances. I hit the gas again and was about to peel out of the lot when a thought hit me. "Geez! Do you think Winnie's all right in there with him?"

"If he's got a beef, it's with us, not her," Goober said.

"She'll be all right," Winky said. "Winnie done told me she's used to handling skunk apes on a daily basis."

Goober and I eyed each other again.

"I believe that," I said, and turned out of the lot. "Guys...if he's at the donut shop, you know what that means?"

"That he's not on a gluten free diet?" Goober asked.

"No! That he's not at home."

"Brilliant deduction," Goober deadpanned.

"Argh!" I grunted. "It means we can take a look around his place. He's not there to chase us with a meat cleaver and slap us on a grille."

"Well then, shake a leg, Val," Winky said. "All this talk about food is making me hungry."

"YOU WERE RIGHT, WINKY," I whispered. "It's a little graveyard, just like you said."

The three of us had scaled a ladder over my neighbor's chain link fence. Once we'd gotten through the tangle of hedges, we'd followed a worn-down trail in the waist-high weeds. The gap in the overgrowth had led to a dilapidated shed. Next to it, a small patch of ground had been cleared down to the soil. We stood around the bare plot of sand, staring at the handful of crudely-carved limestone headstones, each baring a different name.

"This is worse than I thought!" I said, swallowing hard. "He's only been out a week or two...and there's already what...six graves here?"

"You think he murdered all these people?" Goober asked.

"Why else would he hide them back here?" I asked.

"'Cause he's ashamed 'a his poor engravature skills?" Winky asked.

I blew out a breath. "Look. I'm gonna get some pictures of the headstones to show Tom. You guys look around. See if there's anything else we should tell him about." I snapped a few pictures of the plot and individual headstones. Bob. Ralf. Peggy. Jon-Jon. Lance. Mable.

Mable? Wait a minute. Wasn't that his mother's *name?*

A spine-chilling creak pierced the air, followed by a loud bang. I nearly jumped out of my skin.

"Hey y'all!" Winky called out. "Come take a look in here."

Winky had pried open the shed door and was peeking inside. I walked over and cautiously stuck my head in for a look. Inside was an old wooden bench. On the bench lay a hammer and a chisel—beside another half-finished gravestone. Carved into the slab were the letters B U and S.

"Oh my lord!" I cried out. "Do you know what this means?"

"He's done kilt a bus driver?" Winky asked.

Winky's phone rang, scaring the bejeesus out of Goober and me. Winky answered it nonchalantly. "Uh huh. Yeah. All right. Thanks for calling." He hung up and put the phone back in his pocket.

"Well?" I asked.

"Oh. That was Winnie. She just wanted me to let you know that hairy guy just left."

My heart dropped to my knees. "We need to get the hell out of here! Now!"

Weeds batted me in the face as we scrambled down the path and scrabbled through the hedges. I bit my nails as Goober scaled the ladder straddling the fence. He hopped off and held it for me as I crawled over. I jumped and landed in my yard next to Goober.

"Did you shut the shed door?" I asked Winky as he stepped a bare foot on the first rung of the ladder.

"Crap!" he hollered, and ran back into the thicket.

"My work here is done," Goober said, and ran off.

I heard a loud creak and a bang. Winky's face poked through the bushes a moment later.

"Hurry up, already!" I screeched.

"Hold your horses!" he grumbled. "I'm having testicle difficulties!"

"Technical," I hissed as he climbed the rungs.

"Nope. *Testicle*, Val. I got me a major wedgie in the works."

THE THREE OF US WERE on the street, standing around the open hood of Goober's Chevette, still panting from our getaway sprint. Once we'd made it safely back over the fence, Goober had confessed he might have left a Zagnut wrapper at the scene of our crime. In a panic, I'd ordered them to establish an alibi by pretending to fix Goober's car.

"Try to look innocent," I whispered as ape man drove slowly by in his white SUV.

He pulled his Bronco up in his driveway, climbed out and stared at us. I got a bad case of the willies.

"What's he doing now?" Goober asked. From their vantage point under the hood, he and Winky only had a view of the Chevette's puny engine.

"He's going to the back of his SUV," I said. "He's pulling out a box. Oh lord! He's coming our way!"

I panicked, jumped in the driver's seat of the Chevette and tried the ignition. Nothing.

"What's in the box?" Goober asked.

"A gaul-dang meat cleaver with my name on it!" Winky said. "We got to get outta here. Lemme try bangin' on the solenoid." I heard Winky hit something hard with the socket wrench he'd been toting for protection.

"Try it now!" Goober yelled.

I bit my lip and tried the ignition again. Nothing. Ape man was only twenty feet away.

"Do something!" I screamed.

Winky gave the engine another blow with the wrench. I tried the ignition again. The Chevette belched to life.

"Get in!" I ordered needlessly. The guys' torsos were already halfway inside the open windows. I hit the gas. The Chevette lurched forward. Winky and Goober tumbled the rest of the way onto the backseat. My eyes shifted from the rear-view mirror to the windshield. Ape man was just a few feet away. He reached into his pocket for something....

"Punch it!" Goober shouted.

I hit the gas and whizzed by ape man. Then I remembered I live in a cul-de-sac.

Crap on a saltine cracker!

I did a one-eighty in somebody's driveway. We squealed past ape man again. He was staring us down like a stone-age serial killer.

Chapter Twenty-Six

G oober wasn't one to waste money filling a gas tank. There was just enough fuel in the rusty old Chevette to make it to the turn-in for Davie's Donuts before it sputtered out and died. If we hadn't had to wait on a nearly fossilized old guy from Ontario to finally make a left-hand turn, we probably would have made it. As it was, we had to get out and push the stalled hulk into the lot next to Winnie's old Dodge van.

Yep. Just another glamorous day in St. Pete Beach.

"Can you spare a spill?" Goober asked Winky as I wiped dirt and rust from my hands onto my jeans.

"Sure...thang," Winky said between gasps for air. "I'll fetch...the gas can...out of the van."

My cellphone pinged. The display read, "Tom."

"I gotta take this," I said. "I'll meet you guys inside."

I walked a safe distance away from the guys' potentially flammable endeavor and clicked on the phone.

"Hey, Tom!" I said, trying to sound cheerful. My heart was still thumping from pushing the dead Chevette.

"Hey there! How's my favorite dog sitter?"

I gulped. "Uh...great."

"Everything running smoothly?"

I glanced over at Winky and Goober playing tug-of-war with the gas can. I walked a little further away, out of obscenity range. "Well, uh, you could say that."

"Good. You holding down the fort with Buster?"

"Uh, yeah. No problems there."

"That's good. Because...I won't be home tonight. The meeting got extended for another day."

"Oh..." I said, trying to sound disappointed. Actually, I was elated. It gave me one more day to find Buster! "That's too bad."

"I'm still waiting on that picture of you in the earrings," Tom said in his sexy-time voice.

"You didn't get it?" I asked coyly. "Huh. Something goofy must be going on with my phone. Oh, I know. There's been some bad storms the last two days. A cell tower might be down."

"Oh. Any damage at our place?"

Our place? "Just the usual. Chairs blown around and stuff."

"Good. Send me the picture, okay? I want to show it to some buds here."

"Oh. Right. Will do."

"Hey, I got something for Buster."

Crap! "You did? What?"

"I'll show it to you when I get home tomorrow night. We can celebrate."

"Sure. That sounds great."

"I miss you, Val. Don't forget to send the picture."

"I won't. I miss you, too. Bye."

"Wait! I know it's a day early, but...happy anniversary. Can you believe it's been two years since we met?"

"No," I said. "I can't believe it. Bye."

I clicked off the phone. Geez! Tomorrow was May 22 already? With everything else going on, I'd forgotten all about it. Tom had gotten me diamond earrings. I'd gotten him squat. And I'd lost the earrings and his dog to boot! It was official. I was a terrible girlfriend.

I racked my brain. What can I get Tom to soften the blow? I can't just have him come back to find Buster and my earrings gone! I looked over toward the van. The guys were nowhere to be seen. I punched #3 on my speed dial. Cold Cuts picked up.

"Hey, Val! Long time no see. What's up?"

"Not a lot," I lied. "How are you and Bill?"

"Doing great. It's been a blast helping him out here at the resort."

"You're there now?"

"Yeah. I'm telling you, Val, it's like living on a permanent vacation at the beach."

I chewed my bottom lip. "That sounds really cool. I wish *I* was there."

"Me, too. Bill and I took the old RV out camping last week. We actually stopped by your place the other day, but you weren't home."

"That's too bad. I'd love to see you."

"Why don't you come down? Stay a few days?"

"Seriously?"

"Sure!"

"Well, I have to admit, that's why I was calling. Do you happen to have a cottage free tomorrow night? I wanted to do something nice for Tom. It's our anniversary."

"Cool! How long's it been?"

"Two years."

"Wow. Congrats. Let me check the books. Ooops! The resort line's ringing. Hold on."

I listened as Cold Cuts picked up the other line and said, "Sunset Sailaway Resort. Yes. No. I'm sorry. I just booked the last room available for tomorrow. Yes. No. Well, thanks for giving us a call. Goodbye. Val?"

"Yes, I'm here. So, you booked up?"

"Nope. You're in luck. Got you your favorite cottage, too. Number twenty-two. Come and stay the weekend. We can catch up!"

I nearly jumped for joy. "Thanks so much! You're a life saver, Cold Cuts! Okay. We'll—"

"Uh-oh. A customer just walked in. I gotta go. Come on down any-time tomorrow. We'll talk then! Bye!"

The line went dead. I smiled and hit speed dial #7. Tom picked up right away.

"Hey," he said. "I thought you might be sending me a sexy picture of you in your new earrings."

"Nope. Sorry to disappoint you."

Tom laughed. "I can wait. So, what's up? You miss me already?"

"Yes," I teased. "And I wasn't going to say anything, but since you're not coming back until tomorrow, I have to. I booked us for a weekend at the Sunset Sailaway Resort."

"What? Really? That's great! When?"

"Starting tomorrow. For our anniversary."

"Val, tomorrow's Wednesday. I'll have to check if I can...uh...get the time off work."

"Just ask for comp time. You worked all last weekend, right?"

"Right. Sure."

"So, just meet me down there tomorrow."

"But...okay. Next time, give me a little more notice, okay?"

"You don't give people notice when it's supposed to be a surprise, Tom. And it's hard to pull anything over on you, Detective Foreman."

WHEN I WALKED INTO Davie's Donuts, Winky and Goober were chowing down on a selection of donut discards compliments of the head waitress, Winnie. I ordered a coffee and tried not to look as they scarfed down the half-eaten leftovers of earlier patrons.

"Don't you want any?" Winky asked, and shoved the plate my way.

"No, thanks." I patted my stomach. "Saving my donut calories for the peanut butter bombs waiting for me at home."

"Can't blame ya there," Winky said, and popped a piece of powdered donut in his mouth.

A dish shattered on the floor. I spun around to see Winnie grimacing and shaking her head so hard her black bob was swaying.

"I'm nervous as a mouse in a rat-trap store," Winnie said. "I hope I hear from that contest soon, or I just might break every darn dish in this place."

"Don't worry," I said. "I can't imagine anything being better than those donuts you came up with."

"We sure could use the winnings," Winnie said as she unhooked a dustpan from the wall. "We sunk all our savings into fishing tackle and jewelry what-not for Playing Hooky. You know, those tackle earrings we make."

"Yeah," I said. "Oh! That reminds me. Winky, you got a call this morning. The jewelry you left at Old Joe's Bait Shop needs to be picked up."

"Old Joe called me?" Winky asked, his eyebrows almost touching his ginger buzz cut. He must have been astonished, because he forgot all about the piece of donut hovering in his hand next to his right cheek.

"Uh...no," I clarified. "Old Joe is dead, Winky."

"Whew!" he said, and let his hand drop. "I seen this show on TV where somebody got a phone call from their dead paw-paw, and—"

"It was Finkerman, Winky," I said, cutting him off. "Ferrol Finkerman called. He's handling distribution of Old Joe's worldly possessions."

"Oh. Well, that was mighty thoughtful of him," Winky said.

"I'm sure he's being remunerated for his troubles," I said.

"Sorry to hear that," Winky said and shook his head. "Hope he gets over it quick."

"We had us a sizable inventory in the shop," Winnie said. "I was gonna give a pair of hard-bodied grub earrings to Sherryl. You know, like the ones we gave you, Val. But I haven't had time to make any, what with the contest and all."

"All you need to do is call Finkerman and make an appointment to pick them up," I said. "I'll go with you if you want."

"Uh, okay," said Winky. He gave Winnie the eye. "I'll let you know."

"So, who's Sherryl?" I asked Winnie. She looked down.

I glanced around. Winky's and Goober's eyes found somewhere new to look. I cleared my throat. "I said, who's Sherryl?"

"Jorge's girlfriend," Goober said.

"Oh!" I smiled. "You mean Jorge's hot girlfriend."

"You know about her?" Winky asked.

"Well, sure. The guys told me already."

"And you're okay with it?" Winnie asked.

"What? Why wouldn't I be okay with it?"

"Well, Sherryl is the cousin of Darryl," Goober explained.

"The near identical cousin," Winnie added.

"Oh," I said. I sensed there was more to this story than they were letting on.

"I got a cousin looks near identical to Popeye the Sailor Man," Winky offered.

Goober rolled his eyes. "Look," he said. He reached a long arm over and showed me a cellphone picture of Jorge and Sherryl. She was J-Lo gorgeous, and spot on a match for Tom's breathtaking ex-wife, Darryl.

"I think it's pretty cool," Winnie said. "Going all the way up to Tallahassee to meet her family."

"Tallahassee?" I asked. My internal radar pinged to life.

"Yes...?" Winnie said.

"Let me see that picture again." I grabbed the cellphone out of Goober's hand and started flipping through the photos.

"Hey! Give that back," Goober protested. "Those are private!" He tried to wrestle the phone back from me. But three flips in, I found what I was looking for. It was a picture of Darryl, Tom's ex, looking sexier than a woman had a right to be. Sitting next to her, holding her hand, a huge grin on his handsome, boyish face, was Tom, my soon-to-be ex-boyfriend.

Chapter Twenty-Seven

I gave Goober back his phone and pretended not to see the picture of Tom cozying up to Darryl on their secret rendezvous. The one that he'd lied through his teeth to me about! *That cheating jerk!*

I forced a smile, even though I was seething with the anger of betrayal. I excused myself and walked as calmly out of Davie's Donuts as I could, hoping my teeth wouldn't crack from the strain of holding back the motherlode of obscenities tumbling like an avalanche through my mind.

I stomped through the parking lot looking for Maggie. When I saw Goober's old Chevette, my blinding rage lifted enough for me to remember I'd arrived in that rusted-out hulk. Cinderella's carriage, it was not. *Crap.* I could either call a cab or walk, because I sure as hell wasn't going to go begging a ride from those jerks back inside. I pictured them having a laugh on me, casually eating donuts while my world crumbled around me.

Did everybody know about Tom's affair with Darryl except me?

I hitched my purse up on my shoulder and marched in the direction of home, fueled by rage and righteous anger—and the frenetic energy generated by my inner thighs rubbing together. If I could've harnessed the power of *that*, I could've quite possibly become the next Nobel Prize laureate.

But at the moment, I had other more important goals on my mind. And I needed to see a woman about a couple of dogs....

AFTER I'D TRUDGED ALL the way back home, I'd jumped in Maggie to run a few errands. Along the way, I'd called Judy Bloomers and asked her to meet me for coffee at a diner down the road. I needed an objective opinion about how to dispose of Tom, the murderous barbecue guy next door, and the fake diamond earrings I'd just picked up at the Dollar Store. We were sitting in a booth sipping lousy coffee. I'd just spilled my guts about Tom's affair.

"Affairs with ex's are the worst," Judy said as she twirled a lock of black hair poking out beneath her bleach-blonde bouffant. "But look on the bright side, Val. It solves your problem about Tom moving in with you."

I looked up from my coffee cup. "You know, you're right, Judy!" I pursed my lips and shook my head. "Can you believe it? I just made plans for a beach getaway for our anniversary. Why did I even bother?"

"Men," Judy sneered. "Almost never worth the effort." She eyed a plate of nachos headed for another table and snagged the waitress. "I'll take one of those, please."

"Nachos? At ten in the morning?" I asked.

"I just took a picture of you wearing fake earrings to impress your cheating boyfriend," Judy said. "Don't judge me and I won't judge you."

I bit my lip and sighed. "Deal. Mind if I ask you a question?"

"Sure. What?"

"What's with the dark hair under the blonde?"

"You mean my 'secret hair'?"

"Uh...yeah."

"It's there to annoy people. Works pretty good, huh?"

I coughed out a laugh. "Yeah. I guess so."

Judy eyed me up and down. "Look, Val. Why should I have to try and look pretty for other people? I tell you now, the world's being overrun by *beauty terrorism!* And we women are the only victims. Look around. Guys don't even have to shave their faces anymore. Or cut their hair. Look at mister man-bun over there."

I glanced over at a guy who was a poster child for Judy's cause. "You have a point, there."

"They get to let it all hang out," Judy continued. "Meanwhile, we gals have to shave and wax and...and geez!" She leaned in toward me and lowered her voice. "We're not even allowed to have *pubes* anymore!" She sat back in the booth and showed me her palms. "I give up. Forget it! Call me ugly if you want. I'm gonna live the rest of my life to please me, myself and I."

The waitress delivered the nachos. I eyed them *and* Judy with growing envy.

Judy picked up a tortilla chip and waved it like a pointer. "If I want nachos for breakfast, so be it. I mean, really. Who cares?"

I responded with a shrug. "I dunno."

"Look at it this way," Judy continued. "I have two choices. I can choose to *not* eat the nachos and starve myself in the one-in-a-million chance prince charming comes along and thinks I look good in a pair of jeans *and* has the balls to sweep me off my feet. Or, two, I can eat nachos and be *one-hundred percent sure* of enjoying myself *now*. And as the Buddhists say, all we've got is the *now* moment. Five thousand years later and that truth still stands, Val."

Judy shoved the chip in her mouth and crunched down on it. She cocked her head and smiled. "Hey, in a way, eating these nachos is kind of like practicing my religious beliefs."

"You've got a pretty good point there," I admitted. "Mind if I practice along with you?"

Judy grinned. "Be my guest. I never say 'no' to new converts."

I reached for a chip. "I have to confess—"

"No you don't," Judy said, putting a hand up. "This is Buddhism. Not Catholicism."

I laughed. "I called you because I wanted to ask you about my neighbor. The guy who bought 1333 Bimini Circle?"

"Yeah? What about him?"

"He's pretty weird. I mean...he's *really, really, really* weird."

Judy grinned and leaned in for the juicy details. "What kind of weird we talking here?"

"Serial-killer weird. Dogs are missing. He barbecues in a Speedo. We found graves in his yard!"

"I knew it!" Judy said, straightening up in the booth. "I did some digging." Judy caught her own pun and laughed. "Sorry. Unintentional. Anyway. I found out the guy's name. It's Jake Johnson."

"Yes!" I exclaimed. "He told me once. I couldn't remember. But that's it. I'm sure of it."

"Not good," Judy said, shaking her head.

"What do you mean?"

"It's the same guy, Val. The one who murdered his mother."

My jaw went slack. "And now he's living next door to me."

Judy nodded solemnly.

"I'm telling you, Judy. He's burning bodies in his backyard. He's got to be! He's been out of the slammer for what? Two weeks? I've seen at least two dogs over at his place. Now they're both missing. And so is Buster, the dog Tom brought home."

Judy stared at me with eyes as big as plums. "And you're still staying in your house? Alone?"

"Good thing I don't have four legs, huh?" I joked nervously.

Judy shook her head. "I doubt his mother did, either."

I GLANCED AT THE CLOCK on the kitchen wall. It was 9:30 p.m. Old-lady midnight. I set down the rolling pin in my hand and reached for the phone. I almost called Tom again for the eight-millionth time.

It was pitch dark outside. I'd turned on every bulb and checked the locks on every door and window fifteen times. Still, I couldn't shake the portent of impending doom that hung thick in the air around me. I was at home alone. *Utterly* alone. With nothing for company except an overactive imagination and a bag full of donuts. Correction—a bag that *used* to be full of donuts.

It also didn't help that I'd just finished watching *The Shining*.

"Dumb move," I muttered to myself. I shut off the TV and walked to the kitchen. I tossed the empty Davies Donuts bag in the bin and stared out the sliding glass doors into the black night. At least there was no storm tonight. And no howling. I breathed a sigh of relief.

Then I spotted them. A pair of red, glowing eyes stared back at me from inside the doghouse Tom had built.

I stifled a scream and scrambled to grab hold of the rolling pin. "Get a grip, Val," I said, trying to reassure myself. "It's probably just a possum." *Or an alligator. Or a hideous brain-eating demon from hell!*

One of the red eyes blinked. I gulped and grabbed my cellphone. My hands were shaking so badly I dropped the rolling pin. Who could I call? I dialed 'nine' with a trembling finger. I looked back out the door. I could have sworn the eyes in the doghouse were bigger! I looked down and stabbed 'one' with a jerking finger. I tried to hit 'one' again, but I missed and dialed 'two.'

Crap on a cracker! Fresh panic shot through me. I tried to hit the 'back' button, but my hands were nearly paralyzed. A movement outside sent my eyeballs swinging back to the doghouse. The red, glowing eyes were on the move!

A long, low squeal escaped between my lips. The eyes lurched forward and a huge toad hopped out of the dark doghouse into the glow of the porch light. My knees buckled with relief. I put a hand on the sliding door to steady myself and giggled nervously. But another movement outside silenced me like a knife to the throat.

Someone was in my back yard. Digging a hole. And this time, whoever it was, was way too tall to be J.D.

The hair on the top of my head stood on end. I slapped a hand around on the wall until I found the light switch. I turned off the kitchen light and dove to my knees. As my eyes adjusted to the dim porch light, I could make out the silhouette of someone in a dark cape and hood. Whoever it was stopped digging. They put the shovel down and placed something into the hole. I blinked hard, straining to make out what it was. I moved forward on my knees. Pain shot through my kneecap. I winced and held my tongue. When I opened my eyes again, whoever it was had disappeared.

Following the lead of every dimwit in every scary movie I'd ever seen, I cracked open the sliding door and went out to investigate. I crept through the yard, armed with a rolling pin and the garden spade I tripped over on my way out the door. When I got to the area where the digger had been, I saw a fresh hole. It had been filled in.

I should have known better, but I'd already come this far. I dropped to my knees and started digging with the spade like someone under a voodoo spell. About six inches in, by spade hit something that made a hollow sound. I dug around it. It was a wooden box. No! It was a little coffin in a shallow grave!

I pulled the box out of the ground and turned it over. In the moonlight, I saw a little head pop out of the coffin. It sputtered out a horrible, squeaking moan.

Oh, dear lord! This poor creature's been buried alive!

A twig cracked behind me. I whipped around. The horrible, hooded creature was back! It towered over me, its hideous face a ghostly, greenish shade of death. Snakes twisted in its hair. It reached its bloody claws toward me. I was a goner.

I opened my mouth to scream and the world went black.

Chapter Twenty-Eight

Something had a hold of my leg, pulling me across my back lawn. I cracked open an eye and shut it again. It was the horrid, hooded demon! I screamed and kicked my leg like a mule. It let go and whirled around, the bulging eyes in its long, putrid-green face bored into mine like a cobra mesmerizing its prey. Its hideous slit of a mouth opened and said,

"Are you all right, honey?"

I blinked in disbelief. Had I been transported to some surreal dimension? Had Winky been right all along and I was being abducted by aliens? I blinked again. My eyes and mind found a bit more focus. Standing over me, wearing an avocado face mask and a hooded bathrobe, was Laverne, her strawberry curls done up in twist rollers.

"Geez, Laverne! What are you doing out here?"

"Nothing," she said coyly. "What are *you* doing out here?"

"I thought you were some kind of hideous demon!"

Laverne wilted. "Do I really look that bad?"

"What? No," I said, sitting up in the grass. "It's just.... The coffin! Why did you bury some poor creature in my backyard?"

"Coffin?" Laverne asked, and cocked her horsey green face. Peeking out of the long, hooded robe, she looked like that ghostly creep in *Scream*—sporting curlers and red lipstick.

"Oh. That's not a coffin, Val. It's that dad-burned cuckoo clock of J.D.'s. I figured if you got rid of Tom's dog, I could get rid of the cuckoo clock. I buried it in your yard to make it look like someone else did it. Like you did with the dog."

As inanely absurd as her explanation was, I didn't care at the moment. I was crestfallen. "Laverne, you think I got rid of Buster?"

"Well, didn't you?"

"No! How could you think such a thing?"

"Well, *you* thought *I* killed someone and buried them."

My pout disappeared along with my self-pity. "Oh my gawd!" I said. "You're right, Laverne. I'm sorry. Geez! What a bumbling mess this all is!"

I struggled to my feet. "Come on. Let's go inside. We've got to figure out a way to get rid of Tom and J.D. that doesn't involve us going to prison."

"I STILL CAN'T BELIEVE Tom's cheatin' on you, Val," Laverne said. She'd washed off her avocado mask and was enthusiastically helping me belt back a matching set of Tanqueray and tonics.

"And it gets worse," I said. "I spoke to Judy Bloomer, the real estate lady. The guy next door is the same guy who killed his mother. He's got a whole graveyard in his backyard, Laverne."

Laverne drained her cocktail and set it on the counter. "When you think about getting blown to smithereens by your own son, putting up with a cuckoo clock doesn't seem like such a big deal anymore."

"Too bad that isn't *Tom's* worst offence."

Laverne rattled the ice cubes in her glass. "What else has he done? Besides this cheating, I mean."

"He leaves the toothpaste cap off, okay?" I pouted. I grabbed her glass and went about fixing us another round. "He wants me to quit my job. So I can...stay home and write," I groused and stabbed at the lime with a knife.

"Monster," Laverne said, and gave me a sympathetic smile as I poured a generous slug of gin in both glasses.

"Crap, Laverne!" I yelled and slammed the gin bottle on the counter. "I finally meet a man who wants to help me follow *my* dreams. And now he's gone and done *this!*"

"Well, honey, sounds to me like you got to choose."

I topped off the glasses with tonic. "Choose?"

"Yeah. Life ain't always a fairytale. You should know that by now." Laverne took the drink I offered. "What's more important to you, Val? Fidelity or having someone who really gets you?"

I bit my lip. "But why should I have to choose just one?"

Laverne shrugged. "Sometimes, we just have to. And you don't fool me, missy. I know you really care about him."

"How do you know that?" I asked, and took a sip of my gin and tonic.

"Easy. Because if you didn't care, you wouldn't care he was cheating. And it works both ways. If he didn't care about you, he wouldn't care about your dreams."

"My dreams don't involve another lover," I said.

"Whose do? Everybody's dreams are different, Val. And men's dreams are a lot different than women's. Lord knows I've learned that over the years. How else do you explain cigars?"

Laverne smiled weakly and drained her drink. She stood up and gave me a hug. "Well, I better get on back home," she said. "I've got a keep an eye on J.D. or he'll be out in the backyard again. He sleepwalks, you know."

I bit my lip. "No. I didn't know."

Chapter Twenty-Nine

"It's not *what* you know. It's *who* you know. And first you've got to know *yourself*," chirped the syrupy DJ on the clock radio. I slapped the snooze button. What I *really* wanted was to slap whoever's face had just uttered that optimistic flapdoodle. At least I knew *that much* about myself.

I sighed, rolled out of bed and stomped to the bathroom. One glance in the vanity mirror and I had a little come-to-bejeezus meeting with myself.

What's it gonna be, Val? Like Laverne said, relationships take compromise. But a woman on the side? Is Tom worth it?

I stared at my sorry reflection. My hair was a frizzy rat's nest. I could stand to lose twenty pounds. My jowls were starting to sag like a hound dog. I put on some cheater glasses and studied my face. Growing out of my chin like some alien life form was a black hair about half an inch long! *Crapola!* Who was I kidding? Compared to Darryl, I looked like the victim of a botched sex-change operation.

Judy was right. Beauty terror is real!

I plucked the hair on my chin and stomped into the kitchen to make a cappuccino. I needed caffeine courage. Today I would have to face the ultimate showdown with Tom. My stomach flopped at the thought. Judging by the sunlight outside, I should have been at work already. I reached for my phone and begged off with a text to Milly. At this low point, I just couldn't face Milly and her perfect life. She had the perfect button nose. The perfect husband. The perfect wedding ring. The perfect house. Even the perfect dog! No wonder it didn't like me! At least Buster did. Or had. The thought of never seeing the little Bark-mitzva-basher made me burst into tears.

The only perfect thing I had to offer was a *perfect mess*.

AFTER A GOOD, LONG, hot, ugly cry, I blew my nose and put on my big-girl panties. I finished perking a cappuccino and plopped on a barstool to pull myself together. The clock on the wall read 9:33 a.m. I was supposed to go with Winky to meet Ferrol Finkerman at ten this morning.

Awesome. Can't wait. But at least when I make promises I keep them.

Thankfully, when that stupid meeting was over, all I'd have left to do was pack a suitcase and drive down to the Sunset Sailaway Resort. To confront my cheating boyfriend. And to tell him I'd lost his earrings *and* his dog. Oh. And one more thing.

To punch Thomas Foreman right in his big, fat nose!

I took a slurp of cold cappuccino and noticed something lying on the other side of the kitchen counter. It was the notebook the guys and I had used the other night to write down ideas about what might have happened to Buster. I leaned over and drug it toward me. I scanned the list and crossed off J.D. and Laverne. I'd already marked through skateboard kid the other night. If a gator or shark had gotten him, there was nothing I could do about it. I marked through them. Only two scenarios remained on the list. Abduction by aliens or by my psycho next-door neighbor. After what I'd learned about him over the last couple of days, I prayed for alien abduction. Not just for my sake, but for Buster's, too.

I'd planned on waiting until I had Tom for back-up before I confronted the guy who'd cremated his own mother. But having Tom's support seemed as unlikely now as getting Buster back within the next three hours. I looked around for the newspaper. I wanted to check the "lost and found pets" column one more time. I couldn't find it.

Oh yeah. Tom usually brought in the paper. Crap!

I climbed off my stool and cracked open the front door. I was still in my nightgown, so I peeked around to see if the coast was clear. With no one in sight, I tiptoed outside.

Drat! As luck would have it, the paper was at the end of the driveway. I scurried my way alongside Maggie, then bent down and grabbed the newspaper by the plastic bag it was wrapped in. As my head bobbed back up, I spied something hairy out of the corner of my left eye. I nearly fell backward. It was the missing link—naked except for a pair of shorts. And he was headed my way!

Crap on a cracker! All I had to defend myself was a rolled-up newspaper to swat him with!

I stood and tried to make a run for the front door, but the man was cutting through the grass on a collision course for me. There was no way I was going to make it! He positioned himself between me and my house. I braced myself and held *The St. Petersburg Times* in a death grip. I was about to club him with it when ape man spoke.

"We haven't been properly introduced," he said and held out a hairy hand. "I'm Jake—"

"Johnson," I interrupted. My voice shook with fear and adrenaline. "I know who you are."

He let his unshaken hand fall. "So you really *did* remember me from the donut shop."

"Uh huh."

"And *you* are?"

"Val Fremden."

He smiled, revealing a beautiful set of white teeth. "Buster's mom. Speaking of which, how's he doing? I haven't seen him around the past couple of days."

Is that some kind of sick joke? "He's been...indisposed."

Jake's eyes looked genuinely sorrowful. "Oh. I'm sorry to hear that." He reached into the pocket of his shorts. "Take this," he said. A hairy paw jerked toward me. I flinched in horror, expecting a knife, or maybe a body part.

In his palm was a baggie full of brown wafers.

"I make my own special doggy biscuits," he said. "They should perk Buster right up."

I stared at the cookies with dread. *Were they made from real dogs? Or maybe his "special" ingredient was cyanide....*

He pressed the bag of biscuits into my hand as I stood motionless, helpless, paralyzed with fear. He eyed me intently.

"I sense you're filled with a deep-seated distrust of strangers," he said. "But there's more to it than that. Hmmm...."

That's an extremely odd thing to say to someone. I stared at the biscuits, afraid to look into his primitive, animal face.

"Val pal!" I heard Winky holler. "You ready to go?"

His voice snapped me out of my trance. I looked up and saw the blue van parked a few yards away in the street. "I...uh...gotta go," I said to Jake. I turned and took off toward the old Dodge van, flung open the door and climbed into the passenger seat.

"What's goin' on here, Val?" Winky asked. "Did that ape feller show you his banana?"

"What?" I whispered, hoarse with fear. I looked over. Jake the ape had disappeared.

Winky threw up a hand. "What you do in yore spare time is yore business, Val." He eyed me up and down. "You gonna wear that? I don't think it's legal. Less'n we're goin' to Walmarts."

I looked down. I was still in my nightgown, still holding the baggie of dog biscuits. I flung the baggie on the floorboard and opened the van door. "Give me five minutes."

WHEN I GOT BACK TO the van, Winky was eating the last biscuit in the baggie. I opened my mouth to object, but then thought better of it. If the dog treats really were laced with cyanide, there was nothing I could do about it now.

Winky read my face wrong and handed me the last half of a bitten biscuit. "Sorry. You want it?"

"No thanks. Winky, you really shouldn't have eaten those."

"I thought they was waitin' snacks."

"You're right. They are." *Now we just have to wait and see if they do you in.*

THE BISCUITS WEREN'T lethal after all. Winky was still alive and kicking when we pulled into the lot at Finkerman's. Unsurprisingly, one of Finkerman's clients was in the middle of being busted and hauled away in the parking lot. A police car was angled over three parking spots, its lights flashing. The cop's K-9 partner was waiting patiently for him in the backseat of it while the suspect was being shackled on the hood with a set of handcuffs.

"Why I Suwannee," Winky said as we climbed out of the van.

"Typical," I said. "Finkerman's clientele are cheats and personal injury scammers."

Winky nodded toward the dog in the squad car. "What do you think he done?"

"Maybe he ate too many biscuits," I sneered.

Winky's eyes widened and he rubbed his stomach. Then he made a visor with his hand to shade his face from the cop. I grabbed his arm and led him through the front door of Finkerman's office. A woman who looked as if she'd been sucking on a Pine-Sol-flavored lollipop asked, "May I help you?"

"We're here about...." I began, then looked over at Winky. He still had his hand over his face. I slapped it down. "Winky!" I turned back to the sour-faced woman. "We're here about...." I turned back to Winky. "Ugh! What's your name again?"

"Wallace J. Winchly," a voice sounded. A pasty-faced, frizzy-headed, bean-pole of a man in a cheap suit walked into the lobby carrying a cardboard box full of mangled fishing tackle. "Your consolation prizes."

"Finkerman," I sneered.

Finkerman looked at Winky and nodded in my direction. "A friend of yours?"

"Yes'm," Winky said.

"My condolences," Finkerman said.

Winky shot me a look. "It really *is* condolences. Huh. Who would 'a thunk it?" He grabbed the box with his pudgy, freckled hands. "Thanky. This here looks like my stuff all right. But what's in that there envelope?"

"I couldn't say," Finkerman said. "It was sealed."

"And you're telling us you didn't open it?" I sneered. "Yeah, right."

"Client attorney privilege," Finkerman sneered back. He shrugged. "Okay. You got me. I thought at first it was just gonna be a list of the junk...uh...*retail items*...in the box. But it turns out that Joseph Bateman left your friend Wallace here a lot more than that.

"Who's Joseph Bateman?" Winky asked.

Finkerman sighed. "Old Joe. He must have been short of relatives, because he signed over the deed to his bait house to one Wallace J. Winchly."

"Which one?" Winky asked, with genuine interest.

"You," Finkerman said. He turned to face Winky directly. He leaned over and spoke slowly, as if to a very slow-witted goat. "The...Bait...Shack...by...Caddy's...is...yours."

"Mine? Whoo hooo!" Winky cheered.

"I wouldn't celebrate just yet," Finkerman said. "Once the deed is transferred, Old Joe's Bait House will lose its grandfathered property tax exemptions. I figure the beachfront taxes on that little patch of land will cost you around sixty-five thousand a year."

"Holy smokes!" Winky said. "That's more money than I've made in my natural born lifetime!"

"Shocking," Finkerman deadpanned.

"What's it worth if he sold it?" I asked.

"I don't know. I'm an attorney, not a real estate agent. Now, if you don't mind, I'm busy."

Finkerman turned to go. "Uh...Mr. Finkerman," I began.

He turned around. His evil smile told me he's picked up on my gaff. I'd been polite.

"Yes?" he asked, drawing the syllable out four seconds.

"Uh...have you ever handled a dog poisoning case?" I asked.

"Sure. For a hundred-fifty an hour. Plus expenses. But for you, I'd do it for two hundred an hour."

"Thanks," I said sourly. "I'll let you know."

Finkerman turned and left the lobby. Winky had opened the envelope and was staring at the deed to the bait shop.

"What do you think it's worth, Val?"

"I dunno. But I think I know someone who can find out."

Winky folded the deed and tapped his forehead with it. "You know what, Val? If it's worth enough, I'm gonna get me a doublewide!"

Chapter Thirty

It's weird how your whole life can change in the shake of a dog's leg. In under the space of a day, I was soon to be short one boyfriend, and Winky had inherited a place worth a half a million dollars.

"Are you sure about that?" I asked Judy Bloomers.

"Well, it depends on what someone will pay for the property, of course."

I clicked off my cellphone and turned to Winky. "I think you can afford that doublewide."

"Woo hoo!" Winky cheered. "And maybe a Camaro, too?"

I grinned. "Maybe."

"Then let's get her done, Val. Put that bad boy on the market."

"Okay. I'll make an appointment with Judy for when I get back."

"Where you goin'?"

"To Sunset Sailaway. To meet Tom."

"Oh, I get it," Winky grinned. "A romantical getaway, huh?"

"Yeah. Something like that." I opened the van door and climbed out. "See you soon. I'm really happy for you, Winky."

"Thanks Val. Looks like life is lookin' up for us all."

"Yeah," I repeated. "Some more than others."

It felt as if I were wearing lead pants as I walked up my driveway toward the front door. I knew nothing else even remotely good was going to come of this day. Maybe even the rest of my life. As if to prove my point, when I closed the front door and walked into my living room, what I saw through the sliding glass doors made me drop my purse. Jake Johnson, the psycho murderer, was wandering around in my back yard!

The hair on the back of my neck stood up. But like a moth to a flame, I found myself inexplicably drawn across the living room to the sliding glass doors. This was supposed to be my home. My sanctuary. My port in a storm! My safe place! Anger mowed over my fear like a runaway John Deere. I grabbed the empty gin bottle from the counter and slid open the door.

"What are you doing out there?" I shouted.

"Oh! Hi," he said. "Sorry to barge in on you. I lost something. Ah. Just found it!" He bent over and picked up something from my lawn.

How convenient that you just *found it.* "I would prefer you ask next time, before you come into my yard," I said indignantly.

"I'd like to make the same request of you," he replied.

My face grew hot. "Look, I don't need..." My eyes fell on the object in his hand. It looked like some kind of...*restraint collar!*

"What have you got there? In your hand?" I gulped, and took a step back.

"It's a...*training device,*" he said as he walked toward me. "See?"

"Training?"

"Listen, we got off on the wrong foot. I'm barbequing for lunch. You hungry?"

"Is it gonna be another wrong foot?" I hissed.

"Huh?" he asked, and cocked his hairy face sideways.

"I'm not hungry," I replied, and tested my grip on the gin bottle I was packing, concealed behind the door frame.

"Come on," Jake insisted, and took another step forward. "You haven't tasted real meat until you've tried my barbecue."

I turned and glanced around inside the house for my cellphone. I needed to call Laverne. Or 911. Where was that blasted phone?

I felt a hand wrap around my left wrist. I turned my head slowly back to face my neighbor. The convicted murderer was smiling at me, but not like any smiley face I'd ever seen.

"I'm from New Jersey," Jake said, and tugged on my arm. "We don't take no for an answer."

I tried to jerk my arm away, but that horrific paralysis had returned. I no longer had any will of my own. "I'm in a hurry," I whispered with my last bit of strength.

He eyed me playfully, like a cat with a mouse. "Just a quick bite then. It won't take long."

As he pulled me out of my house and tugged me toward his back-yard, I only hoped Jake Johnson would be true to his word...that he would be merciful, and make it quick.

Chapter Thirty-One

I was sitting, half-paralyzed, in a lawn chair by a huge fire pit. A round grille was suspended over the flames from a rusty tripod of metal. A beverage was in my right hand, but I was afraid to drink it. I was pretty sure it was how Jake had drugged all his other murder victims.

He ambled up beside me and set a box on the ground by my feet. He smiled and my blood ran cold. It was the same box he'd gotten out of his SUV and had carried toward Winky, Goober and me yesterday, when we'd escaped in Goober's rusty old Chevette.

Oh dear lord! What has he got inside that thing? A knife? Zip ties? A rope to throttle me with?

I heard the lock click. I gulped and dared a downward glance. Jake took out a huge screwdriver and pointed it at me. "You're in a lot of danger, you know," he said. He bent over me, his hot, horrid breath in my face. "The arm on this chair's a little loose." He leaned over and tightened a screw on the chair.

He's taunting me. What's he going to tighten next? A noose around my neck?

I let out a weak, pathetic scream. "Aaaahhhgh!"

Jake looked at me and shook his head. "Intimacy issues, too," he muttered. "Boy, are you ever wound up tight."

"Of course I am!" I panted breathlessly. My lungs were so tight I could barely draw enough air to speak. "You're a mur...uh...." *Oh no!*

Shut up, Val! If you say it, he'll know you know. Then you'll be doomed for sure!

Jake dropped the wrench back in the box and scowled. "Go ahead and say it. *Murderer.* I'm a *murderer.*"

I started whimpering.

"You're not the only one I've had to deal with," he said. "Everyone thinks I am."

"Is that why you killed them?" I whined.

"What?"

"All the graves. Behind your shed. I saw them!"

Jake's black eyes narrowed to slits. "You did?"

"Yes," I huffed. "And so did my friends. If you kill me, they'll know it was you!"

A grimace nearly swallowed Jake's hairy face. "Kill you? I was just hoping to eat lunch with you! If that's how you feel, forget it. Just go."

Jake hung his head and shuffled back toward his house. I tried to get up and flee, but something inside me wouldn't let me.

"Then you're not...a...murderer?" I gasped.

"No!" he shouted back.

"You promise?" I asked.

Jake stopped and turned around. "Yes, I promise, for what *that's* worth."

"I...It's just that...how the hell do you explain all those graves, then?"

"They're my childhood pets," he said, and took a step back toward me. "After I hit puberty and this hair showed up, they were my only friends."

"Oh," I said sheepishly.

"After twenty years, the wooden markers had rotted away. I wanted them to have new tombstones. I'm almost done, too. All I've got left to finish is Buskers, my turtle, and I'm done." Jake sat down on a chair next to me. "I know it may sound weird, but it's not against the law to bury your pets in your yard. Believe me, I've had plenty of time to research the laws."

"Twenty years, I'm guessing."

"Bingo."

"So you didn't...I mean...your mom really...*exploded?*"

Jake sighed. "Spontaneously combusted. Yes, it's a real thing. Look it up on the internet."

"Actually, I already did," I confessed. "Lots of people agree with you. That it's a real thing, I mean."

"Do you?" he asked. His beady eyes looked almost pleading.

"I'm getting there."

"Thanks."

"But tell me, what about the missing dogs? You had that hound, and now you don't. Then a Doberman. Where is it? What happened to them?"

"You really *are* nosy," Jake said. "And paranoid, too."

"I like to think I'm cautious," I argued.

"Right," he said sarcastically. "Have it your way. If you must know, they were clients."

"Clients?"

"While I was...*away*...I took a correspondence course in psychology. I'm a certified animal counselor. A dog psychologist, if you will."

"*That's* a real thing?"

"Yes, it's a real thing."

"Wow. So, why did you choose *that?*"

Jake sighed. "When you look more like a beast than a human being, it's easier to sympathize with the animals."

I looked down at my feet. "I get that. Sorry I misjudged you." I looked up to see Jake shrug. "So, how does it work?"

"The therapy?" Jake asked. "I introduce patients to their triggers. Their *antagonists*."

"What do you mean?"

Jake stood up and used his hands as he spoke like the world's hairiest Italian. "Take the hound and the Dobie. Both were terrified of thunderstorms. So I did a group session the other night. Remember when we had those storms?"

"Uh...yeah," I said and coughed. "I vaguely recall them."

"The Dobie was a hard case. Poor thing. His owner was ready to put him down. Can you believe it? They'd had to keep him locked in their garage during storms. He'd go bananas. Well, the last straw came when he actually busted out a tiny garage window in a panic to escape the storm. His owners found him cowering under the neighbor's pool cabana the next morning. The garage window frame was still stuck around his middle."

"That's horrible!" I said.

"Psychological trauma can break anybody. Believe me. But it doesn't mean you have to *stay* broken. Thanks to my therapy, Gus the Dobie is back home now, weathering the storm, so to speak."

"Wow. I'm sorry...and impressed. I had no idea."

Jake nodded. "Not too many people do."

"Wait a minute," I said. "Why were you banging on my door the other night in the middle of a storm?"

"I'd tried your doorbell. It didn't work."

"It got fried the night before," I explained. "During the first storm, when the lights went out. But why in the world were you out in a storm in the first place?"

"I needed to borrow a cup of milk," Jake said. "I was in the middle of making a batch of doggy biscuits and knocked over my carton."

"Oh. Those would be the same...biscuits...you gave me for Buster."

"Right. Did they do the trick? How is he?"

I slumped in my chair. "To be honest, Jake, he's not sick. At least, I don't *think* so. He's *missing*. He disappeared the night of the second storm. Goober had him on a leash.... We heard this horrible howling, then a cracking sound...like bones crunching. The leash went slack...and he was gone."

Jake studied my guilty face. "And you thought what? That I ate him alive?"

I shriveled. "No. Not alive. Well, yes, maybe alive."

Jake rolled his eyes. "And people think *I've* got mental problems. Let me give you a recommendation, Ms. Fremden. Never have a mother who spontaneously combusts. It's a real lifestyle cramper."

I shrunk in my chair. "Sorry."

"You know, that cracking noise was probably the limbs that broke on that tree over there." Jake nodded toward a small tree that was missing a few limbs about as thick as my wrist. "Wind damage."

"Oh."

"Now, as to what happened to Buster, I couldn't tell you. He might suffer from astraphobia, too. A lot of dogs do."

"Astraphobia?"

"Fear of thunder and lightning. If so, he probably freaked out and ran off. If a dog can bust out a window, a dog can slip off a leash."

I sat up in my chair. "That's true. Tom found him wandering around. It could be—"

Jake's doorbell rang. "Excuse me for a moment. That may be my next client. She's a little early."

After Jake left, I took a tentative sip of my drink. It didn't taste like arsenic. It tasted like a gin and tonic. I gulped half of it down. I heard the back door open again. A moment later, a little white poodle skipped down the path, put its paws on my shins and wiggled its bobtailed rear excitedly.

"Hey! Get down, you dirty little rat!" I said, and scrambled to my feet.

"Oh my word," Jake said. "I get it now. *You hate dogs.*"

"No I don't," I said, and pursed my lips. "I mean, not really. Not *all* dogs."

"Admitting a problem is halfway to solving it," Jake said.

"I don't hate dogs!" I insisted.

"Come on, Val. Why don't you want to admit it?"

"Because dog haters are right up there with serial killers!" I blurted.

Jake shot me a wry look. "Tell me about it," he said.

Chapter Thirty-Two

"You are without a doubt the most insecure, distrustful, jealous and paranoid piece of work I've seen in a while," Jake said.

"I hope you're talking to the dog," I sneered, and sat back down in the lawn chair by Jake's fire pit grille.

Jake hugged his latest client, the little white poodle, and whispered in its ear. "Don't listen to her."

"All I said was the dog stinks," I repeated.

"Well, for your information, to a dog, you're a walking stink bomb."

"I beg your pardon?"

Jake let go of the dog and used a pair of tongs to turn the meat on the grill. It smelled so good my stomach growled.

"You can wear as much deodorant or perfume as you want," he said, waving the tongs for emphasis. "A dog can smell right through it. In fact, the human armpit is the smelliest thing in the animal kingdom. Our breath? Woo boy. And don't even get me started on the genital region."

I grimaced. "Don't worry. I won't."

Jake laughed. "But the biggest source of smell, believe it or not, is our skin. We're literally churning out a boatload of sweat and oils. It's our signature scent. That's what a dog picks up on when it's sniffing you out."

"I thought it was our scurf."

Jake stopped dead and smiled. "You know about scurf?"

"Yeah. It's a real thing."

Jake grinned. "You know, I've got an idea, if you're game. Here. Take Trixie."

He shoved the little poodle into my arms. I held it like it was wearing a poo-poo diaper.

"Just as I thought," he said. "You're stiff. A dog can sense that."

"How? Are they psychic?"

"No. They can smell fear. And anxiety. Some say they even know when you're sad."

I looked at Trixie. She tried to lick my face. *Gross.* "How is that possible?"

"Hormones, mostly," Jake explained. "Adrenaline especially. It's the fight-or-flight hormone. We can't smell it, but dogs can. And when you're agitated, you're heart rate goes up. That shoots smelly chemical messages coursing through your skin."

"Sounds nasty," I said.

"Maybe. But it's honest. You might be able to smile and fool your friends, but you can't fool man's best friend."

"A dog's never been *my* best friend."

"That's too bad," Jake said.

"Can I put her down now?" I asked.

"Wait a minute. Just look at Trixie. You don't like her. She knows it. But still, she keeps on trying."

Trixie lunged to lick my face again. I jerked her away just in time. "Yeah. It's kind of cute and disgusting at the same time."

Jake chuckled. "You have any idea why dogs are so quick to wag their tails, Val? Even when they feel abused? Or even when they've been betrayed?"

My heart pinged. "Betrayed, too? Really? No. I don't know why."

"Because in some ways, they're higher animals than us," Jake said.

"Higher? What do you mean?"

"Well, it's kind of funny, but no matter what the world shows them, dogs never seem to forget they came to this earth to be loved by God, and needed by man. People sometimes forget this, but a dog never does."

"Wow, Jake. That's actually kind of profound."

"Yeah. Why do you think dog is God spelled backward? They're the only two beings I know of that are capable of unconditional love."

I looked at Trixie and grimaced. "Well, I guess I'm gonna have to wait until I meet up with God, then."

Jake shook his head. "Not necessarily."

"No?"

"I think I can help you get there sooner."

"Uh...meeting God?" I said. "That's okay. I can wait."

Jake laughed. "Funny gal. I like that. Now listen carefully, and do as I say."

"THEN I GOT KNOCKED over by Dad's horrible old hound dog," I said, wiping back a tear. Jake, dressed in a doctor's white smock, was behind me, his hairy fingers massaging my shaking shoulders. Trixie the poodle looked on sympathetically.

"Good. Let it all out," he coaxed.

"He made me drop my ice cream!" I bellowed. "Then he nearly licked me to death with his nasty tongue. My birthday was ruined! That's when I decided dogs were just dumb, horrible animals. I hated them all!"

"Good job, Val," Dr. Jake said encouragingly. "Now, you just sit and rest for a minute."

I dabbed my eyes. Dr. Jake moved to the next lawn chair arranged around the fire pit. Trixie was waiting her turn patiently. She wagged her tail as he approached, and he patted her on her eager head.

"Trixie will demonstrate how it's done, won't you girl?" Dr. Jake looked over at me. "She's here to overcome her fear of shoes." He looked back at the dog. "Aren't you, little Trixie?"

She didn't speak, but from the way her rear end was wiggling, I could tell she was ready.

"Is that why dogs chew shoes?" I whispered. "Because they're afraid of them?"

"I don't get into psychoanalysis," Dr. Jake replied in a hushed tone. "I find it's too judgmental."

"Oh," I said. "Just one more question." I fingered the thick leather strap around my neck. "Is the restraint collar really necessary?"

"Yes. Until I can determine the extent of your psychosis."

"*My* psy...uh. Okay. And the white lab coat?"

"Listen," Dr. Jake instructed. "It's better if you just sit. And stay. And don't speak."

"Okay."

I watched as Jake tied an old shoe to the end of a fishing line attached to a short cane pole. He placed a paper bag over Trixie's head. A hole had been cut in it where her nose could poke out. She could smell, but she couldn't see. He checked the harness holding her in place in the chair. He seemed satisfied. "Ready," he said to himself.

"Sit, Trixie! Stay," he commanded. Trixie sat up at attention, the bag over her head. Jake picked up the pole and swung the old shoe to within an inch or two of her nose.

Trixie went ballistic. She growled and snapped at the shoe, tugging so hard on the collar strapped to the chair that I thought she might pull her own head off.

"That's it, Trixie girl!" Dr. Jake said. "Get it out! Get it all out!"

Trixie howled and snapped and yelped herself half-hoarse. After a while, exhausted, she lay down on the chair and sighed. Dr. Jake removed the paper bag over her head and placed the shoe by her nose. Trixie sniffed the shoe, then licked it once, half-heartedly.

"Is she cured?" I whispered in amazement.

"For the most part, yes," Dr. Jake said. "She's learned through primal screaming that the shoe is not the problem."

"Primal screaming?"

Jake shrugged. "Well, in this case, primal howling. Now it's your turn. Remember to use your words, Val. And by that, I mean your *doggy* words. Did you bring the object that symbolizes your deepest fears?"

"Yes sir. I mean...woof woof!" I handed him the object.

Dr. Johnson tied it onto a fishing line, then covered my head with a paper bag. He positioned it until it fit snug on my head. I couldn't see, but my nose poked out of one hole and my lips out of another.

"Okay," he said. "Ready? Here we go."

I heard the sway of the fishing line in the breeze. I figured if I could get rid of my fear of dogs, maybe I could get rid of my fear of relationships, too. Suddenly, I felt a small tap on my face as my mother's old wedding ring bopped me gently on the nose.

I opened my jowls and howled my brains out.

Chapter Thirty-Three

It was a miracle. I was crossing the Sunshine Skyway Bridge with the top down on Maggie, the wind blowing through my hair, and not a care in the world. I felt like a million bucks. A million *empowered* bucks.

Who knew screaming could be such powerful medicine? Forty-five years of loathing gone in five short—albeit very *loud*—minutes.

Jake Johnson might not have completely cured me of my loathing of dogs and marriage, but he'd come darn close. After my therapy session had ended, I'd hugged both him *and* Trixie, and felt as light as a helium balloon in outer space.

I looked out over the sparkling Gulf of Mexico. My future seemed just as bright and limitless. Jake's primal scream treatment had released my fears and given me a whole new attitude about life.

This was a dog-eat-dog world, and Tom Foreman was about to get rabies.

I PULLED INTO THE LOT of the Sunset Sailaway Resort still flying high. I was ready to face anything! My plan was in place. I was unstoppable! I was going to march right up to Tom Foreman and tell him I'd lost Buster, his diamond earrings, *and* my respect for him.

Then I was going to go eat a plate of nachos.

I cut Maggie's ignition and opened the car door. Before I could swing my legs around and out, I was accosted by a Chihuahua with short fur the color of butter.

"Ooops! Sorry about that!" Cold Cuts called from across the lot. "I can't seem to get him to stop jumping into people's cars!"

"No worries," I said. I tousled the little dog's head as Cold Cuts made her way toward me. "I love dogs."

"Well, it looks like he loves you, too," Cold Cuts said, grinning.

"Where did you get him?" I asked.

"That's a long story. Come on in and I'll tell you all about it."

I grabbed my suitcase out of the trunk and followed Cold Cuts across the lot, the little Chihuahua trotting happily beside us.

"YOU'RE KIDDING," I said and set my mango margarita down on the cabana bar. The beach breeze blew my bangs around. I tucked my hair behind my ear.

"Nope," Cold Cuts said. "When we got back here, I went to get our suitcases out of the back of the RV and found him asleep on the bed."

"When did you say you went camping?"

"Well, Bill and I'd planned to stay all this week at Fort DeSoto. But three rainy nights in a row finally drove us away."

"You should have come by to see me."

"We did. I rang your bell, but I don't think it was working. So I pounded on the door. You didn't answer. It was raining like mad and my umbrella was about to give up the ghost. So I got back in the RV and Bill and I drove back here. That's when I found this little stowaway back there, snoozing away."

"That's so odd, Cold Cuts. That's the same time I lost Buster."

"Buster?"

"*My* dog."

"You have a dog?" Cold Cuts asked, incredulous.

"*Had* a dog. He's been missing for three days. That's the night you stopped by, right?"

"Yes. You don't think...."

"No. Buster has long, fluffy hair. And it's more reddish gold."

"Oh good grief, Val! So did this dog when we found him. But he got all snarled up in a patch of sandspurs and by the time I cut them all out...well, I decided he'd be better off if I just shaved him."

"Oh my word!" I stuttered.

"I had no idea, Val! If I'd known, I would have.... I don't know how he got in the RV. And I had no idea where we might have picked him up along the way. The campground...a gas station. Oh, good grief! I'm sorry! Are you sure it's him?"

"No. Not one hundred percent. I mean, when I think about it, Milly's dog looks just like him, too. And I'd only had him a few days myself. Where is he now?"

"Probably with Bill's dad. He's nuts for him. How can we figure out if it's him?"

"Well, I know Buster loves to go for a ride. And he loves to eat. By the way, you didn't happen to...." I thought about the diamonds and shook my head. "Never mind. Wait! I think there's one pretty sure way to find out. Do you happen to have a can of smoked oysters?"

Cold Cuts crinkled her nose. "Gross. Really? No. I mean, who would?"

I looked away. "Nobody I guess. On another note, do you happen to have another room free tonight?"

"Why? Is someone else coming?"

"No. It's just that...since we last spoke...I found out Tom had a secret rendezvous with his ex-wife, Darryl. He lied and told me he had a business trip in Tallahassee. But Goober slipped up and showed me a picture of him sitting next to her. He was holding her hand and smiling like the cheating jerk he is!"

Cold Cuts shrunk back. "Oh, Val! That's awful!"

"Can I ask you something? Do you think that cheating is okay? I mean, if a man is great in so many other ways. Is it something we should put up with?"

Cold Cuts' chin met her neck. "Oh, hell no!" she bellowed. She saw my expression and softened her voice. "I mean, not for me, anyway. Are *you* okay with it?"

"Not in the slightest," I said. "I thought I might could make myself be. But...I just came out of therapy....and I know what I want now."

Cold Cuts hugged me. "Good for you."

"Thanks." I looked up and spotted Tom coming out of the lobby door. My resolve evaporated. "Oh crap! He's here! Hide me!" I whispered and ducked under the bar.

"Okay," Cold Cuts agreed. "But just promise me that if he finds you, you won't start anything in front of the resort guests, okay?"

"I promise. Just hide me. Hurry!"

"Climb in the beer fridge. It's broken."

She slid one side of the lid over and I stuffed myself in. Cold Cuts slid the glass lid back and covered it with a couple of bar towels. A moment later, I heard her voice. Then Tom the weasel's.

"Hi Tom," she said coolly.

"Hi, Cold Cuts. How are you?"

"Great. You?"

"Never better, thanks."

Never better my ass! My left foot was going to sleep. I shifted in the cooler.

"Have you seen Val?"

"Uh...she was here a minute ago. She went to the restroom. Should be back in a minute. So, what's new with you?"

I strained to hear through the plastic cooler-coffin.

"Not much. Just got back from a little trip."

"Really? Business or pleasure?" Cold Cuts asked.

"A bit of both, actually."

"Yeah?"

"I had to go help my boss with a presentation in Tallahassee. Then a friend of mine...oh. You know Jorge, right?"

"Sure."

"He works in my office now. Well, about a month ago, he started dating my ex's cousin, Sherryl. Come to find out, she lives just up the block from him in St. Pete. Anyway, her family is all up near Tallahassee. They planned this big get together to meet him. He was so nervous about it, he could barely make it through his work shifts. He knew I was going to be nearby working this past weekend, so he asked me to come along with him...you know, for moral support. He's been a little fragile these past few years. I couldn't say no. I wanted to vouch for him to her family as a good guy. You know, and be there if he needed me."

"Oh. Wow," Cold Cuts said loudly. "That's so thoughtful of you, Tom. Hey, have you checked in yet?"

"No."

"Go take care of that with Bill. When you get back I'll get you something out of the beer case. At the moment, though, it still needs a few minutes to cool off."

I winced and hoped Tom couldn't hear me cringe inside the cooler.

"Great," Tom said. "Tell Val I'll be back in a minute."

"Don't worry. I will."

The bar towel lifted, providing me a good look at the expression on Cold Cut's face. If a stitch in time saved nine, I was gonna need about nine-hundred stitches.

Chapter Thirty-Four

"Play nice, now," Cold Cuts smirked as Tom walked toward us at the bar. I waved to him. He waved back with one hand. In his other he carried a bag of citrus. The big lug had remembered to get my Minneola tangelos. In exchange, I'd lost his diamond earrings and told my friends he was a lying, cheating dirt bag. The jury was still out on whether I'd lost the dog, too.

It wasn't one of my high points.

"I have a confession to make," I blurted as soon as Tom got within earshot.

"Me first," he said, and set the tangelos on the bar. "Be kind and hear me out, Val. I come bearing gifts."

I glanced at the bag. "You remembered my tangelos."

"Of course," he said. "And I got you these, too." He reached in his shirt pocket and flashed a tin of smoked oysters.

I started laughing. It got snagged up in my throat and turned into crying. I'd been such a jerk!

"What's wrong?" Tom asked. "I promise what I did wasn't that bad."

"I know," I said between sobs. "You went to help Jorge. Why didn't you just tell me?"

Tom put his hands on my waist. "I'm sorry. I was afraid you'd do something stupid."

I pursed my lips and looked up guiltily. "Who? Me?"

Tom fought back a smirk. "So, what's *your* confession?"

"I lost your earrings," I wailed. Tom looked at me funny. Cold Cuts slapped a tissue in my hand.

"I don't understand," Tom said. "Then how are you wearing them?"

Oh, crap! I'd forgotten I'd worn the Dollar Store knockoffs. "I...I was going to lie about it," I confessed.

Tom shook his head. "Val, sometimes I honestly don't know what to do with you."

"I have an idea," Cold Cuts said. "Why don't you make her eat those smoked oysters?"

"Good idea," Tom said. He fished the tin out of his pocket and set them on the bar.

"I have to tell you something else," I said to Tom.

"What?"

"I lost Bust—a"

Tom cracked opened the tin. From the corner of my eye, I saw a little golden dog running my way. It stopped, winked at me, then jumped up and pranced around in a circle, begging for an oyster.

"Buster!" I cried out.

"I didn't expect to see *you* here!" Tom said.

Cold Cuts looked over at me and said, "Nobody did."

TOM AND I WERE SITTING at the cabana bar on the beach, admiring the sunset and the way hard-nosed Cold Cuts and easy-going Bill toyed with each other like a pair of silly lovebirds. They seemed perfect for each other, despite being complete opposites in so many ways.

"You two were so lucky to find each other," I said.

"So were you," Cold Cuts reminded me.

"I guess every couple is," Tom said.

"True," Bill chimed in. "And while we're on the subject of couples, odd as they may be, I have a huge favor to ask of you two."

"What?" I asked.

"Look over there," Bill said, and pointed to an old man sitting in the sand about twenty feet away. Buster was frolicking around him as he laughed.

"My dad Fred is crazy about Buster," Bill said. "Only he's named him, The Colonel."

"I didn't know that," I said.

"His dementia is getting worse," Bill said. "I see him shrinking away more every day. He's forgotten all about fishing. Sometimes, he even forgets who I am."

"I'm so sorry," Tom said.

"It's okay. The favor I ask isn't for me. You see, in the past few days, my dad has been happier than I've seen him in ages. I guess The Colonel has given him a purpose. When he saw him the first time, his eyes lit up. Now he lives for that dog. He plans his life around feeding him, going for a walk on the beach. I guess The Colonel gives him something of his own. I know he's your dog. There's no doubt about that. But I'd be really grateful if you would consider leaving him here with dad. He's got a good home here, I assure you."

Tom and I looked at each other. Tom nodded.

"Then The Colonel's gotta stay," Tom said.

"Are you sure?" Bill said. "It would mean the world to my dad."

"Yes. We can get another dog," Tom said.

"When we're ready," I added.

"Yes," Tom agreed, and squeezed my hand. "When the time is right."

"Besides," I said, looking at Cold Cuts. "He belongs here. He's a master of disguise, just like you."

AFTER A WALK ON THE beach, Tom and I slipped away together to our little cottage by the sea.

"Seeing Bill's dad got me thinking, Val," Tom said as he unbuttoned his shirt. "Who knows how much time we have? I don't want to waste it."

"What do you mean?"

"I don't need a dog, Val. If you don't want one, just say so." He unbuttoned the last button and let his shirt fall open. "What we need is *honesty* if we're gonna make it."

I walked up to Tom and toyed with the hair on his chest. "You think I don't love dogs, don't you?"

Tom smirked and took my hand. "With you, I can never be sure. I mean, it took you over a year to say you loved *me*."

I sighed. "Okay. You're right. When it comes to dogs, I'll admit I have my reservations. Right now, I only have room for one old dog in my place."

Tom grinned. "You talking about yourself?"

"Ha ha," I sneered. "No. I mean you."

Tom cocked his head to one side. "Wait. Does that mean you want me to move in?"

"Yes. You've been a good dog. You can stay."

Tom let out a silly yip and kissed me.

"And I'm gonna take you up on your offer, too. I'm gonna stay home and write. I mean, I've always wanted to. And like you said, life is short. We shouldn't waste it."

"I only see one problem with this plan," Tom said, and furrowed his brow.

"What?"

"There's something wrong with your clothes."

"My clothes?" I asked, and looked down at my dress.

"Yes," Tom whispered in my ear. "They're still on."

Chapter Thirty-Five

Nearly two months have passed since I broke the news to Milly that I'd be leaving my post at Griffith & Maas to stay home and try my hand at writing novels. Winnie didn't win the Dollars for Desserts contest. That went to a deep-fried Twinkie full of peanut M&Ms. But she and Winky did hit a different kind of jackpot. Winky got an offer for Old Joe's Bait House from the guy who owned Caddy's. The really cool thing was, the guy wanted to keep it as a bait shop and put Winky in charge. Judy Bloomers helped negotiate the contract.

Winky started running the place last week with Winnie by his side. The place still looks like an old shack, but it has a new sign. Old Joe's Bait Shop is now Winnie and Winky's Bait & Donut Shop. Davie's Donuts lost Winnie as head waitress and manager, but she worked it out with Davie so she can still make her peanut-butter bacon bombs there and sell them at the bait store, kind of like a franchise.

J.D. finally confessed to Laverne that he wasn't sleepwalking, but burying her food in the backyard in an attempt to extend his lifespan. In turn, Laverne confessed to burying J.D.'s cuckoo clock, then, after I un-buried it, to throwing it away in a nearby dumpster. Every once in a while, I still think about the crazy night Laverne and that clock scared the wits out of me. When I do, I like to think that somewhere, in a dumpster far, far away, that mangled old cuckoo clock still gargles out a rancid chirp every hour on the hour.

Bill and Cold Cuts are doing well at the Sunset Sailaway Resort. Business is good, and Bill's dad Freddie is still enjoying whiling away his golden years with Buster, aka The Colonel, by his side.

Tom and I had dinner with Jorge and his girlfriend Sherryl. She truly was the spitting image of Darryl, Tom's gorgeous ex. She was also fun and flirty, and I could tell Jorge was crazy about her. She told me she made a pretty good living doing YouTube makeup demonstration videos. She offered to do my makeup, so I let her. When she got done, Tom whispered in my ear that he liked me better without it. How could I *not* love this man?

Tom also made good on his promise to get me a new couch. It got delivered last Friday. When the guys picked up the old one to haul it away, I found my earrings underneath it, still in the little card thingy. I guess Winky was right. I really should clean under my couch more often.

I wore the earrings today on my last day on the job at Griffith & Maas. I was a good friend and didn't leave Milly in the lurch. I'd found and trained my replacement, even though, honestly, a trained chimp could make better coffee.

"Did you add four scoops like I said?" I asked the new guy.

"What do I look like, some kind of idiot?" Goober asked.

Dressed in short pants, a short-sleeved dress shirt and a bow tie, yeah, he kind of did. I smirked. "Well, now that you mention it..."

"It's time! It's time!" Milly shrieked as she ran in the break room.

Goober dropped the coffee can. I dropped everything else and ran out the door after her. We left Goober in charge at the accounting firm and piled into Milly's red Beemer. She drove like a mad woman while I hung onto the doorknob to keep from ending up on her lap. A few minutes later, we were at her Tudor mansion. Vance met us at the big mahogany door.

"There's six," he said. "And they're all beautiful."

We ran down the hall to the bedroom I'd caught Buster and Charmine in at the Barkmitzva. In a beautiful wicker basket, Charmine was busy nursing six tiny, reddish-gold balls of fluff.

"They're Buster's, all right," Milly said. "Charmine isn't the kind of girl to sleep around."

I fought back a grin. I wasn't about to argue with that.

"I promised one to Mr. Griffith," Milly said. "But if you want, Val, you can take your pick."

A little golden ball stretched out its legs, yawned, and winked at me.

"I'll take that one," I said. "The one with the white paw." I snapped a picture of it to send to Tom, who was busy moving the rest of his stuff in with me today.

I sighed and smiled at the sleeping puppies. It was official. My life would soon be going to the dogs. And, for the moment at least, I was okay with that.

DEAR READER,

Thanks so much for reading Six Tricks! I hope you enjoyed the story. It's actually based on some of my own life experiences—including fear of dogs. Like most families, growing up we had a menagerie of dogs and cats. We and even had a pet lizard! Some were great. Others? Not so much.

Like Val, I spent summers on a farm and was traumatized by the hound dogs my grandfather let roam loose on his property. They never did me any harm. Not physically, anyway. But psychologically? The jury's still out on that one! By the way, Charmine was based on a dear friend of mine's Pomeranian. The dog actually likes me, but absolutely hates my friend's daughter. Go figure?

While I was writing Six Tricks, a friend asked me to take care of her dog Watson for four days. I don't know if it was life imitating art or vice versa, but it was odd timing, for sure. I haven't had a dog in my life in years. Like most of us, Val has her phobias. Dogs are a big responsibility. And we all know how Val feels about commitment....

If you'd like to know when my future novels come out, please subscribe to my newsletter. I won't sell your name or send too many notices to your inbox.

Newletter Link: https://dl.bookfunnel.com/fuw7rbfx21

Thanks again for reading my book! Sometimes life really can be a bit hairy. ;)

Sincerely,

Margaret Lashley

P.S. I live for reviews! The link to leave yours is right here: https://www.amazon.com/dp/B07BPMC22T#customerReviews

Want to get in touch? Here's How:

Website: https://www.margaretlashley.com

Email: contact@margaretlashley.com

Facebook: https://www.facebook.com/valandpalspage/

What's Next for Val?

First of All, Thanks for Reading Six Tricks!

I hope you enjoyed Six Tricks: Doggone Disaster. If you did, it would be wonderful if you could take a minute and leave a review on Amazon. I appreciate every single one!

https://www.amazon.com/dp/B07BPMC22T#customerReviews

Follow me on Amazon and BookBub and you'll be notified of each new release. Thanks so much for being a fan!

Follow me on Amazon:

https://www.amazon.com/-/e/B06XKJ3YD8

Follow me on BookBub:

https://www.bookbub.com/search/authors?search=Margaret%20Lashley

Ready for more Val?

Get set for a vacation of last resort in **Seven Daze**! Val survived a potential canine calamity. But here comes the next one! Tom's about to move in. Will the pressure of cohabitation prove too much for Val?

Enjoy the following excerpt from the next Val Fremden Midlife Mystery:

Seven Daze!

A Sneak Peek at Seven Daze:

<u>Chapter One</u>

I thought seven was supposed to be a lucky number. Maybe it was...for *dwarves*.

But *me?* Not so much.

In fact, every time that number popped up in my life, I gave it a little side-eye. Seven wasn't lucky. It was a boil on my buttocks. An ugly reminder of how close I'd come to living in a cardboard box, wrestling alley cats for empty tuna cans.

A few years back, before I returned to Florida, I'd spent seven years in Germany. That's when I found out that seven years abroad was exactly how long it took to destroy my life savings *and* my life in general. I'd washed up back on the shores of my hometown, St. Pete Beach, not just broke and homeless. I'd also been pretty much erased from the hearts, minds and credit histories of every person and place I'd ever thought I could count on.

Geez. Even my *name* had become a stranger. Literally. The old Val Jolly I'd been before I left for Europe was gone. A bad marriage had changed it to Val *Fremden*—a word that meant "stranger" in German. It's almost scary to think how apropos *that* had turned out to be....

So screw you, seven.

Come to think of it, six was no good, either. It reminded me of what a magnet for mayhem I could be. Six times now, I've ended up smack-dab in the middle of a nut-fest of squirrelly shenanigans no sane person could have imagined. Like hobgoblins inhabiting an unsound mind, bulldog-faced bullies, shady shysters, fruitcake relatives and nutty neighbors seemed to track me down and stick to me like Crazy Glue.

Don't even get me started on five. It was the number of years I've had to lick my wounds since I got torpedoed by a German dreamboat. *Anchors away, dirtbag.*

Four wasn't much better. That was how many times I've had to start my life over. *With nothing.*

As far as three went...well, that was the number of times I've been married. Or, perhaps more accurately, it was the number of times I've been *divorced*.

Over the years, I'd become deeply suspicious of the numeral two, as well. Two was a pair. A matched set. If you don't get my drift, go back and read number three.

I never have understood eight, either. To me, it always looked like an infinity symbol that had been stood on its head. No thanks. My life didn't need any more help going off-kilter.

And nine? Nine sounded like German for "no." A non-starter on both counts.

Nope. In my book, the luckiest number was one. *Numero uno.* As in me, myself and I. During my extended tutelage at the School of Hard Knocks, I'd learned that *one* was the single digit I could consistently rely on.

Even if it was odd.

JUST WHEN I THOUGHT everything in my life had returned to a semblance of normalcy, I opened the mailbox and screamed. Inside was a letter from the AARP. It was official. The world had just declared me "old."

"You all right over there?"

I glanced over my left shoulder. My neighbor, Laverne Cowens, was waving at me from the other side of her mailbox. In the full light of day, the radiant glare rocketing off her gold-lame jumpsuit nearly blinded me. Either that, or I'd succumbed to cataracts. I squinted and waved the letter back at her.

"Ugh! Laverne, I've just been 'AARPed.'"

"Oh," she grinned and shook her horsey head. "That ain't nothin'. Wait 'til you get your first coupons for Depends. *Then* we've got something to talk about."

My upper lip snarled involuntarily. "Can't wait." I turned toward the house, then changed my mind. I was stalling. I knew it, but I didn't care. Anything was better than going back inside to face "it."

Up to now, I'd made a point of trying to steer clear of Laverne's personal life, but I was out of ideas and just desperate enough to push the scales in her favor. I forced a smile. "Hey Laverne, how are things going with you and J.D.?"

Laverne's grin faded like a cheap tattoo at the mention of her boyfriend's name.

"We haven't killed each other yet, so there's that," she joked half-heartedly. One of her penciled-on eyebrows jerked upward. "How about you? I noticed a bunch of moving boxes going into your house yesterday."

"Yeah," I sighed as I made my way along the sidewalk toward her. "Tom's almost moved in."

"Boy howdy. He's not wasting any time, is he?"

"No." I blew out a breath. "I guess it's like lancing a boil. Better to just dig in and get it over with."

Laverne's red lips twisted into a smirk. "How romantic."

I shook my head. "Sorry. Sometimes, I really think I should just be taken out and shot."

Laverne snorted, giving me a gander at her dentures. "We can't all be hopeless romantics now, can we?"

"No, I suppose not. But why is it I only ever seem to get the 'hopeless' part down pat?"

"Ha ha! Honey, you always make me laugh. Want to come in for a drink?"

"It's ten-thirty in the morning, Laverne."

Laverne shrugged. "So?"

I glanced around at the neighbors' houses. Nobody was around. "Okay. What the heck."

I FOLLOWED THE SKINNY old woman up her driveway toward her modest, ranch-style house. Built in the 1950s, it was a mirror image of my own little abode. If our homes hadn't butted up to the Intracoastal Waterway leading out to the Gulf of Mexico, most people wouldn't have given the low-slung, concrete-block boxes a second glance. In fact, nowadays, the only reason anyone bought a place like ours was to doze it and build a McMansion on the lot.

But folks like Laverne and me preferred character over modern conveniences. At least that's the story I told myself. I didn't have enough money to remodel my vintage kitchen, much less rebuild the whole house. And I kind of liked that my place had a "lived in" appearance. The delicate pallor of impending poverty came in handy. It kept away would-be door-to-door solicitors and Halloween trick-or-treaters.

On the outside, Laverne's place was just like mine. A tad faded, and as non-descript as an out-of-shape, ball-capped man at a sports bar. But *inside*? Now, *that* was a different story.

Amongst the hallowed rooms of Laverne's lair lurked the biggest collection of Vegas memorabilia outside Madame Tussauds' wax museum in Las Vegas proper. As I followed her inside the door and waded past bookshelves cluttered with tacky souvenirs, I noticed that something was off. Laverne's living room, once an unabridged shrine to all things happy, glitzy and glittery, had been infiltrated by an army of somber, humorless invaders.

On the wall beside the stunning, life-sized, color photo of Laverne in her feathery cabaret outfit being kissed on the cheek by Elvis, hung a black-and-white picture of a dour group of short, angry-looking men dressed in lederhosen. Their expressions seemed to convey they were recent graduates of the Sauerkraut Club. Laverne's bookcase, once chock-a-block with shiny celebrity figurines like a mini Oscar-Awards after-party, now had dull-hued, kerchief-wearing Hummel figures milling about in the crowd like babushka-headed party poopers.

I shot a worried glance at Laverne as she pulled a couple of beers from her fridge. "How far has J.D. gotten with this?" I asked.

"What?" she asked.

"This...I dunno...*hostile takeover* of your space."

"You noticed, huh?" Laverne shook her head. "Sheesh. He wants me to drink beer out of stein, Val. A *stein!* I got my doubts, honey. I'm not so sure it's gonna work out with us."

"Why? I know you like beer."

"Sure. But I only drink it out of the bottle...or my lucky Marilyn Monroe leg." Laverne opened a kitchen cabinet and pulled out a flesh-colored, leg-shaped glass complete with white high-heel and fishnet stocking. "I don't do steins," she muttered. "And I'm beginning to think I don't do roommates, either."

"Oh," I said, and slumped in my stool. "Sorry to hear that. Well, I guess it's good you two didn't tie the knot. At least you and J.D. can dial back the living-together thing pretty easily, right?"

Laverne cracked open a can of beer and began to fill the shapely leg with golden liquid and foam. "I guess. I mean, he's still got his place on the beach and all."

My chin met my neck. "J.D.'s got a house on the beach?"

"Yeah. Sunset Beach." Laverne sulked at the leg, as if it might have been Marilyn's fault.

I glanced around with fresh eyes at the garish clutter crammed in every crevice of Laverne's kitchen. A bobble-headed Dean Martin winked at me. "And he chose to live *here* instead? Why?"

"Beats me," Laverne answered. She shoved a shamrock-covered glass full of beer across the counter toward me. "Because *I'm* here, I guess. And because I don't want to live on the beach."

I couldn't have been more incredulous if Laverne had confessed she wanted to live in a dumpster with Frosty the Snowman. "Why not?"

"Because *this* is my home, Val." Laverne looked around her place with sad, puppy-dog eyes. "And *you're* next door. I like having you near-by. I don't feel like I'm all alone."

Laverne's words tapped a nerve. Hard. Like a spike hammered into a beer keg. The fact that J.D.'s memorabilia had distinctly German roots reminded me of all the lonely, soul-sucking years I'd spent in Germany, forlorn and friendless. My heart flinched at the rush of painful memories of feeling hollowed out, vulnerable and fragile. Then I realized, to my great relief, that I hadn't felt that way in a long, long time.

My gut instinct was to warn Laverne. But of what? Geez, given my track record, I was in no position to give relationship advice.

"Compromise is hard," I offered, trying to put a positive spin on the personal dread that had begun to churn like sour milk in my stomach. "But, you know, it's not like you'd be moving to another *country* or something. Sunset Beach is only a few minutes' drive from here."

"True. But it's not *here*." Laverne pouted and stared at me with her endearing pug eyes. "I know it sounds corny, but home is where your *heart* is, Val. And my heart's *right here*."

My eyes stung. "Then *here* is where you should stay. After all, it's *your* life." I sniffed back a totally unexpected tear. Was I getting sentimental in my old age, or just going senile? What next? Crying at dog-food commercials?

I grabbed my glass. "Hey, how about a toast?"

"To what?" Laverne asked.

"To knowing where your home is."

Laverne grinned. "To knowing home when you see it," She hoisted Marilyn's leg.

I sipped my beer and watched her take a long, throat-bobbing chug. Her grin returned. She set the leg-mug down on the counter and asked, "You got any super glue?"

I nearly spewed my beer. "What?"

Laverne opened a drawer and pulled out a baggie containing the shattered remains of what appeared to have once been a Hummel figurine.

"I...uh...accidently dropped this."

I stifled a smirk. "I don't have any glue. I used it up fixing Tom's acrylic baseball case. I...uh...accidently dropped *it* yesterday."

We eyed each other and burst out laughing.

"It would appear that great minds think alike," I said, and drained the beer from my Shamrock Casino glass.

Laverne wiped the corners of her eyes with a paper towel. "Thanks, honey. I needed a good laugh."

"I think we both did. Boyfriend business can be tough." I set my empty mug on the counter and looked around her place again. "I'm curious, Laverne. What exactly do you *do* all day?"

Laverne shrugged nonchalantly. "Whatever I want."

I nodded appreciatively. "Huh."

Laverne picked up Marilyn's leg and finished off her beer, blissfully unaware she'd created a scene perfect for a flesh-eating zombie spoof. She set the empty leg on the counter and grinned at me. "So, how's the writing going?"

My smirk faded. "Slow. I'm still setting up my writing space in the second bedroom."

"Give it time, honey," Laverne said.

I blew out a sigh. "You're right. I shouldn't press myself. Now that Tom's living with me, he's helping out with the bills. I hope that'll take the pressure off my savings account."

"I hear that." Laverne stepped over to the sink to give Marilyn's leg a rinse. The sight of a fishnet-clad shin in the drain-board was unsettling enough, but Laverne upped the ante. She slid a plate across the counter at me and asked, "Want a cookie? Snickerdoodles. I made them in cooking class."

I'd never been startled by a cookie before. Not even one of Laverne's. I eyed the misshapen, hideous globs of dough. Pale, gooey middles surrounded by charred edges. They reminded me of petrified splats of vomit with eyeballs in it. I thought about J.D., who faced trials like this on a daily basis. I wished I'd had one of his baggies tucked in my waistband, so I could fake eating one, smuggle out its remains, and dispose of it in a toxic waste container.

"I'm on a diet," I lied.

"Suit yourself." Laverne picked up a cookie.

"Wait a minute," I said. "I thought you got banned from cooking classes at the senior center."

Laverne shrugged. "You set one little oven on fire and you're blackballed for life. I'm telling you, Val, those old folks got no sense of humor."

She poked the horrid cookie at me for emphasis. My body shrunk back involuntarily.

"Nope. This new class is down at St. Pete College. Continuing ed."

Laverne put down the cookie and picked up a brochure. She reached a long, skinny arm across the counter and handed it to me. "See? They've got all kinds of classes. And the best thing is, not everybody there's got a blue rinse in their hair and a stick up their butt."

I glanced through the brochure. "Huh. It says here they have a writer's class. *Mystery Writing for Fun and Profit.* Meets Thursday nights from six to eight."

"That's tomorrow!" Laverne squealed. "Same time as my cooking class!"

"But it started last week," I muttered.

"So? You've only missed one class. Why don't you take it? We can ride over together. It'll be fun!"

"I dunno."

"What have you got to lose? And Val, it's in the *evening*. Think about it. That's free time *away from the guys*. And like the brochure says, you can 'Explore Your Inner Aptitudes.'"

"Or *inept*itudes." I bit my lip and read the brief syllabus.

Laverne drummed her red-lacquered nails on the counter. "Thirty-five bucks buys seven weeks of 'Thursday evening do-as-you-damn-well-please' time."

I looked up at Laverne with a new admiration. "Excellent point, my friend. Mind if I use your phone?"

Keep reading! Pick up your copy of Seven Daze on Amazon now!
https://www.amazon.com/dp/B07D6FGMPC

About the Author

Like the characters in my novels, I haven't lead a life of wealth or luxury. In fact, as it stands now, I'm set to inherit a half-eaten jar of Cheez Whiz...if my siblings don't beat me to it.

During my illustrious career, I've been a roller-skating waitress, an actuarial assistant, an advertising copywriter, a real estate agent, a house flipper, an organic farmer, and a traveling vagabond/truth seeker. But no matter where I've gone or what I've done, I've always felt like a weirdo.

I've learned a heck of a lot in my life. But getting to know myself has been my greatest journey. Today, I know I'm smart. I'm direct. I'm jaded. I'm hopeful. I'm funny. I'm fierce. I'm a pushover. And I have a laugh that makes strangers come up and want to join in the fun. In other words, I'm a jumble of opposing talents and flaws and emotions. And it's all good.

In some ways, I'm a lot like Val Fremden. My books featuring Val are not autobiographical, but what comes out of her mouth was first formed in my mind, and sometimes the parallels are undeniable. I drink TNTs. I had a car like Shabby Maggie. And I've started my life over four times, driving away with whatever earthly possessions fit in my car. And, perhaps most importantly, I've learned that friends come from unexpected places.